THE SEDUCTION OF
JAMES GRAY

MOONLIGHT FALLS BOOK ONE

COLETTE RIVERA

Mystery, temptation,
and risking it all.

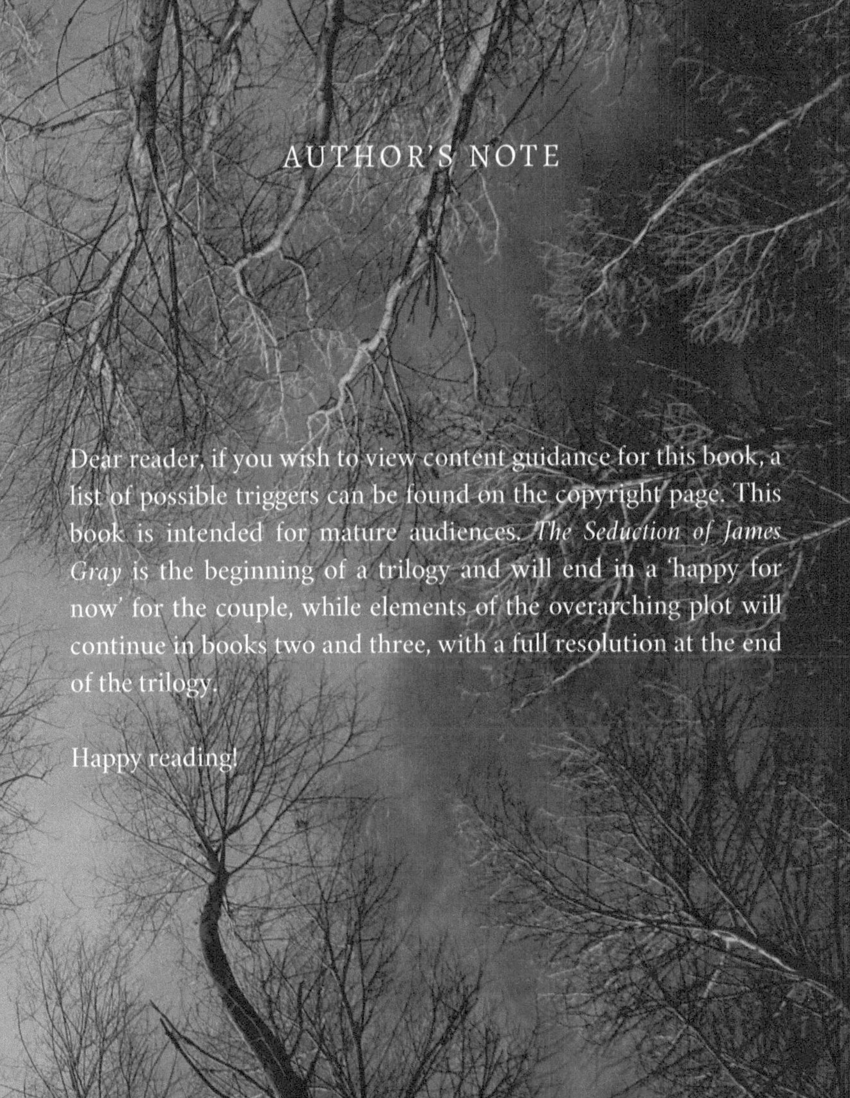

AUTHOR'S NOTE

Dear reader, if you wish to view content guidance for this book, a list of possible triggers can be found on the copyright page. This book is intended for mature audiences. *The Seduction of James Gray* is the beginning of a trilogy and will end in a 'happy for now' for the couple, while elements of the overarching plot will continue in books two and three, with a full resolution at the end of the trilogy.

Happy reading!

Storm Family Tree
Selma Nock — Tony Storm
Nelson Storm   Sullivan Storm — Marilyn Dalton
Claire Bates — Simon Storm
Stephen Storm   Samantha Storm — undisclosed
Kira Storm   Sebastian Storm

MOONLIGHT FALLS

The Fall of Elijah Gray

The Seduction of James Gray
The Cursed Sebastian Storm
The Heart of Moonlight Falls

THE SEDUCTION OF
JAMES GRAY

MOONLIGHT FALLS BOOK ONE

COLETTE RIVERA

James Gray held trouble in his hand. He felt it down to his bones. Even at first glance, he hadn't liked the look of the letter, but upon closer inspection, the return address on the dark-green envelope didn't bode well.

"Are you going to open it or just stare at it all day?" Hazel Delgado asked as she peered at him from across the workroom, amusement making her lips twitch. She was almost smiling.

"I'm opening it, hold on. Just can't remember the last time I got mail that wasn't a bill." James eyed the wax seal and curly script displaying the sender's name.

Sebastian Storm. Why the hell was that man writing to him?

James tore open the envelope. Inside was a single sheet of good quality paper, thick and a soft cream color rather than white. He unfolded it to find the stationary was personalized with S. *Storm* and a small depiction of the infamous Storm House centered at the top. James frowned in distaste but couldn't say he was surprised. It fit what he remembered of Sebastian's personality.

His eyes trailed down to the message, written in the same frilly cursive as the address. Had Sebastian used some sort of fancy pen? It certainly didn't look like it'd been written with a ballpoint.

"What century is this guy living in?" James muttered. Hazel ignored him. She knew him well enough to judge which grumbles weren't worth responding to.

For all its flair, the letter wasn't very long. At first, James had feared it might be an invitation of some kind—that would explain the pretty packaging—but it didn't seem to be that kind of trouble after all.

James,

I was so pleased to hear about the reopening of Gray Electrical and was hoping to engage your services. I'd be grateful if you came out to Storm Manor at your earliest convenience.

Regards,

Sebastian

James flipped the note over. The back was blank.

"So?" Hazel, who co-owned Gray Electrical with him, crossed her arms and leaned back in her chair, obviously waiting to hear why a mysterious letter had arrived at their business.

James tossed the note onto his desk. It was much tidier than Hazel's, though she always kept the shared work area pristine. "He needs an electrician."

Hazel raised her brows, clearly finding Sebastian's methods of hiring them as unusual as James did. "Couldn't he have just called?"

"You'd think." James was annoyed by the whole thing. "He didn't say what the problem is, and it's like he's only just heard we've opened."

James had reopened his grandparents' magical electrical business two years ago. You could hardly call that a recent event.

Hazel shrugged. "I hadn't even realized Sebastian had moved back to Moonlight Falls."

James hadn't either, and James had been back for six years. The town was small, and he knew almost all the residents by sight and most by name. He couldn't remember the last time he'd seen Sebastian. James knew the guy from when they were kids. Sebastian was a couple of years younger than James, so they hadn't crossed paths much, yet he stood out in James's memories. Sebastian had always seemed unique—even by Moonlight Falls standards—and had never done things quite like anyone else.

Case in point: this silly letter.

"Wonder what he's been up to." James peered out the window beside him as a car drove past, heading into town.

"Now that I'm thinking about it, I'm pretty sure I heard somewhere that he inherited the house from his uncle." Hazel stood and stretched, throwing away the paper that had wrapped her lunch.

That tidbit of town gossip didn't exactly answer the question of why Sebastian had only now come back to Moonlight Falls. James couldn't quite remember how long ago the older Storm— whose name James had forgotten—had passed away, but again, it wasn't a recent event. Maybe Sebastian hadn't spent much time in Moonlight Falls since inheriting the house and had put off returning to deal with it until now. That would explain why he was commending James for reopening his business years after the fact.

If James had inherited a place like Storm House, he certainly wouldn't have moved in. Even with Sebastian's penchant for going against the grain, it was hard to imagine him embracing the creepiest house in a town known for what lurked in the shadows.

"So, what, the haunted house has faulty wiring?" Hazel walked out from behind the counter that separated the workroom from the Gray Electrical storefront.

James picked up the note. "He didn't say. Just requested I come over."

Hazel *hmphed*. "I'm glad the letter isn't addressed to me."

James narrowed his eyes. "Doesn't mean I have to go. I'm due to look after the pumps this afternoon. So, really, you should go see what he wants."

"Hard pass." Hazel redid her ponytail, gathering all the loose strands of dark-brown hair that had escaped since that morning. She grabbed a box cutter and sliced open the package that had been delivered along with the damned letter.

James got up and joined Hazel in the shop, where they sold everything from tools to small circuit boards and wires. Hazel began stocking a display with the new batteries that had been in the package. They were the latest Nelson model, smaller than any other magical energy sources created to date. The things weren't cheap.

"You looked after the pumps this morning." James picked up a battery. He could feel the energy trapped within. It glowed faintly green. "It's against regulation to have one person working the pumps for a full day."

Hazel rolled her eyes. "Only one customer came by before lunch, and you know it. Regulation says I can perform ten full refilling spells in a shift. I'd be surprised if we get that many today."

A service station was attached to Gray Electrical. It was the main reason a business like theirs could stay open in such a small town.

Magic was the energy source the world ran on, from electrical power plants to the batteries installed in cars and the small ones they sold in the shop. James had never been interested in working with the sources of magical power. He liked the order of mundane energy flow, electrons, and wires, the kind of work someone without any magical ability could do. He had little interest in performing the powerful spells that harnessed and stored energy. Besides, all that technology was guarded by companies like Nelson Power. It was intellectual property the world at large wasn't allowed access to, and no one had figured out how to make magical power work like Nelson had.

Gray Electrical was all James had ever wanted, keeping the community ticking along just as his grandparents had.

"I'll go see what Sebastian wants tomorrow." James put the battery on the shelf.

"Do you not like him or something?" Hazel looked at James more shrewdly than before. "I can go if you two have history."

"It's nothing like that," James said quickly. "You've known me my whole life. You know he and I were never friends. Never anything." As he denied it, a memory returned to him: seeing Sebastian sitting in the park when they were teens and getting a fluttery feeling in his chest. Not that it had ever developed into a full-on crush. He remembered thinking Sebastian was cute, that was all.

Hazel narrowed her eyes. "I don't know *everything* about you."

James walked away and grabbed his jacket from the workroom. "It's just the creepy house I don't feel like dealing with," he lied.

"Fair, but you have to admit it's kind of intriguing." Hazel put the last battery on the display as James returned to the shop side of the room. "I haven't been that far up North Road in ages. Actually, I'm surprised we haven't been asked to install more lights up that way."

"Scaring the shades away would ruin the ambiance."

Hazel laughed. "Speaking of shade-lights, we've got more to do on Cedar Street in the morning, so you can't see Sebastian then."

"I know. I'm going now. Text me if you need anything." James checked his jeans pocket for his keys. Putting off Sebastian wouldn't help anything. Better to get it over with.

CHAPTER TWO

James had forgotten how far out of town Storm House was. His truck wound along the road leading north, surrounded by nothing but forest. Most people would probably find it scenic, even if the tall redwoods blocked a lot of the daylight.

James wasn't most people. Knowing bad things had happened out here always made it feel sinister. No matter how old he got, he couldn't seem to forgive this stretch of road or see it as just another place, so he didn't come up this way much.

Moonlight Falls was a tiny dot on the map a couple of hours south of the Oregon-California border. Despite his aversion to North Road's shady atmosphere, James liked living in a town amid a sea of trees. The town was peaceful for the most part, and the area had a magic that comforted James. Outsiders found the energy unsettling, but that was Moonlight Falls for you.

Magic was always said to be strongest out in the wilderness. Maybe people had naturally settled in places far from the veins of power running through the earth, or maybe, the flow of power avoided people. Either way, cities didn't feel like Moonlight Falls. It was why true citizens of the town were always drawn back. Moonlight Falls called you home.

James had always known he'd return to this place and hadn't gone very far when he'd left. Maybe Sebastian had felt the same gnawing restlessness that being away from Moonlight Falls had triggered in James, and that's why he was back, staying at a place like Storm House. Maybe the house didn't faze Sebastian. The residents of Moonlight Falls had a higher tolerance than outsiders for things that went bump in the night, and the Storms were some of the most tolerant among them.

The town seemed to draw shades as much as the people it had claimed as its own. Everyone here embraced a magical life and a few oddities, but in James's mind, there were limits, even here, and most people's lines were drawn around Storm House.

The radio in James's truck turned to static, so he switched it off. His destination should be coming up. The notorious house was the last building on the edge of a vast expanse of logging land. There were no other driveways out here, no other homes, only a forest that slowly turned from redwood to pine, so he wanted to ensure he didn't miss the turnoff.

There wasn't much north of Moonlight Falls. The town spread in a southern direction as if trying to reach out to its closest—albeit not that close—neighbor. The woods out here were claimed by other things, and the people working the logging land had the strangest stories of anyone in town.

James came upon the driveway at last and noticed the gate was shut. He let out an annoyed sound as he made a U-turn and stopped. At least he was able to pull completely off the road.

James hopped out of his truck, but as he went to open the gate, he spotted a chain and padlock. "Oh, for fuck's sake." James shoved the metal gates and the chain clinked. They were embellished Gothic-style iron monstrosities and looked ridiculous. A gargoyle sat on either side of the gate, perched on the stone wall that ran the length of the property in both directions.

He could just see the blasted house at the end of the long driveway, though a mix of redwoods and pine trees blocked the rest of the property from view. It looked as creepy as ever, weather-worn and dripping with an air of general abandonment.

Who painted a house forest green? Whoever had designed the place had made some odd choices. All the ornate trim and Victorian details clashed with the stone gargoyles lining the north side of the driveway, to say nothing of the gate. It was all distinctly unwelcoming.

James thought about driving back to town. Sebastian hadn't left a phone number, so perhaps James should write him a letter back, asking Sebastian to arrange a time for him to stop by when the damn gate wasn't locked. Or he could get this over with now and climb the wall.

He could have used a spell to unlock the gate, manipulating the air inside the simple locking mechanism until force clicked it open, but that would technically be breaking the law. It was a good thing the wall wasn't very high.

The stones weren't cut flat, so they provided good footholds. James just hoped he wouldn't scuff his jacket. It was his nice leather one, and if the fall air wasn't so brisk, he might have left it in his truck just to be safe.

James landed on the grass on the other side of the wall and brushed himself off, the sleeves of his jacket looking no worse for wear. He stepped around the gargoyles and walked up the unpaved driveway.

The house might have looked foreboding, a large two-story mansion with a tower at the back, dark windows, and a shadowy porch, but the property seemed well-tended, not creepy or neglected. The lawns he passed were neat, and no trees crowded the house. It wasn't as James remembered, though he'd been a kid the last time he'd ventured up to the gate.

There was an off feeling about the place, like the energy was wrong. You could groom the land, not change its nature, and being on the property had always made people anxious. James's heart rate had picked up as soon as he'd come over the wall. He had the sense of being alone yet watched, an unsettling but well-known sensation that could always be felt here. It was why people said Storm House was haunted.

As James reached the porch, he glanced to his left. Beyond the lawn lining the driveway was a paddock housing a single cow.

That was odd.

James stared. It wasn't the kind of odd he expected from Storm House. The gargoyles, fine, whatever. The skin-crawling sensation, yes, he'd anticipated that. But the cow made James pause. What was it doing here? This wasn't a farm or anything like that. The animal didn't fit the haunted aesthetic. It seemed happy and not even remotely possessed.

The cow ignored James, busy munching the grass. He turned away and proceeded up the steps, crossing the covered porch to the front door. There didn't seem to be a doorbell, so he knocked.

James waited, his annoyance with the situation growing as his patience thinned. The house was so damn big that he doubted anyone would hear him knocking. He rapped his knuckles on the door again. What if Sebastian wasn't home? That could have been why the gate was locked. A possibility James hadn't thought of before he'd climbed the wall.

After several more minutes of knocking and waiting, he pounded on the door. "Hello?" he called out as loud as he could. The air seemed to swallow the word. It was still out here, like being in the middle of the forest with no signs of civilization. Maybe no one was home.

James shivered. In addition to the anxiety-inducing energy that hung around the property, there was a chill in the air, the kind that shades seemed to like. He hoped one of the nasty beasts wasn't about to pop out from under the front porch. There were enough shadows around here for one to be out on a cloudy day like today.

Shades were creatures from Beyond. As the name suggested, they drew power from shadows and darkness and couldn't materialize in direct sunlight. Most shades weren't actually dangerous. Their ghostly forms frightened people who weren't used to them, city folk mostly. To people in Moonlight Falls, they were pests, more than anything, mischievous little devils. The kind of nuisance James didn't need to deal with right now.

He knocked one last time, mostly because he didn't want to have to come back here.

To James's surprise, the door swung open. The small success did not wipe the scowl from his face.

"Hello!" Sebastian stood before him, sounding delighted to find James on his doorstep. He was a bit breathless, as if he'd come running. It didn't stop him from beaming at James, his pale cheeks cut by the sort of dimples people found endearing.

James clenched his teeth. He was not endeared and had a renewed sense that this guy was going to be nothing but trouble.

"I wasn't expecting you." Sebastian swept ginger curls back from his face with slender fingers. He was taller than James, poised, and cut an elegant, trim figure, his muscles lean and stomach flat. A fact James couldn't help noticing because Sebastian wasn't wearing a shirt.

"You sent a letter asking me to stop by." James's eyes ran down Sebastian's body without him wanting them to, annoyance at how eye-catching Sebastian was prickling at his senses.

Sebastian wore slim-cut jeans, no shoes or socks, and what looked like a robe. Not a fuzzy bathrobe, but some sort of sophisticated thing with silk accents on the cuffs and lapels. Did robes even have lapels? James had no idea. The garment, whatever it was, was dark purple and made Sebastian's expanse of pale freckled skin pop in contrast.

James found himself captivated, mostly wondering *why?* Why to any and all of this.

Sebastian leaned against the doorframe, resting one arm above his head. The position stretched his body languidly.

"You're right. I did ask you to come by. Now that you're here, you've got me thinking it's my lucky day."

"What?" James's gaze shot back to Sebastian's face. Was there a flirtatious edge to his voice? James narrowed his eyes. "I doubt that. I assume you called me because you have a problem for me to look at. Sounds like bad luck to me." He kept his gaze fixed on Sebastian's.

He shouldn't have let himself look, but he'd been caught off guard by Sebastian's unusual appearance. James wasn't in the mood for flirting or finding anyone attractive. Especially Sebastian. However, he had to admit—grudgingly—that Sebastian was good-looking.

"I've got a few things you could take a look at if you're interested." This time, there was no doubt that the line was meant to be flirty. Sebastian's purring tone was over the top, and he seemed to be enjoying himself, going by his sly little smile.

James didn't allow himself to react. He wondered if Sebastian was just messing with him after catching him staring. It served James right and seemed like the kind of thing Sebastian might do. He'd been a boy who'd liked causing trouble and riling people up. In other words, the opposite of James.

James hadn't changed much, even though he was twenty-eight and not the boy he'd once been. Unfortunately, he was remembering more and more instances when Sebastian had caught his eye in the past, both for appealing and annoying reasons. It seemed that being in Sebastian's presence was bringing it all back.

"Why don't you come in?" Sebastian stepped back from the door and gestured inside with a flourish, purple sleeve flapping. "Can I tempt you with a lemonade or something *else*?"

James stepped inside, looking away from Sebastian. "I'm fine, thanks."

The large entryway was dim, the only light coming in from

the open door and skylights in the vaulted ceiling. The floor was tiled and looked cold, especially for Sebastian's bare feet.

Narrow tables covered in unlit candles lined the walls. At the center of the space was another table housing several old-fashioned oil lamps and a row of leatherbound books. James had a sudden urge to push the two bookends closer together to better hold the volumes on display. The ones in the middle leaned to the side, leaving enough space for at least one more book between them.

Beyond the table was a grand set of stairs tiled to match the entry floor. Gargoyles guarded the banisters on either side.

"I can't get you anything? You're sure?" Sebastian sashayed forward, heading toward a hallway to the left of the stairs. He'd left the front door wide open.

Wasn't he cold? The temperature in here didn't seem much warmer than outside.

James followed Sebastian. "I had to climb your wall, you know."

"I'm sorry, had to? Says who?" Sebastian turned to face him, tone teasing. He bit his bottom lip, making it look like he was trying not to laugh.

James didn't reply. Sebastian's cheekiness wasn't endearing. It was infuriating, and James was annoyed by how much effort he'd had to expend just to get here.

Sebastian's soft hazel eyes lit up as something seemed to occur to him. "You must have been eager to see me if a locked gate couldn't keep you out."

"Why would I be eager to see you?" James couldn't keep the frustration from his tone. "I don't even know you."

All of Sebastian's playfulness died. "No?" He crossed his arms over the open front of his robe, sleeves falling back to his elbows. His voice turned sneering. "Never seen me around before? No idea who I am? I thought everyone knew *everyone* in Moonlight

Falls. All looking out for one another, more like a family than a town. Not that it ever seemed to apply to me."

James opened his mouth, but nothing came out. He felt a twinge of guilt for being a grumpy ass for no real reason and maybe even a smidge of guilt for ignoring Sebastian when they were young.

"Look." James ran a hand through his short hair. "Why don't you fill me in on why you need an electrician?"

Sebastian marched down the hall in a huff. James reluctantly followed. He *didn't* know Sebastian, not really, and saying so shouldn't have been a big deal. James hadn't seen him in at least ten years. Still, he knew enough for this interaction to feel familiar.

Sebastian had kept to himself back in high school, and James hadn't hung out with many younger kids. There were at least two years between them if he remembered correctly. He shouldn't have to feel bad for never really talking to the guy. Most of the times he remembered noticing Sebastian, the younger boy had been creeping around town alone, acting out, or messing around with magic when he wasn't supposed to be.

James was pretty sure Sebastian had set the park bench on fire once.

It's not like James had wanted to get involved with any of that. He'd never been *that* much of a sucker for a cute face and was proud to say he still wasn't. James didn't want anything to do with Sebastian Storm now, any more than before.

Sebastian stopped halfway down the darkened hallway. James looked around at even more unlit candles and faded green wallpaper. Sebastian flicked a light switch. Nothing happened. He flicked it off and on rapidly before turning to give James an exasperated look.

"The light doesn't work." James glanced at the ceiling to see a bare bulb hanging above them.

"Not the light." Sebastian's exasperation had reached his voice.

It was as if he thought James was dumb for needing the problem pointed out.

Why was he acting like this? It's not like James knew what was going on. Explaining what needed fixing was standard and shouldn't be an annoyance. Not like climbing a wall was.

"So the power isn't working?" James guessed.

Sebastian smiled. It was toothy and appeared genuinely heartfelt, a jarring contrast to his mood a second before and nothing like the heavy-handed flirtation from the doorway. "Can you fix it?"

James suspected this guy was going to give him a headache. "Sure. Do you know why it's not working?"

The happiness left Sebastian's features. "Isn't that your job to figure out?"

It was going to be a long afternoon.

CHAPTER THREE

The hairs on the back of James's neck prickled as he looked at the fuse box. He was used to some customers wanting to keep him within sight when he worked in their homes, but casually keeping an eye wasn't what Sebastian was doing. The two of them were outside, around the back of the house, in an alcove used to store firewood. Sebastian was watching every move James made.

The attention made James squirm. He didn't like it at all. So what if he found Sebastian attractive? He didn't want the interest returned. Sebastian wasn't the kind of guy James wanted to be involved with in any capacity. Which was just as well because he wasn't entirely sure Sebastian wasn't messing with him. If any interest on his part was feigned for a reaction.

It wasn't that James doubted Sebastian was interested in men in general. Unless Sebastian's identity had changed over the years, they were both bisexual and had each come out in high school. It was probably the only thing the two of them had in common.

But Sebastian had only started acting flirty after he'd caught

James looking, and the way Sebastian was staring at him now wasn't the usual sort of looking-at-someone-you-liked behavior. It was too intense for that. He had to be messing with James.

James tried to concentrate on the disaster in front of him. "So none of the power is working?"

"Nope." Sebastian popped the *P*, and James imagined the shape his lips would have made doing it.

He didn't turn around and continued to picture Sebastian in his mind, conjuring up an infuriatingly innocent look that matched the man's refusal to be even remotely helpful. Couldn't he just leave James to get his work done alone?

"When was the wiring last updated?" James eyed the corroded fuses. They were old and should have been replaced with modern circuit breakers long before now.

Sebastian hummed as if he were thinking. "When the house was built?"

The nonchalant shrug James imagined accompanying Sebastian's words was as graceful as it was careless.

James turned around, pushing away fictional images of Sebastian and gaping at the man himself. "You're telling me this is original?" He was appalled.

"Yeah. That's bad, isn't it?" Sebastian seemed completely unconcerned about the state of the wiring, unlike most homeowners, who would bemoan a problem of this magnitude.

James closed the fuse box. "When was this place built exactly?"

Sebastian raised one lazy shoulder. "Nineteen forty-ish."

It was hard to believe nothing had been updated since then. James eyed Sebastian, wondering if there was something he wasn't saying. He noticed goosebumps on Sebastian's chest. So he *was* cold out here without a shirt or shoes.

Thinking about the goosebumps was his first mistake. From there, James couldn't help looking Sebastian over a second time. Sebastian seemed graceful even when he wasn't moving, making it hard to look away from him. The combination of his annoyingly high cheekbones, enough freckles for James to get lost in, a pointy little nose, and lips that looked tender had James admitting Sebastian had grown out of his cuteness and into something more dangerous.

Trouble, this was going to be nothing but trouble.

"Am I distracting you?" Sebastian asked, his teasing tone making a reappearance.

James's face heated. "This wiring isn't up to code."

Sebastian nodded in a way that could only be described as mock-serious. He bit his lip like he was trying not to laugh again.

James cleared his throat. "It's probably a good thing nothing's running. It could be a fire hazard."

"But you can fix it?" Sebastian asked more seriously, pulling his robe tighter around himself.

James nodded. "The whole house will need to be rewired."

"Manor."

"I'm sorry, what?"

"Manor." Sebastian gestured toward the house. "This is Storm Manor."

James snorted. It was almost a laugh. "Everyone in town calls it Storm House."

"Well, everyone in town is rude." Sebastian flicked his long bangs back with a shake of his head. He looked so indignant. It was adorable.

"Right." James closed the fuse box. "The *manor* will need to be rewired."

"See, you said it in a snide way. That doesn't count."

James ignored that. There were so many more pressing things to discuss. "Are you staying here without power?"

Sebastian seemed to swallow whatever silly thing he'd planned to say about the house. He frowned. "Looks that way, doesn't it?"

James didn't like that. Had Sebastian been here long? Surly not, if he was so blasé about getting things fixed, writing letters, and being all mysterious about it. But then, who had been keeping the yard so tidy and feeding the cow? James shook his worry off. A gardener had probably been looking after the property. No one would be living here. "You should see if the B&B has a room free until the work is done."

"Aw." Sebastian swatted at James's shoulder. "Are you worried about me being out here in the dark?"

"No." James cleared his throat, his voice gruff. "But it's not going to be a quick job. It'll be too long to go without power."

"I'll manage." Sebastian dismissed James's concern, sounding careless.

They stared at each other for a long moment. James wanted to argue, but it wasn't really his business.

"I'm not going to be able to start today." James shifted his weight and shoved his hands in his jacket pockets. "I'll need to do a bit of planning first. I assume the interior walls here are plaster, going by the age of the building, and you probably don't want to have me ripping them off, so it's going to be fiddly work."

Sebastian's eyes glazed over. Was he even listening? "Mm-hmm," he hummed in detached agreement.

James asked the powers that be for patience. "Do you have any of the old plans for the house? It would be helpful if I could look at the schematic for the original wiring."

Sebastian frowned. "There are probably plans laying around somewhere."

"Great." James thought about smiling but couldn't be bothered dredging up his customer service skills. "We can look at those and figure out the best way forward. Hopefully, I'll be able to start disconnecting the existing wiring tomorrow."

Feeling like things were done for now, James began walking toward the front of the house. Sebastian followed. They passed a well-tended garden and greenhouse. The gardener must have a lot of work to do around here.

"So, how about that lemonade?" Sebastian offered as they reached the front porch.

"No thanks. I should get going. Gather everything I'll need so we can get working on this."

"Right, of course." Sebastian turned away.

Too late, James realized the offer had been made without snark or overdone flirtiness, as if Sebastian simply wanted James to stay and chat for a bit.

Before James could say anything, Sebastian went on, "I suppose I should walk you to the gate, or else I really will be forcing you to climb over the wall." He sounded put out but made his way down the driveway without further comment, purple robe billowing behind him.

Overall, James didn't think Sebastian liked him much. The flirting and offer of lemonade didn't necessarily mean anything, and James needed to get his wandering eyes in check before he came back here. There was no need to encourage whatever games Sebastian might be playing.

At the gate, Sebastian pulled keys out of his pocket and unlocked the chain. He eyed James's truck. "Not much has changed, has it? Different jacket, different truck, but hardly."

James didn't like the judgment in his tone. "Yeah, well, you're about as I remember too."

Sebastian opened the gate. "I thought we didn't know each other. Surprised you remember me at all."

James walked out, not particularly looking forward to coming back.

AFTER CLOSING Gray Electrical and wishing Hazel a good night, James walked down the block to Moonlight Diner.

The center of town was small. Main Street ran in a circle

around an eight-foot-tall gray stone marking the founding of Moonlight Falls that stuck out of a landscaped patch of grass. The street was lined with shops, eateries, the library, the post office, and the town hall. Gray Electrical was located just off the town circle's north end, next to the thrift store. There were a few more businesses off the south end, but the whole place was about two blocks. It hadn't changed much since James had been born, which was one of his favorite things about the town.

James liked going to the diner for an early dinner. It gave him a chance to socialize with the staff before the place got busy.

At ten past five, the only other customers in Moonlight Diner were Mr. and Mrs. Billings, an elderly couple who lived in the neighborhood east of the town center. They waved to James, and he gave them a smile before sliding onto one of the stools at the counter.

"Always sitting by the pies." James's younger brother, Elijah, abandoned the cutlery he'd been sorting near the register and came over.

"How's things?" James asked.

Eli rolled his eyes. "Pretty much the same as they were when I saw you this morning."

"You had a good day then?" James pressed. Eli hadn't been back in town long, and even though he'd moved in with James, and they saw each other every day, James liked to check in. He wanted Eli to be happy here. Helping his brother rebuild his connection to Moonlight Falls felt key to James's happiness. Not everything had to be stained by bad memories.

"I had a great day, actually." Eli beamed, proving that James often worried unnecessarily. His brother was fine. "Parker and I went for a hike before work. I got some good data too."

Eli pulled a map from his back pocket and unfolded it on the counter. A red line ran straight through Moonlight Falls and the rock in the town center. The line stopped a little way beyond the road leading north, past the last houses out that way. Eli pointed to a new red line he'd drawn on the map. This one was smaller. "The river trail takes you across this point here. It's a straight shot to the vein in town."

Eli was studying the vein of magical power running through Moonlight Falls and working at the diner part-time. He was conducting research as a part of his master's degree and had been sent here by his supervisor to investigate the unique magical properties of Moonlight Falls. Apparently, the vein running through town was different from most other fixed veins of power around the world.

James wasn't up on all the current research that had been done on natural magical forces. He'd always enjoyed the practical side of magic more. He had a stronger-than-average magical ability, while his brother had none. Not that Eli seemed bothered about his inability to practice magic. He loved studying it.

James looked up from the map. "How far do you think the vein goes in a straight line?" He knew straight lines were rare but couldn't quite remember why.

Magical energy flowed through the earth, but the intricacies of how it worked were complicated. James had a better grasp on the straightforward principles governing human use of magical power. All magic required a transfer of energy. With the right spell, you could expend your energy to harness magical forces and manipulate the physical world around you.

James tried to remember how strong Sebastian's magical ability was, but he wasn't sure. Maybe moderate? Surely, Sebastian wouldn't stay in a house without power if his magic was faint. Either way, it wasn't James's problem, and he shouldn't worry about it. He'd be back to start rewiring the house—*manor* —tomorrow. He had no obligation to Sebastian other than that. He could take care of himself.

"I'd love to keep following the line and see how far it goes. I have no idea how long it stays straight." Eli looked at the map longingly. "But the paths up there don't align very well, and Parker doesn't want me traipsing around off-trail."

"You could get lost. Or twist your ankle and fall down a ravine. No one would ever find you again," Parker called from the kitchen.

Eli huffed and folded the map. James had to agree with Parker, not that he said so aloud.

Parker Hayes was the head chef at the diner and had been a good friend of James's over the past several years. His family had owned the diner for decades, and he'd taken over most of the daily operations from his mother. Parker was also Eli's boyfriend. James couldn't have chosen a better match if he'd tried. Unlike James, Eli seemed to have no trouble with attachments and was already swept up in planning a future with Parker.

Eli turned toward the kitchen as Parker set the Billings' order on the passthrough. The food smelled delicious, making James's stomach growl.

Parker came out from the kitchen as Eli took the meals to his customers. "Those lights out back and in the park have been good."

James nodded. "Glad to hear it."

The number of shades appearing in Moonlight Falls had recently increased, which was becoming a problem. Their mischievousness seemed to be shifting from annoying antics toward more aggressive behavior. As a result, the mayor had ordered more lights installed to keep the shades away from populated areas at night.

There had been an incident a month ago that had actually turned dangerous. Luckily, Parker had handled it, and it had been late enough that no one was around the diner. Just Eli leaving work.

James's gut pinched at the memory. If anything ever happened to Eli, he didn't know what he'd do. He couldn't even think about losing his brother and suspected it would be the death that did him in. He couldn't lose anyone else he loved.

Not that anything bad was going to happen. James had gotten a handle on his fear of unexpected disasters and lived his life happily, for the most part. Surely, the Grays had experienced enough tragedy and everything would be good for him and his brother going forward.

Still, James didn't like to take risks and didn't particularly relish the idea of getting emotionally attached to more people than he currently had in his life. Eli, Hazel, and Parker were all he ever needed, and he hoped like hell he'd never lose any of them.

"Do you know much about Storm House?" James asked. There weren't many people who knew more about what went on in Moonlight Falls than Parker.

The cook paused, scratching his chin. He was taller and broader than James—who had the build of a lifelong swimmer—and seemed intimidating to anyone who didn't know him. "Sure. What do you want to know?"

"Sebastian sent me a letter." James paused, trying to figure out if he wanted more information on the house or the man staying there.

Parker nodded knowingly. "I see."

"What do you mean, you see?" James narrowed his eyes in confusion.

"Oh, I've had a few letters from Sebastian too."

Eli appeared at Parker's elbow. "What about Sebastian's letters?"

Parker raised his dark brows. "He's written to your brother."

"Right." Eli sounded nonplussed.

James pushed aside a prickle of annoyance. It wasn't like he'd thought Sebastian's letter to him was special. He didn't want it to be anything like that. He was just surprised. Writing to people wasn't common in this day and age.

"So you knew Sebastian was back in Moonlight Falls?" James asked the two of them.

Parker shrugged. "Sure. Guy's been back for years. He came into the diner a few times when he first turned up but hasn't been back for a meal since. I'm thinking that house has got a hold of him. He's turned into a total recluse. Not that it's so much of a surprise. He was always a bit like that—off on his own, avoiding people."

James frowned. "Sebastian has been in Moonlight Falls for years? Living at Storm House?"

"Yeah, so?" Parker didn't seem fazed, but then, he'd never left Moonlight Falls and didn't often bat an eye at anything that happened here. He was as much a part of the town as the stone in the center of Main Street.

"So…" James's concern for Sebastian returned. "He's got no power out there, and it didn't look like a new problem. He can't have been living in that house for years."

"Well, he has been." Parker took the lid off one of the pie stands to better arrange the pieces on display. "I don't know anything about the power, but the diner's been delivering bulk groceries out there for fucking ages."

"Yeah, I do the delivery now," Eli added, eyeing the apple pie.

James's frown turned into a scowl. "You never told me that."

"Why would I? I don't tell you every little thing I do at work." Eli poked Parker in the side and leaned his head against the other man's shoulder.

Parker gave Eli an affectionate grin and put a piece of pie on a plate for him. "Sebastian likes my pies too. Always orders one to go with his deliveries."

"So he wants you to fix his electricity?" Eli asked around a mouthful of flaky pastry.

James nodded. Hearing that Sebastian didn't come into town wasn't totally surprising. Parker was right. Sebastian had always been a loner, but surely he could have found a better place to hold up and avoid the world than a house with such an unsettling atmosphere.

And what about all his flirty comments that afternoon? Sebastian had seemed to want James's attention during most of their encounter. That wasn't the behavior of a recluse. Was it?

"Sebastian's hard to get a read on." Eli licked his fork. "Last time I was there, he asked me to come in and have a drink. As if I wasn't working and might want to check out the house. It was a total personality switch after he'd been rude to me the first time I went out there. He was super interested in Gray Electrical though."

"I bet."

James could understand not wanting to go grocery shopping, but Sebastian seemed to have taken avoiding human contact to the extreme. Why hadn't he hired someone to fix his house before now? Was he that averse to dealing with people? It hadn't seemed that way today, but according to Parker, Sebastian had been avoiding town for years, so he must not like being around anyone. But again, if that was true, why had he invited Eli in for a drink? From where James was sitting, Sebastian's behavior seemed all over the place, to a much greater degree than what James remembered of Sebastian when they were kids.

James experienced another pang of worry. Was Sebastian all right? Maybe he'd have to stay and talk next time to get a better idea of what was up. Being alone at that creepy house for so long couldn't be good for anyone.

James tried not to feel guilty for turning down Sebastian's lemonade offer.

"Sebastian seemed interested in you the last time he was in the diner," Parker said, pulling James from his thoughts. "He couldn't stop staring at your picture."

James groaned and glanced at the wall he had his back to.

The diner was decorated with photographs. They ranged throughout the town's history but were mostly focused on the diner and familiar faces. There was a picture of James above one of the booths. He hated it, but Parker refused to take it down, saying everyone would miss seeing such a key local achievement celebrated.

It was a picture of James from high school. The closest one was down in Apple Valley, Moonlight Falls nearest neighbor. James had been on the swim team and won a lot of races. Apparently, that meant the diner needed a blown-up picture of him in his letterman jacket holding a medal with an old swim team T-shirt bearing his name displayed in a matching frame beside it.

It was ridiculous.

James tried to ignore the display and mostly succeeded. The thing had been there for ten damn years, but it was always embarrassing when someone drew attention to it. And what? Sebastian had been staring at the picture? Why? He hadn't been on the swim team with James. There was no reason for him to care about an old state championship race.

"I think the passing of the ten-year anniversary is a good time to take that shit down," James grumbled, turning back to Parker and Eli, who were grinning like devils.

"Not a chance." Parker inched back toward the kitchen. James suspected he liked keeping it up simply because James hated it. Their friendship was like that.

"Yeah, we can't get rid of it." Eli put his empty pie plate on the passthrough. "Remember how proud Grandma was every time we came in here after they put it up?"

Ah, damn. James couldn't argue with that. Their grandmother had died at the start of Eli's last year of high school. It had been hard on both of them, especially because their parents had died in a car accident eight years before and their grandfather shortly after. There was no way James could moan about the photo now, not if having it there gave Eli good memories of their family.

CHAPTER FOUR

The gate was locked again.

James couldn't believe it. Barring the entrance made sense in light of Parker's claim that Sebastian wanted no contact with the rest of the town, but Sebastian had known James was coming back today, which made locking him out feel deliberate and unfriendly.

"It's not like I'm here trying to disturb his peace for no reason," James muttered to himself.

He got out of his truck and slammed the door. There was a persistent drizzle that afternoon, meaning the wall would be slippery. He should have left but couldn't stand the idea of Sebastian living out here with no one around, in a house without basic amenities.

James grabbed his toolbelt and buckled it before tossing his jacket back into the truck and pulling on an old hoodie. He wouldn't be able to carry all his tools over the wall. He'd have to drag Sebastian down here so he could get his truck inside.

As he climbed the wall, James thought of a few choice things to say to Sebastian about locking him out. Shouldn't the guy be desperate for someone to fix his stupid old house? There was no way James was putting up with this sort of nonsense for the duration of the job.

The same anxious feeling from the day before hit James the moment he was over the wall. Pissed off and on edge was never a great combo. Even the manicured lawns didn't brighten the atmosphere around the place. It was miserable, shrouded in mist, and James was sure he caught a flash of movement in the shadowy trees behind the house.

The porch steps creaked under his boots. He hadn't noticed that yesterday. There seemed to be something else different about the house too, but James couldn't put his finger on it.

Just as he was about to knock, the door opened.

"Oh, hello." Sebastian grinned at him, eyes going wide. He was wearing the same outfit as yesterday, though there was now a black shirt underneath the robe. His red hair looked significantly more tangled than before, like it hadn't been brushed.

"Yes, hello." James crossed his arms. "You locked me out again."

"Huh?" Sebastian peered past him, down the driveway. "Oh. Well, I wasn't expecting you here so early."

"It's the afternoon."

Sebastian rubbed his eyes. Had he been sleeping? "Sorry. Sorry. I swear I didn't do it on purpose." Sebastian didn't sound very sorry. He seemed too happy about the whole situation, and James wondered if he was lying. "Come inside. It's gross out here."

James entered the house, putting off getting his truck until he absolutely needed it. The front door closed with a thud. The entry was even dimmer than yesterday, and looking around, James figured Sebastian had all the candles for light rather than playing up the spooky aesthetics.

"Did you manage to find the electrical plans?" James asked.

Sebastian yawned. "Plans?"

James ran a hand through his hair. "The plans for the house. You said you might have them."

"Plans for the *manor*, right. I totally forgot we talked about that." Sebastian shrugged and made a cringy oops face. "We can go look for them now."

James wasn't sure how something like that had slipped Sebastian's mind. It was as if he wasn't that concerned about getting things fixed, which didn't make sense at all.

"Is that really what you want me doing? I charge hourly," James said as a not-so-subtle way of reminding Sebastian that paying him to help look for the plans wasn't the best use of anyone's money.

"Makes sense." Sebastian showed no concern. He turned away and began walking up the grand staircase. "Payment won't be a problem. Come help me."

James didn't have much choice but to follow. He wasn't thrilled about going farther into the darkened house, but he'd have to get to know it eventually.

As he climbed the steps, James noticed a row of books on the floor off to the right. They were on a step about halfway up the staircase and tucked to the side. Not exactly a tripping hazard, but a strange sight, given there was no other clutter. It looked like they'd been placed there deliberately, bookends and all. They were just as sloppily displayed as the ones on the entry table.

James glanced over his shoulder. The books that had been next to the oil lamps yesterday weren't there. Had Sebastian moved them to the stairs?

"You coming?" Sebastian called from the top landing.

James walked past the books, deciding not to ask about them. Any explanation Sebastian gave would probably annoy him.

The stairs ended at a carpeted landing. Green again. An unattractive choice in James's opinion. The landing surrounded the stairwell on all four sides, complete with a dark wooden railing to keep you from falling. If there hadn't been skylights above the stairs, it'd have been unmanageably dark. There were no other windows, only doors leading to the upstairs rooms. Opposite the stairs was an open arch that looked like it led to a sitting room, though from what James could see, all the drapes were shut.

Sebastian led James to the left, where the hall extended beyond the landing, leaving the minimal light behind. He'd never seen so many shadowy corners in his life. It didn't even look like there were light switches or fixtures along here. He would have to put some in.

James was led into what looked like an office. It smelled musty and was, of course, dark and unwelcoming. Sebastian went straight to the opposite end of the room and threw open the dark drapes, which helped a bit.

"So I'm thinking the desk is a good place to start." Sebastian sat behind it. "There's also lots of papers, folders, and shit over on that shelf." He pointed behind James.

"You really want me going through your personal stuff?"

"It's not my stuff." Sebastian yanked open a drawer without much care for what looked like a quality piece of vintage furniture. "This is all previous Storm junk."

"Still…" James hesitated. "It doesn't feel right to poke around."

Sebastian plopped a pile of papers on the desk. "Your polite intentions have been noted."

"As has your sarcasm." James didn't smile, but Sebastian huffed a laugh anyway. "There's nothing wrong with respecting people's privacy."

Sebastian leaned back in the desk chair, stretching his long legs. "I don't want my privacy respected, so let's just get that out of the way now. Okay?" He batted his lashes.

James turned away, directing his attention to a shelf housing piles of old flat files. "You're impossible."

"Thank you." Sebastian sounded genuinely pleased.

James pushed images of Sebastian's smile from his mind and

opened an old folder that seemed ready to fall apart. It was full of letters. He quickly flicked through them without reading.

"This is useless. It's all correspondence with the lawyer," Sebastian complained after they'd been looking for about ten minutes. "Why did they insist on keeping everything? How could decades-old cash withdrawal receipts be important?"

"I'd say they were important at the time." James set aside more letters and picked up another folder.

"There's too much junk in this house."

"Why not clear it out now that it's yours?" James chanced a glance at Sebastian and found him scowling.

"It's not my job to clean up the previous generations' messes. Just because it was left here doesn't mean I'm obligated."

"Okay." James turned away. Not like he was going to argue. What did he care? All he wanted to do was get his job done.

James grabbed a few more folders and something clinked at the back of the shelf. He reached in without thinking and pulled out a glass jar full of small white—*oh hell*! With a gasp of surprise, he dropped the jar on instinct. It clunked on the thick carpet and thankfully didn't break.

Sebastian appeared at his side, so close their elbows brushed.

"Why the fuck do you have a jar of human teeth laying around?" James asked through tight lips. He wished he hadn't reacted like a squeamish kid, but he couldn't take it back now.

"They aren't *my* teeth," Sebastian said like this somehow made the situation less creepy, which it didn't. "Looks like some great-great—I think it's only two greats—Grandma Storm nonsense."

"She lived here?" James looked away from the teeth, focusing on Sebastian instead.

"Her sons built this place, and she lived here with them. Doubt they're her teeth. They look like baby ones, don't you think?"

"Sure." James poked the jar with his boot. It turned, revealing a faded label on the top bearing two names: *S. Storm* and *N. Storm.* "Why save them?"

"Grandma was into some intense magic, according to Sullivan's journals. Blood and bone, and all that." Sebastian pulled a handkerchief out of his robe pocket and threw it on top of the jar, leaving it on the floor.

Did he not want to touch it? The kind of magic Sebastian had mentioned wasn't anything to joke about or mess with. Dabbling in spells that linked people to magical forces through blood or bone was dangerous.

They stared at the covered jar. James wondered what Sebastian was thinking. He'd never considered the possibility that Storm House had such a haunted atmosphere because of a spell the family had cast or dark magic that had gone wrong. But if the Storm ancestors had saved teeth for spells, anything was possible.

Sebastian picked up the covered jar and placed it back on the shelf. He put the handkerchief back in his pocket, then reconsidered. "Maybe I should wash this off."

James wasn't sure what washing it would do, magically speaking, but he didn't argue. "Is that thing monogrammed?" he asked before he could stop himself.

Sebastian dropped the handkerchief on a side table. "Yeah. Blame Simon Storm for that, not me." He grabbed another folder from the shelf and thrust it into James's hands.

James barely glanced at it, a thought occurring to him. "Was the stationary you used to write to me his too?"

Sebastian shook his head, messy curls getting in his face. "I think my Uncle Stephen ordered the stationary."

There was an awkward pause.

James had an urge to fill the silence and keep Sebastian talking. He didn't seem to mind chatting, which James thought a reclusive person might. "You've all got S names?" He almost smiled at the idea. He'd always liked the name Sebastian.

Sebastian didn't seem pleased by James's question and turned away. "Everyone but my darling sister, Kira." He sounded bitter.

James wasn't sure why and wanted to be encouraging. "Family traditions like that are kind of cool."

Sebastian stiffened, pausing as he looked through the folders on the shelf. "No, they're not." He seemed to be getting upset about something. Maybe he didn't like talking to James after all.

"Sebastian is a much prettier name than Kira. Rolls off the tongue better." James spoke before thinking, only wanting to cheer Sebastian up. His insides fluttered, and he knew it would have been better to keep quiet.

Sebastian turned away from the shelf, a piece of paper falling out of the folder he was holding. "Did you just give me a compliment?"

James squirmed. Sebastian didn't have to make a big deal out of it. "Yeah, I like your name. So what? I compliment people."

"You've never complimented me." Sebastian put a hand to his chest.

James frowned, and for some reason, it took more effort than usual. "Well, when would I have? You keep locking me out of your property. It doesn't put me in the most complimentary mood."

Sebastian seemed to ignore this, the glint in his eye turning devious. "I like the way my name rolls off your tongue too, now that you mention it. I could get used to hearing you say it." He took a step closer.

"Okay." James cleared his throat. "Now that we've established we both like your name, can we find this map?"

"Map?" Sebastian was biting his damned lip again, no doubt holding back laughter.

"Not a map. The plans. You know what I mean." James refused to admit he was flustered and turned his attention to the papers he held. He didn't look up again.

They found the house plans a short time later in a folder with more letters from the Storms' lawyer, or at least their lawyer from eighty years ago.

"Looks like we only have the first floor." James rifled through the rest of the accompanying papers, but none were helpful.

Sebastian flopped onto the couch beside them. A plume of dust wafted up from the cushion. "That might be all there is."

"No problem. Better than nothing." James studied the plans. "I can go around disconnecting everything on the second floor by finding the switches and power points, but having this gives me a better idea of how much work there is. And it might be good for you to take a look and tell me where you want extra outlets put in."

Sebastian wrinkled his nose at the dust still fluffing around him, shooing it with his hands. "I hadn't thought of adding more than what's already here."

It didn't seem like Sebastian had thought of much in relation to this project.

"Homes this old weren't laid out to support all the electrical devices we use now. How about you have a think about what you'll need while I go under the house?"

Sebastian made a face. "Why do you want to go under the house?"

"I don't want to." James handed Sebastian the plans, which he took reluctantly. James pointed to several lines on one of the depictions. "Some of the wiring has been run under there, and it could be good to lay the new stuff down there too, to avoid winding through so many walls in such a big house."

"Right." Sebastian gave him an apprehensive look. "The thing is, I'm pretty sure there are shades in the crawl space. The manor is warded, but I don't think the spells extend past the floorboards. Underneath is technically outside."

Of course there were shades. Damn this place. "I've got my shade-light." James patted the special light on his belt.

Sebastian didn't look convinced.

"I'm not saying you have to come with me," James assured him.

Sebastian's lip curled. "I wasn't going to. Those shifty bastards are territorial."

That struck James as unusual. Shades were transient creatures. They moved between this world and Beyond and didn't stay in one place for long. Moonlight Falls had its fair share of shades, but they were only ever passing through.

"Do the shades give you trouble? You could extend your wards," James suggested.

Sebastian frowned. "*Eh.* I don't know if they can be extended. Unless you're offering to do the spellwork?"

James wasn't. Warding wasn't his specialty, and tackling magic like that, in a place where the energy was all wrong, was a daunting prospect. Extending a warding spell on a house this size would require a lot of energy, maybe more than one person could supply.

Now that James was thinking about it, he realized the anxious sensation he got on the property was absent inside the house. The wards here must be strong, even if they didn't cover the crawl space beneath the house.

That was a relief. James couldn't imagine Sebastian enduring the haunted atmosphere all the time. At least he was saved from some of Storm House's unpleasantness while inside its walls.

CHAPTER FIVE

Sebastian opened a hatch at the side of the house, leading to the crawl space below.

"Feel free to wait inside." James peered into the dark. He'd already double-checked that the power to the house was shut off, even if it wasn't working, and was ready to scope things out.

"I'm good here." Sebastian shivered in the misty rain, droplets clinging to his curls.

James put his hood up. "Suit yourself." He clicked his shade-light on and nothing happened. He tried the button again, but it didn't light up. "Damn."

"Is it not working?" Sebastian asked, sounding almost eager. Did he not want James going under the house? It really wasn't a big deal.

James pressed the charging indicator on the side of the light. None of the little dots lit up. The thing was dead, even though he was sure he'd grabbed it off the charger that morning. Maybe it hadn't been plugged in properly.

"It's fine." James clipped the shade-light back to his belt. He flicked his fingers and said the spell for light. A faint glowing ball appeared, hovering above his hand. "I'll still be able to look around."

James crawled under the house. This was why he'd left his leather jacket in the truck and worn an old hoodie. Dirt and spiderwebs were bound to get all over him.

The space was tall enough for him to crouch in a low squat and walk along. It was better than being on his hands and knees. He'd slipped his work gloves on, but you never knew what could be under a house, broken glass or old rusty metal bits waiting to cut you.

The light floated ahead of him. James hadn't used a light spell like this in years. It wasn't worth the energy when shade-lights were more reliable. He concentrated on maintaining the light and kept the glow low in order not to drain himself.

For a seemingly simple spell, light took a lot of personal energy. James wasn't only using magic to manipulate what was in front of him, like moving air to levitate an object. He was calling the light to him from elsewhere, bringing the sun's rays though negative space to reach him outside the laws of physics.

He was half concentrating on the light as he made his way to where the fuse box was located on the side of the house so he could see the wires coming through into the crawlspace. He couldn't see beyond the area immediately around him and wasn't pleased that the anxious unease the property triggered was back with a vengeance.

James was used to crawling around in tight spaces, not haunted spaces. He hadn't been worried about the potential shades, but now he wondered if they had something to do with Storm House's bad energy. He didn't see how they could. As far as James knew, affecting a place's energy wasn't something shades were capable of, but he didn't really know what was happening at Storm House.

He followed the wires away from the edge of the house,

deeper into the dark. The house creaked, wind whistling through small gaps in the wood. A scuffling sound came from somewhere beyond his sight.

James found the spot where the first lot of wires were sent up through the floor. As he suspected, the whole place was done with the old knob-and-tube method of wiring. Luckily, James could just disconnect it and leave it where it was. He might even run his new stuff in a different pattern. The existing wires didn't seem to have been laid out in the most efficient way.

There was another scuffling sound. Closer this time.

James wasn't scared of shades. They were pests, that was all. However, he didn't usually have to contend with the extra anxiety of being at Storm House. He whispered another spell, ushering his light forward. It floated away, leaving him in darkness but allowing him to see more of the crawl space beyond. There wasn't much down here, only supports for the house and dirt.

A shadow moved in front of his light, blocking it out temporarily. James wasn't surprised. Sebastian had warned him, so he didn't expect the spike of fear that hit him. His skin crawled and a primal part of his brain tried to tell him it was because of the shade he'd just seen, but it wasn't. It had to be the haunted nature of the property getting to him. He wouldn't normally be afraid. Shades were essentially supernatural raccoons.

Okay, they were way more creepy-looking than those little trash bandits, but the basic principle held true: they were both nuisances and were hardly ever dangerous.

The shadow didn't cross the light again, so James decided to move on. He wanted to examine the central line of the house, check that all the wooden beams were in good shape and positioned so he could run things along them. He called the light back to himself and inched his way forward.

There was the scuffling again. The sound was definitely getting closer.

"Can nothing be easy?" he grumbled before increasing the strength of his light.

As more of the space was illuminated, James caught the glint of three sets of eyes peeking out from behind one of the supports. One pair blinked and moved away from the others, coming closer.

It wasn't generally a good thing when a wild animal approached you. This was no different. He didn't want the shades coming too close in such a tight space.

James began to back up, making his way slowly toward the exit while keeping his eyes on the shades. He had no desire to interact directly with the beasts. He wouldn't want to be in a tight space with a raccoon either if he had the choice. Both had grabby little hands and sharp teeth.

At least shades couldn't be rabid.

It was a silly thought, but it triggered something in James's mind, and the unease plaguing him turned to alarm. He became hyperaware of the cold temperature. His heart pounded as the shadow slinked closer. What if the energy at Storm House wasn't the only thing different out here? What if the shades on this land were also altered?

James lost sight of the other two sets of eyes. The shade he could see lunged forward with a woosh and a rush of cold air. James could see its wispy, rail-thin arms and bony hands now. It shifted in the dark, its ghostly form changing and moving unnaturally. Its eyes were shiny black, reflecting the limited light. They blinked at him. Then the thing smiled, showing its pointy onyx teeth.

James sent his light toward it. The shade cringed and backed up, hissing.

Hands grabbed James from behind, icy fingers digging into his arms and neck. Even through his hoodie, he felt the unnatural chill like an electric shock. He gasped, and his haunted-house-induced feelings of alarm turned to panic.

James's concentration broke and his light went out. Another set of hands grabbed his ankles. The shades were clicking their teeth and making whiney hissing sounds. One even emitted a wheezy laugh.

The grip on his ankles was vice-like. The creature yanked him, making him fall on his ass. The other hands began to pull him in the opposite direction, like he was the rope in a game of tug-of-war. James said the words for light, but he faltered, and the spell didn't take.

A sharp twinge of pain pinched his ankle as the sharp points of claws dug into him. This wasn't good, and it wasn't just the house making him unnecessarily scared. Shade didn't usually attack if they weren't provoked.

Sebastian was right. They were territorial.

James thrashed instinctively, trying to shake the shades off. They weren't deterred and kept tugging him from either end. James took a breath, forced himself to concentrate, and cast the spell for light again. This time, he didn't hold back. He pulled as much light to himself as he could.

A blindingly bright flash lit the crawl space, emanating from a point right in front of James's face. He shut his eyes, seeing stars. The shades shrieked and released him instantly. The chill in the air lessened as the shades fled the light, seeking dark corners to hide in. If they couldn't find sufficient darkness or the ball of light made direct contact with their bodies, they would be banished back to Beyond.

James turned over and crawled on his hands and knees. He kept the light behind his head and cracked his eyes open. It was so bright that he could barely see, but he wasn't collected enough to dampen the spell. He didn't need the light going out accidentally.

He made it to the hatch. Once he was an arms-length away, he released his magic and the light went out. He was breathing heavily, exhausted from using so much power all at once. He should have been more careful. He hadn't needed quite that much light, but panic had gotten the better of him.

James popped his head out from under the house. He felt anxious and almost jittery, more scared than he remembered being in years. His sweaty skin prickled as if more shades were watching, lurking, about to grab him. He hated this place. It created all these unjustified emotions, fucked with his head, and caused him to wield magic like an undisciplined child.

"What the hell was that?" Sebastian asked in alarm. "Are you all right?" He reached down, took hold of James's hand, and pulled.

James stood, only to bend forward and rest his hands on his knees to catch his breath. "Shades."

"You drained yourself with that flash-of-fucking-lightning spell."

If James didn't know better, he'd say Sebastian sounded worried. He grunted in response.

Sebastian tugged on his arm. "Come inside."

James straightened and allowed himself to be led into the house. Sebastian took him through a back door into a mud room and then the kitchen. He pushed James into one of the chairs at the small table in the corner.

"I'll be fine." James pulled down his hood and took off his gloves. "I just need to rest for a second."

He hadn't completely drained himself. Not even close. He still had plenty of energy left. He'd just used too much too abruptly and needed a nap, maybe some food. Too bad he couldn't curl up and shut his eyes while on a job. He would be useless for the rest of the day, even for nonmagical things.

A glass of water appeared in front of him. "I won't say I told you so."

James grunted again, hoping it showed his displeasure. He picked up the water and drank it all in one long swallow.

"They don't like anyone going down there," Sebastian continued. "I had some feral cats living at the front of the house for a while, under the steps, but the shades chased them off."

Sebastian sounded almost sad about it, like he missed the cats. James didn't have the energy to comment.

"How about a snack?" Sebastian didn't wait for James to answer before turning toward the counter.

The kitchen was a lot more cheerful than the rest of the house. The cupboards had been painted a soft shade of pink rather than the horrible dark green that covered the rest of the place. There were white tiles under foot and light marble countertops. Flowers were arranged on the table and in vases around the room.

A large cast iron stove sat opposite the table with a basket of firewood beside it. James looked at the kitchen more closely. There was no refrigerator, microwave, or coffee maker. Obviously, the power didn't work, but James had assumed Sebastian had a battery-operated generator to run basic things off of since he'd apparently been living here for a while.

Sebastian was taking cookies out of a tin and putting them on a plate. He grabbed an apple from a fruit bowl and, after a moment of consideration, opened a jar labeled *Nuts* and added a handful of almonds to the plate.

He brought everything over to James. "Want some apple cider?"

"Um." James popped an almond in his mouth and chewed. "Sure. Unless you still have lemonade?" Either would be good for sugar to help perk him up.

"I drank all the lemonade." Sebastian looked down at him, frowning slightly. He turned and disappeared through a door leading off the kitchen without another word.

James ate the almonds quickly, then moved on to the apple. He eyed a line of ten identical jars of peppers on the counter. They all sported handwritten labels, making it look like Sebastian did his own pickling.

Sebastian returned with a bottle of cider, again looking like something homemade rather than anything bought at the store. "It's better warm, if that sounds good?"

"Yeah, thanks." James put down his apple core, already feeling better, his mind clearer. It probably helped to be back in the warded house, away from the emotion-altering effects of the rest of the property.

Sebastian brought the bottle over to a stovetop built into the counter. He lit a match, then turned a knob, lighting the gas with the flame. He blew out the match and poured the contents of the bottle into a small pot, setting it on the stove to heat.

"What?" Sebastian crossed his arms and leaned against the counter.

"Nothing." James glanced around the kitchen again. "You don't have a generator?"

Sebastian narrowed his eyes. "What for?"

Wasn't it obvious? "So you can hook up a fridge and a coffee machine."

"I have a French press." Sebastian gestured to the press sitting by the sink next to a jar labeled *Coffee*.

That was so not the point. "I know generators aren't cheap. The ones with the decent batteries anyway." James paused, not sure how blunt he wanted to be. Sebastian had implied he wasn't worried about the cost of rewiring the house earlier, so surely he could afford to run a fridge and a few small things.

"Do you sell generators at Gray Electrical?" Sebastian turned back to the stove and stirred the cider with a wooden spoon.

"We can order pretty much anything in, but we do have a small one in stock."

"Bring it by."

"Okay, sure," James said carefully. "But why didn't you do that before now? Haven't you been living here a while?"

Sebastian faced him, his expression tight. "I've been here for six years."

"And you haven't figured any of this out?" James's voice rose in disbelief.

Sebastian stared at him, the tension thickening between them. Maybe he was offended at James casting judgment on the way he lived.

"I've hired you to fix the place, haven't I?" Sebastian returned his attention to the cider. "You can sell me a generator too, if you want. But it's not like I haven't managed without it."

But why manage? Why settle if he had the means to afford modern conveniences? What else was going on with Sebastian? It seemed like he was avoiding more than people, hiding out here in this unbearable place.

Sebastian took two mugs out of a cabinet and poured the cider. He brought them both to the table and sat opposite James.

"Thanks." James picked up his steaming mug. Scents of cinnamon, allspice, and sweet apple made his mouth water.

Sebastian assessed James over his own mug, lines crinkling around his eyes. All traces of his previous tension seemed to have disappeared. "Are you feeling better?"

"I'm tired but not about to fall over or anything." James sipped his drink. "Oh, that's good."

"Thanks." Sebastian looked down at the table, almost like the praise made him shy.

James had another sip. "You made it from scratch?"

"Yeah. There are trees out back. Apples, pears, apricots, *lemons*." He looked up with a pointed stare.

"Now I wish I hadn't turned down the lemonade. Should have said it was homemade."

Sebastian *hmphed*. "Eat your cookies."

James obeyed, picking one up. He still had a way to go in restoring his energy, and eating more, sooner rather than later, was always best in these situations. The cookies were peanut butter. He ate the first one in two bites and picked up another.

"I have more, so don't hold back." Sebastian sounded amused, and James thought he caught the hint of a smile hidden behind his mug.

"I love peanut butter cookies." James ate another.

"Me too." Sebastian got up and grabbed the tin, bringing it to the table. "Here. Eat them all. I'll just make more."

James swallowed. "You're good at baking. And cider making."

"Thanks." Sebastian looked away again, staring off into space.

James ate most of the cookies. He felt silly for freaking out about the shades and was glad Sebastian hadn't hassled him. Sebastian was a good man. He had taken good care of James, who would recover from his magical overuse more quickly after the array of snacks, even without a nap.

James found he wanted to do what he could to take care of Sebastian in return. He didn't understand the guy and still found him aggravating most of the time, but he didn't like that Sebastian didn't seem to have anyone looking out for him. There might be a reason he lived out here, avoiding people and not trying very hard to take care of the problems at his house. But James didn't need an explanation to know the situation with Sebastian was likely complicated and Sebastian probably needed somebody.

If Sebastian was okay with accepting help with the house from James, that had to be a good sign. It wasn't his business why Sebastian hadn't gotten things together sooner. He was doing it now, and James would make sure he was taken care of. If that included staying for a chat over lemonade, he could do that too.

James didn't usually get this concerned about his customers, but this was an unusual case. James wouldn't get attached or anything. He didn't exactly want to be friends with Sebastian. He just didn't want the guy to be in the dark without a fridge and no one to talk to. He wanted to make sure the isolation wasn't hurting Sebastian and wasn't a sign of something more serious that might need addressing.

Sebastian had said the community support of Moonlight Falls never seemed to extend to him. James was going to make sure that changed. That was all. It had nothing to do with the unexpected warm feeling he got while sitting at the table with the man.

CHAPTER SIX

JAMES LAID out a plan for the rest of the job and gave Sebastian a quote. It was more of a hassle than usual because his phone had died, so he couldn't use the calculator or double-check material prices, but Sebastian didn't seem to need more than a ballpark estimate. He said to send the bill to his lawyer and handed James a business card.

James disconnected the fuse box and some of the outlets on the first floor before leaving. It wasn't a bad effort, considering he was still yearning to lie down. He'd bet anything he'd sleep hard that night, but not before a big dinner. He was already starving, even after the snacks he'd had.

He made a mental note to bring a hell of a lot more shade-lights for the next time he went under the house. He wouldn't be caught off guard again.

"Do you mind walking me out?" James asked Sebastian when he was done for the day. He hadn't needed to get his truck after all, sticking to his screwdriver and other small tools, so it was still down by the road.

Sebastian bounced up from the chair he'd been sitting in while watching James work. "Sure, I can be a gentleman."

James snorted. "As long as gentlemen unlock gates."

Sebastian made an exasperated face. "Oh, right. The gate."

He'd stayed close to James the whole time he'd been working. This would have annoyed James, but he hadn't had the energy that afternoon. Sebastian had watched everything he'd done, chatting and teasing almost constantly. He kept making suggestive remarks about also being good with his hands and wanting to see James handle *other* things with such attention to detail. The comments had been more ridiculous than serious and had made James laugh.

It hadn't been terrible.

The two of them made their way down the driveway, the mist as wet and unpleasant as it'd been all afternoon. James couldn't help thinking how dark it would be out here in less than an hour.

"You sure you don't want to check the bed and breakfast for a spare room?" James asked as Sebastian unlocked the chain.

"Beyond sure." Sebastian opened the gate and faced James.

He couldn't really argue with that, but he was overcome with the desire not to leave Sebastian here. "What about dinner? Come to the diner with me and grab a meal. I can give you a ride back home."

After all the teasing and silly, flirty remarks, James figured he'd set himself up to be playfully accused of asking Sebastian on a date. Not that he'd intended the offer to be a date or anything.

But Sebastian didn't smile at the offer, flutter his lashes, or do any of the things he'd been doing all afternoon. He closed his eyes for a moment, his face tightening with what looked like anger. His eyes snapped open, and he glared at James, his cheeks darkening with color. "I don't want to go into town, okay?"

"Why not?" James was totally confused, a renewed sense of exhaustion overtaking him.

"I just don't want to." Sebastian's voice rose. He clutched his robe tightly around himself, knuckles going white. "I don't like town and don't want to see the damn people that live there. I don't want to go to the diner. I don't need to."

"Sorry." James put up his hands in surrender.

It was easy to forget Sebastian didn't want people around when he'd been teasing and friendly. James wondered if Sebastian had some sort of social phobia. Whatever it was, it wasn't a joke or an act, not with the way Sebastian was glaring. He must really be more comfortable out here, alone, than anywhere else.

After a long moment, the glare lessened. "It's okay." Sebastian took a breath with apparent effort. The rest of his anger seemed to fade. "I just can't— I'm not going into town. I'm not."

"Got it. I won't ask again," James assured him.

Sebastian nodded, looking toward a part of the property James hadn't been to. His face crumpled into a sudden and surprisingly heartbroken expression. It yanked at James's heart, and for a second, James swore he detected something deeply relatable in the look, but he had no idea why.

Sadness wasn't something James could fix for Sebastian, but he was surprised to find he wished it were possible. He usually only felt that way about Eli, wanting to save his brother from any possible pain or heartache. But, of course, he'd want to do everything he could for Eli. Why did he suddenly feel that way toward Sebastian?

Sebastian was attractive, but that wasn't enough to make James care like this, and it wasn't like he had a crush. He couldn't stand Sebastian a lot of the time. Unless it wasn't really annoyance and he was just trying to push his own feelings away, cover them up with grumbling complaints.

James was usually good at that.

He'd have to try harder. Everyone James cared about made his life better but also caused him stress. Sometimes, he worried irrationally about Eli and even about Hazel and Parker, who were more put-together than him and needed no one's worries. James couldn't handle getting attached to Sebastian as well.

It was why he never dated or allowed himself to develop crushes. He couldn't find happiness in loving someone if it was overshadowed by his fear of losing them, and even if he could handle his fear—he had gotten better at it—that didn't mean he wouldn't lose his partner. Tragedies happened all the time, and James couldn't cope with any more, so he didn't risk adding people to his life.

James was suddenly overcome with anger at having to be at Storm House, in these woods, down this road. He walked through the gate to escape the horrible feeling of the property, but it barely helped. He didn't want to drive through this forest right now. He didn't need the reminder of his loss.

His parents had died in a car accident out here when he was fourteen and Eli was ten. He and his brother had been at their grandparents' house that weekend while his parents visited friends in Oregon. It was lucky they hadn't been in the car with their mom and dad, but James didn't like that they had died out here alone.

"Can you please not lock me out tomorrow?" James asked over his shoulder as he unlocked his truck.

"Fine. If you insist, I'll open the gate in the morning." Sebastian closed the gate, peering through the bars, then, after a pause, said, "You should get tater tots."

"What?" James turned, leaning against his open door. The random comment almost drove the melancholy from his mind.

"From the diner." Sebastian fiddled with the lock. "They're the best."

"Okay, yeah." James was baffled and not sure why Sebastian would suggest he order tater tots after how upset he'd been with the invitation to join James at the diner.

Sebastian only nodded and looked away. James got in his truck and drove off before Sebastian finished relocking the gate.

JAMES HAD plans to meet Eli and Hazel for dinner, so it was probably a good thing Sebastian hadn't wanted to tag along. James was glad his brother didn't mind going to the diner in his free time. It was the only real restaurant in Moonlight Falls, and James had never been enthusiastic about hanging out at the town's bar.

James stopped by home to change out of his work clothes and take a quick shower. The shades had given him a few shallow puncture wounds on his ankles and upper arms, so he washed them and put on some antiseptic ointment. They weren't much more than scratches. The sharp pain he'd felt at the time must have been due to panic and the force of the shades grip more than breaking his skin.

Eli wasn't home and the house was quiet. James had always liked their grandparents' old house, but it was much nicer to live in now that Eli was back. It had felt empty during the years James had lived there alone. He couldn't imagine what being in a place like Storm House by himself would be like. Even discounting the creepy dreariness—which you couldn't—the sheer size of the *manor* would have left James feeling like he was bouncing around in a void, and he hadn't even seen a quarter of the place yet.

Hazel and Eli were already in a booth when James arrived at the diner. Eli had his map out again and was pointing things out to Hazel as she nursed an iced tea. The diner was busy but not packed. Since it was Friday night, James had no doubt it would be soon. A group of kids in the next booth were levitating sugar packets and shooting them at each other. Behind them was a family with two toddlers coloring on placemats.

"Have you ever known shades to be territorial?" James asked as he sat and grabbed a menu off the table.

Hazel set down her tea. "Do they even have territories?"

"Yeah, they're not wolves." Eli laughed.

James eyed his brother. "I know, but you're sure you've never heard anything like that? No cases of shades guarding certain places?"

Eli gave him a confused look. "No. I mean, I don't study supernatural entities, but they're pretty well known to be transitory. Right?"

"Yeah, that's my understanding too." Hazel picked up her menu but didn't look at it. "Why the sudden interest?"

James told them about his afternoon and detailed what happened with the shades under Storm House.

"They weren't necessarily being territorial." Eli began folding his map. "Sounds like they were fucking with you. Which is pretty typical, and even them being aggressive and initiating physical contact isn't a total surprise with the way things have been going in town lately."

At the time, it had felt like the shades had gone after him for being under the house and were trying to chase him off, but now, James wasn't sure. "Sebastian seemed to think these particular shades had been living under the house for a while."

"How would he know?" Eli's confidence didn't waver. "It's more likely he saw shades under there once and they moved on, only for more to turn up."

It was hard to tell individual shades apart. Still, James couldn't shake the feeling Sebastian knew what he was talking about, even in the face of Eli's logic. "I don't know. Something felt weird about it." Unless that had just been the bad energy at the property.

Hazel crossed her arms, menu abandoned. "What happened to you today, unfortunately, sounds like more of what we've already been seeing."

"Yeah, this sounds similar to the shade attacking me behind

the diner. Though not as violent," Eli said quietly, leaning in. "It's not good if incidents like this are becoming more common."

Until now, Eli getting attacked had been an extreme outlier of an incident, which was why James hadn't worried the beasts would attack him before he'd gone under the house. But if the shades today weren't being territorial, their going after him could easily be in line with the shift in their general behavior that had been seen over the last couple of months.

James focused on his brother. "You're right. It's not good if they're moving from scaring people to going after them, especially with more shades around. You haven't found anything in your research to explain why things are changing, have you?"

Eli shook his head. "Having so many shades in Moonlight Falls is actually strange in itself, considering what I know about the vein in town. Shifting veins of power create the passages that allow shades to slip from Beyond into our world. The vein here is fixed. It doesn't move at all, so the energy isn't right for passing between."

Hazel took another sip of her tea. "Couldn't there be a shifting vein out in the woods?"

Eli shrugged. "That's my theory. No one's recorded any evidence, but the forest is huge, especially when you count the logging land and national park. It's not surprising we don't know exactly what's going on with magic out there."

James tapped his menu, thinking. "A shifting vein out in the woods wouldn't have anything to do with the haunted energy at Storm House, would it?"

"No, I doubt it." Eli unfolded his map again. "Storm House is pretty far out, but not *that* remote. I'd say any potential passages the shades are using are way out here." He pointed to a vast expanse of trees with no road access. "Though, if I'm right, it's still interesting that so many of them come all the way to Moonlight Falls."

They ordered food after that. James chose the cheeseburger and added extra fries rather than tater tots. He planned on having pie for dessert and was already looking forward to bed.

A shout came from outside. James and his companions turned quickly to the window beside them.

Hazel pointed. "The light in front of the ice cream shop is out."

There was another yell. The three hurried out of the booth and exited the diner. Across the street, people huddled inside the ice cream shop, visible through the front windows. A shade was outside, pressing itself to the glass front door, hissing.

Eli pulled a flashlight out of his pocket and turned it on. It was like the light James had intended to use under the house that afternoon and had an extra-bright setting for shades. Eli pointed the beam directly at the shade's back. It screeched and shot off into the darkness beside the shop. Eli followed it with the light until it flew up into the night sky and disappeared.

The people in the ice cream shop looked like tourists. They came for the supernatural tours, but they freaked out the moment a shade caught them unaware. It didn't seem like anything worse than a dropped ice cream cone had happened, which was a relief after what had happened to Eli and in light of James's earlier incident.

"I don't know why the light is out." Hazel frowned up at it.

James could understand her frustration. They'd installed new ones along this street just recently and shouldn't be experiencing faults so soon.

"Look." Eli pointed his shade-light beam upward. The bulb above the shop had been smashed.

"The shade did it." A man came out of the ice cream shop now that the coast was clear. "Swooped in and crashed right into it, then came after us in the dark."

James wanted to argue. There was no way a shade would dive

straight into a bright light source. They never tried to fight the light, just ran from it, seeking the safety of shadows, but the shade had been pressed against the glass even when the shop was bright inside. It shouldn't have been doing that either.

Was this another worrying new behavior or a fluke? Whatever was changing, James didn't like it at all.

CHAPTER SEVEN

James slept like a dead man and woke up feeling good. It was later than he'd planned to get up, but he'd purposely not set an alarm. His body had needed rest, and he'd been determined to give it however much it wanted.

Gray Electrical's storefront was closed on the weekends, so James had the whole day to work on rewiring Storm House. Before heading out, he stopped by the shop to pick up the generator for Sebastian. James even had an old mini fridge in his garage, which he'd already loaded into his truck.

He checked all his shade-lights were charged and working before locking the shop and heading out. As his truck idled in the driveway, James had an idea. He turned right instead of left and drove around the town center to park at the back of the diner.

Inside, Parker greeted him at the counter. "Should I be worried you're back so soon? I can't seem to keep you away."

James huffed. "Says the man who practically lives here."

Parker grinned. "Yes, but it's my job."

"And you love it because everyone in town is always stopping by." James matched Parker's grin. "Can I get a coffee and an order of tater tots to go?"

"Breakfast of champions." Parker laughed.

"Something like that," James muttered. The coffee was for him, but the tater tots were for Sebastian. Not that he was about to explain this to Parker, who'd only read something into it and assume it meant more than it did.

Every so often, Parker encouraged James to date. They'd become friends when James moved back to town. Parker was several years older, so they hadn't crossed paths when they were young, but that wasn't a bad thing. When James had come home after his grandma passed away, it had been nice for him to get to know someone new, who was also a Moonlighter. The two saw eye to eye on most things except dating. Parker had never understood James's reluctance to meet people and seek romantic connections.

The last thing James needed was Parker thinking there was any meaning behind him bringing Sebastian some tater tots.

The cab of James's truck smelled pleasantly of coffee and fried potato as he drove out of town, a takeout box full to bursting on his passenger seat. He sipped his coffee. If the gate was locked, he'd sit in his truck and eat all the tots himself.

Turned out he didn't have to. The gate was wide open when James pulled up. For some reason, it made him smile. He drove all the way in and parked next to the front porch.

The front door was open as well, giving him a glimpse of the shadowy entryway. It made the house look even creepier than usual, like it really was abandoned. James tried to ignore his unease. It was just the property's energy fucking with him.

He left his empty coffee cup in the cab and grabbed the warm box of tots, hoping Sebastian wouldn't think the gesture was weird. Surely, bringing him food he'd said he liked from the diner was fine—normal—just a friendly thing to do.

He was overthinking it, almost as if Parker's hypothetical analysis of James's actions wasn't completely irrelevant.

Piano music wafted out of the house as James climbed the

front steps. It sounded eerie, but again, maybe that was the haunted atmosphere ruining things.

James paused on the threshold. "Hello?"

The music didn't stop. He assumed Sebastian hadn't heard him and walked in. The sound seemed to be coming from the back of the house, so he headed that way, down the hall to the left, leading toward the kitchen.

He wasn't sure exactly where he was going and wasn't entirely comfortable snooping around, but Sebastian had made a point of saying not to respect his privacy. It was a curious request. Still, James tried to comply and not let himself feel like he was barging in.

He passed the kitchen and turned down a dark hallway, following the music. There was a partially open door at the end. James pushed it wide and paused. The room before him was massive and mostly empty. He wanted to call the space a ballroom, even if he had no idea why anyone would want something like that in their home.

Large windows lined the far wall, letting in enough light for the space not to be dim. The floor was polished wood, not that the room had passed up the opportunity to sport the dark green found everywhere else. The ornate ceiling had been painted in it, as had the walls.

Sebastian was sitting at a piano in the corner by the window, facing away from the door. The music he played sounded less eerie now. The piece seemed well-practiced, the notes blending together perfectly.

James took a moment to watch the small, graceful movements of Sebastian's arms, the way he leaned in and out with the notes. It was captivating. A light fluttering spread through James's chest.

He forced his gaze away from Sebastian. The piano itself was beautiful and appeared well cared for, unlike many other things in the house. It was big, maybe a grand piano, not that James knew much about instruments. The top was closed and something sat on it in a place that struck James as strange.

"You can come in." Sebastian's hands didn't stop moving as he spoke.

James walked across the ballroom, his steps echoing. "Felt me staring, did you?" He belatedly realized how awkward it was to admit he'd been watching Sebastian, but he couldn't take it back now.

Sebastian stopped playing with a laugh. "No, I smelled"—he sniffed the air—"something yummy and fried."

Sebastian spun around so he was sitting backward on the piano bench. James held out the container, and Sebastian took the box as if it were something delicate, slowly opening the lid. His eyes went wide and he smiled, showing James those lovely dimples.

"You got me tater tots."

"Yep." James shoved his hands in his jacket pockets, trying not to echo Sebastian's wide smile or give away how happy he was to have inspired it. "You said you liked them, so…" He left it at that.

Sebastian popped a tot in his mouth and chewed slowly, savoring it. "I'm in love."

"What? That wasn't—" James stumbled over his words, happiness twisting and turning in his gut, mixing with discomfort. "That's not— It's only potato."

Sebastian threw his head back and laughed. "Oh my god, *panic*. You should see your face right now."

"Yeah, well, yours looks pretty silly too." Only this wasn't true. Sebastian looked gorgeous and full of light. He wasn't in his robe today. Instead, he wore a black button-up shirt that fit him well, paired with dark-wash jeans and polished shoes.

Sebastian ate another tot, giving James a challenging look. "If that's what you think, you must like silly."

Not usually, but James liked this side of Sebastian and couldn't seem to deny it, even to himself. He was disproportionally pleased Sebastian was enjoying his treat, even if no one should be that overjoyed by rapidly cooling diner food. "I'm glad one of us is enjoying themselves." He attempted to grumble, but it hadn't come out that way.

"Me too." Sebastian licked his fingers and hummed in apparent satisfaction.

James looked away.

The thing sitting oddly on the piano was an array of familiar books held up by book ends. Why the hell were they here? James was sure they were the same ones that had been on the stairs. Did Sebastian tote them around the house? James could see the titles better this time. They were leatherbound copies of the classic children's stories: *The Magical Tales*.

"Your favorites?" James gestured to the books. Only six out of the typical seven volumes were there.

"Not at all." Sebastian made a disgusted face. "Never liked the whiney characters. You?"

"I always found them a bit boring," James admitted.

Sebastian laughed before eating another tot. "I thought morality tales would be right up your alley, James Gray."

James's gut twinged. "Just because I followed the rules doesn't mean I was a boring kid." Or a boring adult. He turned his back on Sebastian and the books. Why were they here if Sebastian didn't like the stories? Was it just to set Sebastian up to make that jab at him? He'd thought they were starting to get along better than that.

"No..." Sebastian paused like he was considering. "You aren't boring at all. That wasn't what I meant. You're just very *good*."

James found himself flustered again, not sure what Sebastian's tone meant. It didn't sound like a compliment, but it hadn't felt like an insult either. He decided to let Sebastian eat in peace. He was impossible to decipher, and James didn't need to give himself a headache trying.

Instead, he inspected the rest of the ballroom. More instruments lined the wall beside the door, with chairs interspersed among them, almost like the space was a music classroom waiting for students to show up. Most of the instruments were in cases, except a drum kit and a few guitars. There were even stands holding sheet music off to the side.

"Wanna join my band?" Sebastian asked.

James snorted. "You wouldn't want me to. I'd make you cry."

"I thought you were good at everything."

James turned to face Sebastian, brow furrowed. The comment bothered him as much as the last one had. James couldn't deny he'd had a goodie-goodie reputation as a teenager. Was Sebastian holding on to some bitterness about that, or did it amuse him? And why would he care now? It was all silly. James was far from perfect. The only thing he'd really been good at when he was young was swimming.

"No one's good at everything," he said defensively. "Fixing electrical problems is my only talent these days." He was still a decent swimmer, but he only did it for exercise a few times a week at the rec center.

There was a pause. The only sound was the crunch of tater tots.

"I can't play most of those," Sebastian admitted, gesturing toward the instruments with a tot. "Not that it stops me."

Maybe James was being too touchy. Sebastian liked to tease him, that was all this was, and for the most part, James enjoyed it. He wanted to play along. "If that's the case, I'm glad I arrived while you were at the piano."

Sebastian snorted another laugh. "You're funny today."

James held back his smile. "It's not raining, and it's the weekend. I'm easy to please."

"Come on, now you're just setting me up." Sebastian pointed at him in accusation. "Like I haven't thought of *several* ways to please you, and now you're telling me it should be easy."

James made a shooing gesture with his hand, his grin

breaking through. He turned back toward the door. "Eat your tots. I'll go set up the generator."

Sebastian followed James out of the ballroom. Of course he was going to continue to watch his every move. James hadn't expected any different.

"If you want some of these, speak now. Otherwise, I'm eating them all," Sebastian warned as they crossed the front porch.

"I'm good. Knock yourself out."

"Best. Day. Of. The. Year." Sebastian hopped down the steps and then spun around gleefully, managing not to spill any of his tater tots.

"Wait until we have the generator going. Then it'll really be the best day." James went around the back of his truck and opened the bed. He was in a good mood, like something had warmed his soul. He liked the feeling.

James wasn't annoyed that Sebastian ate his tots and watched him unload the generator and mini fridge without offering to help. James used a bit of magic to levitate the heavy objects, so it wasn't like he needed a hand lifting anything, and he didn't mind if Sebastian wanted to hang out. He'd rather that than Sebastian hiding off in a room alone, and okay, *maybe* Sebastian's company was growing on him.

Not one to use magic unnecessarily, James used a dolly to wheel everything around to the back of the house by the kitchen. A Nelson battery-powered generator didn't create exhaust, but he still had to set it up outside.

He ran a cable through a window to where he'd set the fridge in the kitchen. "I can wire it properly later if you want. But once the house is done, you'll only need the generator for emergencies."

"Whatever you say." Sebastian tossed the empty tot container into his recycling bin. "My stomach is too full to care about anything."

"Don't know why your stomach would care about the generator, but all right."

"Stop making me laugh." Sebastian giggled. "I'm going to burst."

The joke hadn't been that funny, but James found himself laughing along with Sebastian as he flipped the switch on the generator.

The things were quiet, but not this quiet, and the indicator light hadn't come on. *Seriously?* James flipped the switch off and on again. "You're not telling me I dragged this all the way out here and it's broken."

"What's wrong?" Sebastian came closer, their arms almost touching.

"It's not turning on, but the damn thing is new. The battery should be full, ready to run that fridge for a month."

Sebastian didn't say anything.

James wondered if maybe the switch was broken. That he could fix. It also made more sense than the generator being faulty. Nelson was known for quality, and magic didn't lose its charge the way mundane batteries did.

He unscrewed the panel covering the switch and checked it out. Everything seemed fine. James went back to his truck to grab his toolbox, though he wasn't sure there was more he could do. He took out his digital multimeter, but it wouldn't turn on either. "What the hell?" James's good mood slowly turned to frustration.

Sebastian just watched as if he were fascinated.

There was one more way to check the battery's charge. James opened the generator and examined it with his magic. He should be able to sense the trapped magical energy, instead there was nothing.

"It's completely drained." James turned to Sebastian, who was grinning like this was good news. A prickle of annoyance crept up on James. He didn't understand Sebastian at all. He shouldn't be pleased by this. "What's that look for?"

"What look?" Sebastian beamed.

James began closing up the generator. "That sly little smile. Is this some sort of joke?"

"What kind of joke could it possibly be?"

"I don't know." James took a breath. It wasn't like Sebastian knew the generator would be broken. But he seemed to have a devious streak. He liked messing with James and laughing at him. That was probably all this was: entertainment for Sebastian. He hadn't cared about setting up a generator, even if James had no idea why, so maybe it not working was funny to Sebastian rather than disappointing.

Sebastian poked at the toolbox with his toe. "Can't you recharge the battery?"

"Yeah, but I'll have to take it to the pumps at Gray's." James loaded it onto the dolly and took it back to his truck.

Recharging magical batteries could only be done using the master fuel cells inside filling station pumps. James and Hazel performed refilling spells, drawing the power out of the fuel cell and placing it into customers' batteries, but the spell was useless on its own. It was all part of how Nelson Power kept control of its products. Only the company knew how to create and recharge the fuel cells, and only they could train and license refilling technicians to use them.

James tried not to be too annoyed with the generator's failure and got on with the rest of his work. Disconnecting all the existing wires was time-consuming, and James figured Sebastian had to be getting bored watching him. They weren't talking much, but James still didn't mind his presence, especially when he started going into rooms he hadn't been in yet.

On the first floor, there was a receiving room, a billiards room, and a magical study full of jars and boxes James didn't want to inspect too closely. Especially not after the teeth incident.

There was a lot of green wallpaper. Too much, in James's opinion.

At the back of the house, next to the kitchen, was a sun room, or conservatory if you wanted to be fancy. There was no power in that room, just a bunch of house plants and wicker furniture covered in soft cushions and blankets. The sun room matched the kitchen, painted the same soft pink. It was more friendly than the rest of the house. A room James could actually imagine Sebastian relaxing in.

They were in what Sebastian called the front parlor when James suggested they put on some music.

"Sure." Sebastian's indifferent response came from where he lay on a green-and-gold couch, staring at the ceiling.

"Any requests?" James pulled his phone out of his pocket.

"Whatever's hot these days."

James went to unlock his phone. The screen stayed black. "Oh, come on." It was dead.

"You didn't charge it?" Sebastian asked, something odd in his tone.

"I did." James put the phone back in his pocket. He was sure he'd charged it, but he'd been so tired last night that maybe he'd forgotten.

He turned away from the socket he was disconnecting to find Sebastian watching him. It wasn't with the casual air of compan-ionship he'd felt earlier. Sebastian seemed to be waiting for something. His eyes were fixed on James, his expression serious. It was almost creepy.

"Is there something you're not telling me?"

Sebastian's demeanor didn't change. "Like what?"

James wasn't sure what. He just knew something felt off, and it couldn't be the haunted atmosphere affecting him when he was inside the wards. "What are you waiting for?"

Sebastian blinked. "I'm not waiting. I'm watching." His tone seemed flat and unnatural.

James missed Sebastian's usual flirty teasing. This version of him was almost chilling. What was Sebastian playing at? James thought he'd done something good with the tater tots, gained some nice rapport. He even thought he'd built something more between them, his feelings for Sebastian growing warm. They were cold now. James had the sense he'd been tricked somehow but wasn't sure why.

He turned back to the wall, moving to the last switch in the room that needed disconnecting. He used his screwdriver to remove the fixture.

Sebastian continued silently watching him.

CHAPTER EIGHT

James finished disconnecting the wires on the first floor and moved to the second. There was no power in the hallway or landing, so he started with the sitting room he'd seen from the stairs.

James circled the room. There were no switches, no light fixtures hanging from the ceiling, and no outlets. "Did they not run power to this room?"

Sebastian shrugged. "It's only on the first floor."

James ran a hand through his hair in frustration. "Why not tell me that before now?"

Sebastian didn't say anything. He didn't even shrug or dismiss the question, just ignored it.

"Why wouldn't they install power up here?" James pressed, trying to get a reaction.

Sebastian continued to stare. It was freaking James out.

"I just want you to fix it," Sebastian said after a while, his voice quiet. It didn't sound teasing or annoyed. It was like he was upset. But about what?

"Yeah, all right." James rubbed his eyes. "That's the plan, and it hasn't changed." He would take care of Sebastian, even if he didn't understand anything about the man's actions.

James went back downstairs, trailed by his silent host. He wished they hadn't lost the banter from that morning and didn't know how to get it back. Sebastian's playful happiness was nowhere in sight. James reminded himself that he wasn't here to figure Sebastian out, but the strange turn had James worried.

Since he couldn't do anything about Sebastian, James decided to install the new circuit breaker panel. He selected a new location, in the mudroom off the kitchen rather than outside. He'd have to cut a hole in the wall, so he measured, marking things out in pencil.

Sebastian watched from the doorway, arms crossed.

James ignored him for now. He grabbed his reciprocating saw and flicked it on. Nothing happened. This time, James's annoyance was tinged with unease. He looked back at Sebastian, who only stared, unmoving.

The saw shouldn't be dead. James knew it had been fully charged when he'd left the shop that morning. He disconnected the battery pack and tossed it in his toolbox, then grabbed the one off his drill. All his tools were the same model and had interchangeable batteries, but this one was dead too. Just to be sure the saw itself wasn't the problem, James hooked the battery pack onto the drill. It wouldn't turn on either.

James put the tools down and faced Sebastian. "Why does nothing work?"

Sebastian didn't answer the question. Instead, he fixed his gaze on James with fierce concentration, like he was trying to see inside him.

"Why are all my batteries drained?" James couldn't keep the strain from his voice.

Sebastian made an annoyed sound. He closed his eyes momentarily.

James gave in to frustration. "Can you not speak all of the sudden?"

"I can *speak*," Sebastian snapped, his eyes almost bugging out of his head when they flew open.

"So what aren't you saying? What the fuck is up with all my tools? My phone?"

"I hired you," Sebastian said slowly, almost like it pained him. "To fix things for me."

"And I'm trying to." James took a breath. "But it doesn't seem like you've told me the extent of the problem."

Sebastian's eyes flashed. His scowl turned into a grin. It was manic and really not helping James feel good about the situation.

James began to gather his things, leaving the bits for the circuit board where they were. "I'm going to go back to town, get some battery packs with full charges, refill the generator, and be back."

"Sure." Sebastian didn't seem to care. All of his intensity was gone.

James stalked to his truck and put his things in the back. He got in the cab and pushed the ignition button on the dash. Maybe he should have seen it coming, but he couldn't quite believe it when the truck didn't start.

He pushed the button again, irate at what the day had become.

James got out of his truck and slammed the door. Sebastian watched from the porch steps, looking almost eager. James popped the hood of his truck and scoped out the battery with his magic. He should have detected a near-full charge, tons of magical energy stored inside. Instead, it was completely drained.

Everything was dead, but how could that be? James checked every device he had, every shade-light. Nothing would turn on. What the hell was going on today?

He thought back to his previous visits. He hadn't actually used more than a screwdriver before, and his truck had been outside the gated property. James couldn't remember checking his phone on the property before today, other than when he'd gone to use the calculator app and the phone had been dead.

He turned to find Sebastian watching him like James was down to the last second of an important race, anticipation etched into Sebastian's fine features as he waited to see how it would end.

James narrowed his eyes. "You knew this would happen."

Sebastian didn't respond to James's tight words.

"Something is draining all the power out of everything. That's why you don't have a generator." James scowled as it all fell into place. "It's this fucking house. This property. It's sucking everything dry."

Sebastian let out a loud whoop and his hands shot into the air like his team had just won. He jumped off the steps, hopping around like this moment was everything.

James's mouth fell open in shock.

Sebastian began to laugh hysterically, and it freaked James the fuck out. He didn't think Sebastian was completely well and probably shouldn't be out here all alone. Isolation wasn't healthy. Sebastian needed help, *something*, someone other than James to address whatever was going on.

Unless he was wrong and Sebastian was fucking around playing games with him for his own amusement—in which case, screw this—but it really did seem like Sebastian's behavior was something he couldn't help. In that case, it would be better for James to be kind right now than to bite the man's head off for luring him here and lying about what was going on. At least until James knew if there was anything malicious behind Sebastian's actions.

"Sebastian." James took a step toward where Sebastian was doubled over laughing.

"Fuck." Sebastian sucked in a lungful of air and straightened, sweeping his long curls back from his face. "Want some lunch?"

"I—" James felt hopelessly lost. Were they not going to discuss any of this? "I should probably get my truck towed back to town."

"Oh." Sebastian giggled. "And how are you going to do that? How are you going to call a tow truck? Via bat signal? Telepathy?" He dissolved into wheezing laughter.

"*Fuck.*" James growled and kicked his truck's tire in a dramatic display he wasn't proud of. Sebastian was right. There was no way to contact anybody, let alone a tow truck that would have to come all the way from Apple Valley. "You knew my truck would die. You let me get trapped in this damn place on purpose."

Sebastian's laughter died. "You're not trapped."

"No? How am I going to get home then? I can't walk. That road is dangerous. There's no shoulder, and we're way too far from town." James's heart skipped at the thought of walking along North Road and potentially getting hit by a logging truck or someone driving too fast.

"I know it's dangerous," Sebastian said more softly, all traces of laughter gone. It made James wonder if Sebastian knew his parents had died on that damn road. He must because he was looking all pitying now.

"Why didn't you tell me this was happening?" James pleaded.

Sebastian's posture sagged, seeming suddenly tired. "I kept the gate locked, didn't I? You wanted it open today. Stop getting mad at me for doing what you asked."

"But you hired me to rewire a house when that's not even the most pressing problem. What is this place? Some sort of dead zone as well as haunted? Why not tell me everything here gets drained? Would the new lights and things I installed have worked, or would Storm House just suck the power right out of the grid?"

"I hired you to fix a problem," Sebastian corrected, ignoring everything else. "I never said anything about wiring when I contacted you." As if this were a completely reasonable justification, Sebastian turned and walked back into the house, leaving James behind.

CHAPTER NINE

Eventually, someone would realize James was missing and come looking for him. Hazel and Eli knew he was working at Storm House that weekend. Hazel might not miss him until Sunday evening when she, James, and Parker were due to meet for their weekly dinner, but Eli would be worried when he got home from work that night and James wasn't there. Unless Eli spent the night at Parker's and didn't go home. In that case, James was screwed until tomorrow.

He went back inside and found Sebastian in the kitchen.

Sebastian was crouched in front of the cast iron stove, his back to James as he added wood to the low-burning fire. "I had some dough proofing, so I'll probably put that in the oven soon."

"Okay," James said flatly as he sat at the table.

"I'm sorry." Sebastian closed the oven but didn't turn around. "I just need someone to fix things." His tone came out pleading, almost desperate.

James made himself let go of his annoyance. There was no denying how genuinely in need of help Sebastian sounded right now, no matter how he'd acted outside. There had to be a reason

Sebastian was behaving like this, and James wanted to understand.

Since Sebastian was living out here, avoiding everyone, perhaps it had to do with trust. Maybe he'd thought James wouldn't help if he'd known the job was more complicated than rewiring. It also seemed likely Sebastian had some sort of mental health condition that was affecting how he dealt with things, so James was going to give Sebastian the benefit of the doubt and forgive the guy for getting him stuck here.

"I can try my best to fix things," James offered. "But if something is draining all power from the property, that's a magical problem. I'm just an electrician. My magical expertise is limited."

Sebastian was still crouched in front of the oven, facing away. "You said you'd help me."

"I will. I just—you have to tell me what's going on."

"I'll try and do better," Sebastian whispered as if he hadn't meant for things to turn out this way. Then he straightened and went to check the dough resting under a towel on the counter.

"I'm not going to get scared off. No matter what you tell me." James tried for a reassuring tone. "You've got me now. Not figuring out what's sucking up all the power out here is going to bug me until I figure it out." That wasn't even a lie. James liked fixing things and hated leaving anything undone.

Sebastian only nodded, seeming marginally reassured.

"You don't have any theories about what's going on?"

"No theories, no." Sebastian grabbed some mugs from the cupboard.

"Could it be related to the haunting? The energy here feels distorted—wrong—surely it's connected."

"Do you think?" Sebastian stared at James. He seemed startled, almost scared.

James tried not to let that make him nervous. Sebastian lived out here. It couldn't be dangerous, or surely, he would have left. Besides, he'd just promised not to get scared off.

They had a light lunch of fruit, mixed nuts, and hot cider as Sebastian baked his bread. Eli wasn't due home until after ten that night, so James had a long while to wait for someone to come looking for him.

There wasn't much point in continuing his work. He'd need his power tools for one, and even though there were a few jobs he could do without them, there wasn't much point before the draining issue was understood. What if it couldn't be fixed? Power might never work out here.

James tried to remember if he'd ever heard of dead zones like this but came up blank. He couldn't even look anything up without his phone. Maybe he should have gone poking around the property, looking for answers, but he didn't really like that idea. He'd go home and do some research, and then, when he had half a clue where to start, he'd come back and help Sebastian.

The awkwardness between them eased as the bread baked, neither seeming to mind the other's quiet company. James liked watching Sebastian in the kitchen. Sebastian obviously knew what he was doing and seemed to get lost in his tasks in a way James found difficult to look away from. He could almost forget about everything else.

After the bread came out of the oven, Sebastian gracefully chopped garlic and herbs. James had rarely seen someone put so much care into every aspect of food preparation.

Sebastian set his chopped ingredients aside and washed his hands at the sink. "I like you watching me." He turned to face James.

"Oh." James would much rather have enjoyed the moment without Sebastian mentioning it, but he supposed it was a good thing Sebastian liked his attention. It was better than the alternative.

"You like watching me too, I think," Sebastian went on, no trace of embracement anywhere to be seen.

"Um."

"Like with the piano and now." Sebastian waited for a response, but James didn't give him one. His voice dropped lower. "You could watch me do other things if you want."

"I—what?" James sat up straight, startled.

Sebastian gave him a sly smile. "You wanted me to explain things more plainly, so here: I'm considering seducing you."

James swallowed. "Considering?" He could not believe Sebastian was going there after everything else that had happened that day.

Sebastian seemed to bite back a laugh. "Yeah, I've been *considering* it since you first showed up. You're attractive. You like to look at me. I like you looking. Seems like a good combination for some fun."

James's face was hot. What was going on with this guy, and why was James as intrigued as he was confused? "I meant for you to explain things about the house more clearly. Not—" He shook his head.

"I know." Sebastian approached the table. "But it seems we have some idle time on our hands." He leaned forward, palms on the table, towering over James where he sat. "You haven't said you're uninterested, but I'd prefer if you were upfront too. Like a yes or no would be good."

"This isn't a good idea," James said, aware he wasn't strictly declining Sebastian's offer. He couldn't tell Sebastian he wasn't interested when he was, and he didn't want to say no. Sebastian was attractive, there was no questioning that, and the idea of letting Sebastian seduce him was tempting.

But not tempting enough to ignore what a bad idea it was. Something was going on with Sebastian, and James didn't think they should add intimacy to their dynamic until they understood each other better. There was also the faint possibility that Sebastian was playing games with him, that all this was calculated and seduction was part of it. Somehow.

Even if that wasn't what was happening, and Sebastian was

genuine, James still didn't want to get attached. He was too involved already, worrying and promising to solve problems it wasn't his job to fix.

"Bad ideas are usually the best kind." Sebastian's hand moved toward James's, where it rested on the table.

James tucked his hand into his lap, and Sebastian backed up. "I'm the boring guy who follows the rules, remember?"

Sebastian rolled his eyes. "There aren't rules against this."

"No. But I don't embrace bad ideas. That's what I'm saying."

"Suit yourself." Sebastian shrugged like it really didn't matter, and James fought with irrational disappointment. Sebastian cocked his head. "So, am I allowed to try and change your mind? I'm not trying to harass you, you know."

"I'm not saying you are," James responded too quickly. "You're not harassing me. It's fine." He didn't want to lose the companionable moments they had, and he liked the flirting. Which meant he shouldn't let Sebastian keep trying to seduce him, but James wasn't perfect.

"Interesting." Sebastian crossed his arms. "You think I need to work a bit harder at it, do you?"

"It's not that at all." James gave him a stern look. "Let's just focus on the house—I mean, the manor. Act however you want. Just don't expect me to fall for any of it."

"Hmm."

James rushed on before Sebastian could voice whatever he was thinking. "Besides, I'm not exactly dying to kiss you after you let my truck's battery drain away, knowing full well I'd be stuck out here. Feels a bit devious."

"I said I was sorry." Sebastian looked more frustrated than sorry. "And it's adorable that kissing is what you think I want to do with you."

James blushed. Sebastian had something more explicit in mind, no doubt.

TRAPPED in a haunted house with an erratic man trying to get him into bed. James had been in worse situations, but that didn't mean he was pleased.

He didn't want to feel good about Sebastian being attracted to him. He knew he was attractive. People liked his lean, muscular frame and broad shoulders. It didn't matter that Sebastian had noticed his appeal. He should have done a better job of turning Sebastian down, left no room for confusion or hope. But there he was, hoping and toying with the idea in his head. Wondering if there was anything else Sebastian liked about him, beyond his body.

It was all bad. Trouble, just as James had suspected.

Things only got worse when the sun went down. James was thankful for the strong warding as the shadows lengthened. He could already see shades moving around outside the window, coming out of the trees and crossing the lawns, getting closer and closer to the house.

They shut the curtains and lit candles, but it was nowhere near enough light. Sebastian didn't seem to mind as he cooked dinner. James supposed he was used to it.

James would have liked to occupy himself elsewhere while his host cooked to discourage more direct advances. However, he had nothing to do. He also wasn't keen on wandering the house alone, wards or not.

He'd asked Sebastian to explain things but hadn't gotten any more information. It would be silly not to be wary of more surprises or to assume there wasn't more Sebastian was deliberately holding back, for whatever reason. Compulsive or calculated as it may be.

James ended up watching Sebastian cook for them. He enjoyed it more than he should have, given everything else.

Sebastian made pasta with a rich red vegetarian sauce and garlic bread. The kitchen was warm from the stove burning all afternoon and smelled amazing, like a bakery and an Italian restaurant blended together.

Low candlelight flickered around James, dancing on the pink cupboards and white walls. Sebastian had two old oil lamps on the counter next to where he was working so he could see better, but it didn't detract from the mood the candlelight set.

Once Sebastian had dished up the food, he disappeared, lamp in hand, and returned with a bottle of red wine. "Drink?"

"Sure, why not." It was already feeling way too romantic. He might as well go all in.

Sebastian set some nice crystal glasses on the table and poured, then went to retrieve the cooling garlic bread. He sat down, leaving both lamps over on the counter. "Hope you didn't have plans for tonight."

"No." James took a slice of bread. "I'm not even sure if my brother will miss me until morning."

Sebastian sipped his wine. "I didn't have plans either, in case you were wondering."

"Oh, um, that's good then."

Sebastian snorted a stifled laugh. "You're so polite. I was being sarcastic. Obviously, I didn't have plans. Or, pasta was my plan. You just happen to be here for it now."

James took a bite of pasta, deciding he was glad he could provide Sebastian with some company. "What do you do in the evening besides cook?"

Sebastian waved his wine glass. "I read or sometimes play the piano if there's enough moonlight and the shades don't press their noses to the glass in the ballroom. Mostly, I jerk off and try to fall asleep early so I can wake up when it's light again. Especially in winter."

James coughed. "You really didn't have to tell me that."

"I'm being open, remember?" Sebastian turned his attention

to his food as if it had been perfectly reasonable to share something so personal.

Now, James was plagued with images of Sebastian touching himself, as was probably the intent of the comment. He really shouldn't be thinking about it. He normally didn't let people get to him this way, but he suddenly felt frustrated, and not with Sebastian's antics.

"It's boring out here," Sebastian said after a few minutes of them eating in silence.

James didn't doubt that, but maybe it was something he could help with. "If you're bored and want to go somewhere else for a while, I can always give you a lift," he offered.

Sebastian didn't seem to have any way of getting into town, no car parked on the road and anything that might be tucked away on the property would be dead. James hadn't considered transportation to be a potential barrier before. Sebastian hadn't brought it up, but maybe he was self-conscious about it.

James rambled on, hoping he could show Sebastian it wasn't something he had to worry about needing assistance with. "I know you can't call me when you want to go somewhere, at least not before we fix things, but we could arrange something for regular rides. There's also Craig Stills, who fixes up used cars and sells them for reasonable prices. I can set something up with him if you're looking to buy one."

Sebastian's mouth disappeared into a thin line as James spoke, his eyes hard. "I thought you weren't going to keep bugging me about going into town. Didn't I tell you I don't want to go? If I wanted a car, I'd have one. I don't need you offering me rides."

His curt tone gave James an uncomfortable guilty feeling. He had promised not to hassle Sebastian about avoiding town, and Sebastian seemed angry at having to explain himself. Whatever was keeping him away from society must hold more weight than his complaint about boredom.

"Sorry, I didn't mean to bug you about it."

Sebastian took another bite of his food, his rigid posture and shuttered expression making it clear the topic was closed. He didn't tell James it was okay or not to worry about it, so this misstep obviously bothered him more than when James had invited him to the diner.

James ate, casting around in his mind for something else to say. "Do you ever cast magic lights?" he asked as his gaze settled on the candles between them.

Sebastian perked up, as if glad to move on and talk about something else. "Sometimes, but it's too tiring to cast lights all evening. My magic is pretty *meh*." Sebastian grabbed more garlic bread, previous anger nowhere in sight. "Most of the stuff I like doing is outside, other than cooking. I can't go out at night. There's too many shades."

There were significantly more of the pests out here than in town, and Moonlight Falls had lights all over the place to keep the ones that were there away.

Dealing with large numbers of shades was a whole different game than one or two on their own. Any beast was more formidable in large numbers. It was the difference between being trapped in a room with one rat or a swarm. James wasn't planning on setting foot outside until the sun was up. Unless Eli came by with his high beams on.

"You do lots of gardening?" James had seen a few patches and raised beds around the property.

Sebastian nodded. "I grew most of these ingredients. I get flour and dried goods delivered from town, but I don't have to buy produce."

"Wow." James had a new appreciation for his delicious meal. "It doesn't bother you, spending time outside the wards? Growing all this would be a lot of work."

Sebastian cocked his head. "Being outside doesn't bother me."

James put his fork down. "You don't get that skin-crawling feeling?"

"I hardly even know what you mean."

That was strange. Everyone in town knew about the haunted nature of the place, and anyone who'd ever been here had felt it. However, Sebastian being somewhat unaffected explained how he could stand living here. "It's good you're immune."

"I guess." Sebastian didn't sound totally convinced.

"Do you know why you can't feel it?" James asked casually, even though he was dying for any information about Storm House.

Sebastian shrugged and went back to eating. He didn't seem to be acting cagey or like he was hiding anything. Maybe he didn't know much more about the property's strange energy than James and didn't think it was a big deal since he wasn't affected, but James couldn't shake the feeling that there was more to it than that.

CHAPTER TEN

After finishing the bottle of wine together, James helped Sebastian clean up the kitchen. It was comfortably domestic, easy, like they were already familiar with each other's routines. James never would have thought they would work so well together.

"I might go back to the piano," Sebastian said when all the dishes were put away.

"Sounds good." James followed. It was too early to go to bed, and there really wasn't anything else he wanted to do alone in the dark house.

He sat on a chair by the guitars and watched Sebastian play. James wasn't sure if Sebastian realized, but this was doing a much better job of seducing him than the blatant advances. As he watched, it was easy to imagine allowing Sebastian into his life, despite his anxieties.

James had enjoyed the evening with Sebastian in a way he hadn't with anyone in a long time. But James knew getting close to Sebastian wasn't a risk he should take. He didn't trust the man and couldn't ignore that fact outside his fantasies. James found himself wishing things weren't so complicated, that he knew what was going on here with the house and why Sebastian hadn't been forthcoming. Then maybe he could see the two of them together.

James didn't necessarily want to be alone for the rest of his life, romantically speaking. He could accept dealing with his fears for the right person. It was too bad finding that person was so messy. The dating process itself wasn't something James dealt with comfortably, and really, Sebastian was the worst possible person to take those risks with. James didn't know if Sebastian liked him for more than his physical appeal, and even if he ignored all other obstacles, someone hiding out here didn't seem like the type to be looking for companionship.

However, James could watch Sebastian play piano and enjoy the view. He could daydream and fill his head with pretty pictures of Sebastian and himself, even if none of it would ever happen for real.

James blamed his sentimentality on the wine and the lack of distraction his phone typically provided. He wasn't usually like this.

The shades outside drifted up to the ballroom windows. They peered in, dark eyes glinting. It was freaky, far less appealing than the thought of a bunch of raccoons watching them.

It wasn't bright in the ballroom. Sebastian had brought an oil lamp and set it on a table next to the piano, but that was the only illumination other than pale moonlight. It wasn't like the night in town when the shade had been peering into a bright room.

James wondered if they liked the music.

"Okay." Sebastian stopped playing abruptly and pointed at the window in front of him. "That one right there hasn't blinked at all. It's making my eyes dry just looking at it. I'm going to bed."

James followed him from the ballroom, and they headed upstairs.

Sebastian turned clockwise around the landing, past doors James hadn't yet been through. "Here's the spare room." He opened a green door. "Mine is there." He pointed to an identical door at the end of the landing, situated toward the front of the house.

"And if Eli comes out here later?" James was doubtful his brother would be coming tonight. He spent most Saturday nights at Parker's, but just in case, he didn't want to miss him.

"I'll hear any knocking below my room—that's where the front door is—but I've locked the gate already."

"Why?" James hadn't realized Sebastian had done that, not that they'd been inseparable all afternoon.

"I always lock it, especially at night." As Sebastian swung the lamp away from himself, gesturing toward the road and the gate, shadows enveloped him, darkening the color of his eyes. "I don't need people driving onto the property and having their cars die, leaving them with all the shades swooping around."

It was a fair point, but James was more focused on how well the moonlight filtering from the skylight suited Sebastian. He pushed ethereal imaginings out of his mind. "My brother's probably not coming anyway."

"He'll come eventually." Sebastian sounded surprisingly reassuring, like he didn't want James to worry.

James nodded, thinking that was the end of the conversation, but Sebastian continued to hover.

"Bathroom's here." He pointed to the door next to the spare room. "So this is goodnight, unless you need company or don't want to be left in my *scary* house all by yourself." He gave a look of mock concern.

James huffed. "Unless you're making me sleep in a room full of jarred teeth and bits of bone, I think I'll be fine on my own."

Sebastian choked on a laugh. "This was my room when I was in high school. The creepiest thing you'll find in there is all my emo art stacked under the bed."

"You lived *here* during high school?" James was thrown by the realization. "I thought your mom had a house in town."

Sebastian set the lamp on a candle-covered table beside the door and crossed his arms. "Why would you think that?"

"I don't know." It had seemed logical. "You, your mom, and your sister all lived with your uncle?"

Sebastian let out a mean laugh. "My mom hasn't lived in Moonlight Falls since she was in high school herself, and my sister never has. Mom would send me here over the summer to stay with Uncle Stephen when I was little, but she and Kira always stayed in Phoenix. I came to live with my uncle permanently at the start of ninth grade."

"I guess I thought your mom moved back with you." James knew Sebastian hadn't spent his whole childhood in Moonlight Falls and hadn't gone to the elementary school here. He remembered him turning up only during the summer. But the Storms were Moonlighters, and when, one year, Sebastian didn't leave at the end of summer as usual, James assumed the rest of his family had stayed too. He was sure other people in town would have thought the same. Moonlight Falls always called its people home.

Though now he was considering it more closely, he didn't think he'd ever seen Sebastian's sister around and might not have realized Sebastian had a sibling when they were kids. When Sebastian mentioned Kira yesterday, James had assumed he'd just forgotten her over the years, that she must not have been close enough to them in age for her presence to register in his kid brain.

"Funny thing to think." Sebastian narrowed his eyes at James. "Did you ever meet my mom?"

"I don't remember. Maybe not." James didn't think he'd ever met Stephen Storm either. The older owner of Storm House had seemed more like a legend than a real person to James when he was a kid, just another part of the creepy tales of the forbidden property. Sensational stories he'd assumed were all bullshit once he'd gotten older.

"Well." Sebastian picked up the lamp. "There are some candles and a lighter in the room. You can snoop on my art if you want. I'm going to bed."

JAMES DIDN'T LOOK at Sebastian's art. It felt too intrusive, even with the invitation. He wouldn't want anyone to read his high school journal, and art could be just as exposing.

The room wasn't as dreary as the rest of the house, other than the darkness. The walls were white rather than green and there was a well-worn beanbag in the corner. The room didn't have any decoration, making it seem like it had been cleared out when Sebastian left. The desk was bare and closet empty, but the sheets on the bed seemed fresh.

Had Sebastian prepared the bed for him? He'd have to have done it before James got there that morning.

James knew Sebastian had let him get stuck here on purpose and didn't understand it any more now than he had before. Everything was just so fucking strange. Why had Sebastian come to live with his uncle during high school? James didn't know how long the energy-draining problem had been going on here, but he suspected the house was like that back then or the wiring would have been updated. What kind of mother left her kid in a place without power if she had any other option? Why had Stephen Storm lived here at all?

James struggled to fall asleep. It was cold, so he didn't even get undressed. He just took his shoes off and got under the blankets. Leather jackets weren't ideal sleepwear. A hoodie would have been better.

As the night got later, James was no closer to sleep. A creaking sound out on the landing caught his attention. He listened, catching more faint creaking. Could it be footsteps, maybe Sebastian walking around? It probably wasn't anything worth worrying about. The house just freaked him out, even though he knew the wards were strong.

Eventually, James drifted off.

A loud banging woke him with a start. His heart pounded, and he was momentarily disoriented.

There it was again, a loud thud, thud, thud. It didn't sound close, but he couldn't be sure. James sat up in bed. He threw the covers off and pulled his shoes on. Out in the hall, he glanced toward Sebastian's room. The door was open.

"Did you hear that?" he called as he approached.

There was no answer.

Another thud cut through the silence. It sounded like it was coming from downstairs. James ducked his head into the bedroom. "Sebastian?" He scanned the place, not really taking it in other than for the fact that it was empty.

"Sebastian?" James called louder and then grumbled, "Dammit."

James left the bedroom and headed to the stairs. As soon as he turned to go down, he spotted the source of the noise. The front door was open and banging in the wind.

He hurried down to the entryway. "Sebastian?"

The man was nowhere to be seen. Had he gone outside? Surely not. He'd said he didn't go out at night.

James caught the door and held it open. Four shades hovered over the porch, looking at him. The only thing keeping them from floating inside were the wards. They clicked their teeth. James called for Sebastian again and got no response.

He peered out into the yard. Sebastian better not be out there. It was dark, the moon only half-full and the sky partially cloudy. There was no sign of Sebastian, so maybe James should search the rest of the house. *But then why was the door open?*

James called up a light and pushed it though the doorway. It wasn't a blindingly bright one, just enough to usher the shades back, but that wasn't what James was concerned with right now.

He sent his light forth, ignoring the shades, and illuminated the surroundings beyond the porch.

The shades didn't immediately swarm back to the doorway. It seemed like they were watching what he was doing, maybe waiting to see if he would come out.

James sent the light across the yard to the gate. Nothing was down there, and it still looked shut. He moved the light along the edge of the property to his left, running parallel to the wall. Still nothing.

He sent the light toward the cow paddock. A path led along the fence into the redwoods that lay beyond the groomed part of the property. The forest within the grounds was a section of Storm House James hadn't ventured close to. There was some movement over that way, shadows swooping around closer to the trees.

James sent the light toward the disturbance. It was hard to see from where he stood in the doorway, so he half-stepped onto the porch.

Shades swarmed the path to the forest. James crossed the porch to the steps, trying to get a better look. Unease bubbled inside him as he was hit with the haunting effects of the property. He sent his light directly at the swarm of shades, pushing a few out of the way. The ones hanging around the porch moved in closer to him, but James didn't have a thought to spare for them.

Something pale was on the ground in the distance, something the horde of shades seemed to be attacking.

James moved across the yard at a run, fear coursing through him. He cast a spell to increase his light's brightness, and it flared, scattering the swarming shades.

Sebastian was on the ground, in the dirt, face down. He was nearly naked, pale skin covered in what looked like streaks of mud. One of his arms was outstretched, reaching toward the house. He wasn't moving.

"Fuck." James skidded to a stop and knelt. "Sebastian!" He grabbed his shoulder.

Sebastian groaned. James rolled him over, and Sebastian blinked at the light.

"What happened? Are you hurt?" James scanned Sebastian's body. There were scratches amongst the mud but nothing that looked serious.

Sebastian made a small, pained sound.

James scooped him up in his arms, doing his best to manage Sebastian's long limbs. "Let's go inside."

Sebastian didn't respond, didn't even grab a hold of James as he was being carried. James tried not to panic.

He had his light lead the way but dimmed it by half, not wanting to tire himself out. The shades followed, hissing and swooping in front of them. James didn't have time for their antics. As long as they didn't try to grab him, they didn't matter right now.

He made it to the house with Sebastian still limp in his arms. The shades on the porch were blocking the door as if they'd been waiting for him. He sent the light to clear his path, and they scattered. As soon as he crossed the threshold, he let the light go out.

James turned. All the shades seemed to have followed him and were waiting just beyond the doorway, their faces and blinking eyes pressed against the invisible barrier of the house's wards.

James kicked the door shut and headed for the stairs. "Sebastian, can you hear me?"

"Mm," Sebastian groaned, no longer completely still as small tremors wracked his body.

The anxiety gripping James's chest hadn't lessened after coming inside. He took Sebastian to his room and set him in front of a free-standing metal fireplace situated in the center of the room. James didn't let him go completely, lightly holding Sebastian in his lap, pulled close to his chest. The fire was low but much warmer than outside.

Sebastian continued to shiver in small bursts. His eyes were closed, and he still hadn't moved much.

James had to collect himself, think and figure out what to do. Sebastian's shivers could be one of two things: strictly from the cold or due to magic overuse. If Sebastian had drained himself— much more severely than James had under the house—that would explain his semiconsciousness too.

James inspected the cuts on Sebastian's arms more thoroughly, wiping away some of the mud. At least he found no injuries worth serious concern. "What were you doing out there?"

Sebastian opened his eyes. That had to be a good sign. If he'd gone completely unresponsive, that could mean he'd drained himself past the point of recovery. James's throat burned at the thought, but that wasn't happening. Sebastian was responding. Slowly.

James held Sebastian's stare. "Did you use too much magic?"

Sebastian nodded, the motion tiny but unmistakable, then shivered.

Okay, James could deal with this. Everything was going to be fine. He'd believe nothing else. He needed to get Sebastian warm, fed if possible, and into bed. He wasn't worried about hypothermia, but Sebastian's body didn't need to expend extra energy trying to regulate his temperature when he'd drained himself like this. The cold mud on his skin wasn't helping, and while James considered wrapping him up in front of the fire as he was, he thought he could take better care of Sebastian than that.

"Are you up for getting this mud cleaned off?" James asked.

Sebastian grabbed his arm and pulled himself closer to James. He seemed to be becoming more alert as time passed. "Yes."

"Where are your clothes?"

"As if you mind the view," Sebastian muttered just above a whisper.

Relief flooded James. Full, sassy sentences had to be good

news, even if Sebastian closed his eyes and leaned harder into James afterward, shivering and breathing deeply, like the comment had cost him.

"Come on, let's see if we can get some of this mud off you. Then bed." James stood, pulling Sebastian with him. This time, Sebastian was able to move and stood with James's help.

They walked to the ensuite at the end of the room. The bathroom was spacious and much nicer than James expected after seeing the others in the house. With a skylight and large window, there was enough moonlight to see the relatively modern state of things, including the large tiled shower and clawfoot tub. The house had gas hot water, thankfully, but installing these fixtures without power tools would have been a lot of work.

James shook himself. Now wasn't the time to think about the house. "Can you stand in the shower?"

Sebastian shook his head before shivering again.

Maybe cleaning off the mud wasn't such a bright idea. Having Sebastian sit, exposed to the cool air while James washed him with a cloth, would only make him colder.

"Do you want a bath? Or just to get warm and forget about the mud."

"James," Sebastian whined. He sounded frustrated. "Fill the bath— I'm fine."

"You don't seem fine." James reached with his free hand and turned on the hot water to fill the tub.

"No, I'm fucked," Sebastian slurred. "Magic's useless."

At least he was talking more. James told himself again that Sebastian would be okay. He hadn't used so much magic that it would kill him, not if he was more alert now than he'd been when James had first found him. He seemed to have stopped shivering too, meaning his body had enough energy to begin recovering, even without food.

James didn't have to worry, but he still did.

He tested the water temperature. Satisfied, he plugged the tub. "Magic has its moments."

Sebastian snorted in what sounded like indignation. He tucked his face into the side of James's neck, his arms wrapping around James's waist, and held on as the water slowly rose in the bath.

The embrace had James wanting to rub Sebastian's back, to soothe him with touch and hold him close. He resisted. It wouldn't be right to take advantage of the situation when comfort wasn't the only reason James wanted to touch.

He helped Sebastian into the tub, leaving him dressed in his boxer briefs. Sebastian curled against the side, holding on to the edge like he was worried he wouldn't be able to stay upright if he wasn't clinging to something. James took off his muddy jacket and tossed it on the floor, then dipped his cupped hands in the water and poured it over Sebastian, rinsing the mud from his body.

Sebastian didn't move from his position gripping the edge of the tub, but he seemed to relax, his body looking less tense. He closed his eyes and made satisfied sounds as the warm water cascaded over him.

After asking if it would be okay, James ran a soapy washcloth over Sebastian, gently cleaning the cuts on his skin. Sebastian made a small humming noise as James washed his face, eyes still closed, and James's heart skipped. He was still anxious, worried about the man he was taking care of, but he also felt something more tender growing inside him.

He cared about Sebastian a hell of a lot, and there might be no saving him from getting hurt at this point. If anything bad happened to Sebastian, James would be devastated. He almost couldn't bear the thought. And if he lost Sebastian and never admitted he had feelings for him? Yes, he'd been resisting those feelings, but suddenly, it all felt too close to being lost, and James regretted his hesitation.

He brushed a damp ginger curl back from Sebastian's brow. He opened his eyes and gave James a soft smile.

Once Sebastian was free of mud, James undid the stopper and let the dirty water out. He refilled the bath with clean water, adding a bit of lavender oil he'd spotted on a shelf. He couldn't help himself. He wanted to comfort Sebastian, spoil him, wrap him up and keep him safe. Give him whatever he needed.

James was doomed.

CHAPTER ELEVEN

SEBASTIAN LAY BACK in the tub, his long legs stretched out in the confined space. "I'm feeling a bit better now."

"That's good." James shut off the water. "What happened?"

Sebastian didn't say anything. James couldn't tell if he was too exhausted or avoiding the question. It didn't necessarily matter which was the case right now. They could discuss it later. James let Sebastian rest, busying himself by lighting a candle and searching the cabinets for antiseptic ointment for Sebastian's cuts. Once he found some, he put it in his pocket for later and spent some time wiping his jacket and jeans clean.

"You should eat something," James said after a while.

Sebastian opened his eyes. "The food is too far away."

"I'll get it for you, but I'm not leaving you in the water." James had been keeping an eye on Sebastian, not wanting him to doze off and slip under.

"I'm not going to drown." Sebastian attempted to scowl, but it seemed halfhearted. "I should get out anyway. I'm wrinkling." He inspected his fingers before grabbing the sides of the tub and trying to stand. He didn't seem to have the strength.

James stepped forward. "Need a hand?"

"Please." Sebastian reached out.

James helped him stand, taking most of Sebastian's weight as he got him out of the bath. Sebastian grabbed a towel from the rack and dried himself as James held him steady, then they headed back into the bedroom.

James laid a towel down on the bed and Sebastian sat, still in his wet boxer briefs. "You should put this on the scratches." He held out the tube of ointment.

"Sure." Sebastian took it with an odd expression.

James figured he was being overly cautious, but they were shade scratches, and he didn't like to think where their hands had been. "There's some on your back I can help with. If you want."

Sebastian began putting the ointment on his arms and hands. "That'd be good. If you don't mind?" He handed the tube back to James.

James didn't mind. He sat next to Sebastian, who turned enough so James could reach his back. James attended to each scratch carefully. "If I grab you some clothes, will you be able to get them on?"

"Hm?" Sebastian seemed to startle out of a daze. "Yeah, I'm good."

James crossed the room to the dresser next to the door and took a moment to light some candles. Sebastian directed him to the correct drawers, and he gathered the clothes.

The furniture in here was nice and far more modern than the rest of the house. The walls were a familiar shade of light pink and the old green carpet was covered in fluffy yellow rugs.

It was a lovely room. You could almost forget you were in a creepy old house. There were white-trimmed French doors leading to a balcony and enough windows that the room would get a lot of sunlight.

James handed Sebastian a pair of sweats, a shirt, underwear, and socks, then left the room in search of food. He took a candle with him for light, but it was a good thing his eyes were well-adjusted to the dark. In the kitchen, he grabbed the cookie tin and jar of nuts from the counter, then, on second thought, put an apple in his pocket.

Back upstairs, James hovered in the hall. "Can I come in?"

"Yes," Sebastian called, sounding faintly exasperated.

James found him dressed and under the covers. He set the cookies and nuts down on the bedside table, glad to see a water bottle there already, and handed Sebastian the apple. "Need me to refill that?" He pointed to the bottle.

"Nah, it's good." Sebastian took a bite of his apple.

James was relieved to see Sebastian had recovered from his delirious state but didn't want to leave him by himself. He was still worried and knew that if he went to his room, the fear that something might happen to Sebastian would keep him up, whether or not it was rational.

Instead, he went to the free-standing fireplace and added another log to the fire. James was glad Sebastian had heating in his room. There were a couple of inbuilt fireplaces around—in the sitting room, the billiards room, and the receiving room—but none had looked recently used. There was also one in the spare room James had been given, but there hadn't been wood.

The fire gave off a soft glow, bringing out the warmth in all the pinks and yellows. Sebastian had a small sitting area with a couch and armchair opposite his large bed. James wondered if he should just set up there for the remainder of the night.

"Why did you go outside?" James asked after Sebastian seemed to have had his fill of snacks.

Sebastian pulled the covers more tightly around himself. "I don't know."

"You don't know?" James perched, leaning against the arm of the couch, and tried to read Sebastian's expression. "Did something compel you to go out?" He assumed Sebastian had gone out for some reason, but if Sebastian didn't know what was going on any more than James did, that would explain why he hadn't put clothes on first.

Sebastian seemed to think about the possibility he'd been lured outside as if it hadn't occurred to him before now, his eyes crinkling with worry. "I don't— How could I have been compelled?"

"I have no idea. Magic of some kind. Unless you sleepwalk?" Sebastian shook his head at that. James believed he was being genuine but couldn't help pressing. "You really have no idea why you were outside in the middle of the night?"

Sebastian gave him a helpless look.

This wasn't good. They had to figure out what happened tonight so it didn't happen again. "What do you remember?"

Sebastian clutched his blankets. "Digging? Don't ask me why."

James scratched the back of his neck. That explained the mud. "You haven't ever found yourself randomly outside before?"

"No." Sebastian rolled his eyes. He must be feeling better and certainly looked much safer tucked into bed than sprawled on the ground.

"I shouldn't keep you up," James said as a reminder to himself. They could talk more in the morning. "But I'm staying on your couch."

Sebastian let out a ghost of a laugh. "You're such a mother hen."

James wasn't going to deny it. He wasn't ashamed of his nurturing, worrywart ways. "I haven't heard you complaining about being fussed over."

"Touché," Sebastian mumbled as he nestled farther into his pillows.

That warm feeling swelled within James's chest again. Seeing Sebastian safe and well made him happy. He liked taking care of people, not only because it helped push away his anxieties about losing them.

Sebastian had wormed his way into James's life without James deciding to let him in. He hadn't given his permission for things to progress as they had, not consciously. James should be annoyed by this but couldn't muster enough negative emotion. Even if nothing happened romantically between them, James suspected he'd never stop caring about Sebastian now he'd stared.

JAMES WOKE to sunlight spilling through the French doors into Sebastian's bedroom. He shifted, sitting up on the couch. A glance told him Sebastian was still sleeping.

Last night seemed even stranger now he reconsidered it. What were the odds of something like that happening when James was stuck here over night if Sebastian had never found himself unknowingly wandering the property before? It was almost too perfect of a coincidence.

Unless it wasn't a coincidence and Sebastian wasn't telling James the whole truth.

Last night, James had been too concerned to be suspicious, but if Sebastian had been compelled outside, someone would have had to do the compelling. Who would have cast the spell? James might have wondered if it had to do with the magic of the haunting, but Sebastian had said he wasn't affected by the strange energy here. Not to mention the wards drew a firm line between outside and in. How could a spell have plucked Sebastian from his bedroom?

None of it made any sense.

James got up and left the room. He didn't want to wake Sebastian. Regardless of how little James could make of the night before, there was no question that Sebastian had severely drained himself. He needed sleep.

James went to the kitchen to make breakfast. He'd seen where enough things were kept to not need to bother Sebastian. He'd even take Sebastian something to eat if he didn't come down before James was done.

He entered the kitchen and stopped short. There, sitting on the table, were the damn books. The same ones that had been on the piano and the stairs.

James couldn't pretend that wasn't suspicious. He almost wondered if they moved around on their own, but that kind of powerful enchantment seemed wasted on books that did nothing more than appear randomly to annoy him.

Had Sebastian moved them here? He must have, but when? James couldn't remember if they'd been there in the middle of the night. It had been dark—obviously—and he hadn't exactly been looking around, just beelining for the snacks, too worried about Sebastian.

He went to the table and opened the first volume, flipping through the pages. There was nothing tucked inside, nothing odd about the book itself. He checked all six, as well as the bookends. It didn't feel like any magical energy had been stored in them, and if the books moved on their own, James thought he'd be able to detect that level of power but wasn't one hundred percent sure. He wasn't the most well-rounded magical practitioner. The basics were all he bothered with, other than the specialized refueling spell he used at work.

James abandoned the books for the stove. He found a pan, the butter dish, and some eggs sitting in a basket on the counter. He scrambled them, then fried a slice of Sebastian's bread in the buttery pan in lieu of toasting it.

The food made him less grumpy, but only marginally. If Sebastian had moved the books, he would have done it after he'd sent James to the guest room, which made it feel like Sebastian was toying with him. Was anything here what it seemed? Was anything about last night as simple as James had thought, or had his head been clouded by worry? Had Sebastian set the whole thing up on purpose?

James couldn't see why Sebastian would do that and felt guilty for even thinking it. He was being unfair to Sebastian. Fucking around with the books, playing flirty games, and teasing didn't necessarily have anything to do with Sebastian draining all his energy and getting swarmed by shades. Taking things to a more dangerous level didn't make sense, but James wished he was more confident in dismissing the idea. He couldn't ignore the fact that his trust in Sebastian seemed to be diminishing rather than growing.

After washing his plate, James set a kettle to boil on the stove top and cooked another serving of eggs and pan-fried bread. He brewed coffee in the French press, grabbed two mugs—hanging them off his fingers by the handles—and carried everything upstairs.

He might not trust Sebastian, but not offering him breakfast wouldn't get James anywhere.

Sebastian grinned, dimples on full display, as James entered the room. "Careful, you're spoiling me."

All of James's suspicions fled his mind and were replaced by pleasurable embarrassment. He thought he might be getting addicted to the sight of Sebastian smiling, though he tried to act unaffected. "It's only breakfast."

Sebastian reached eagerly for the plate. "In bed."

James set the mugs on the bedside table and poured them both coffee from the press. "You always make a big deal out of things."

Sebastian accepted his coffee. "You always have to go and be thoughtful. I can't act like it's nothing."

There was an awkward pause. James's head filled with images of them sharing toast and coffee in bed on Sunday mornings. He liked the picture a whole damn lot, but he couldn't afford to forget everything else going on and get lost in dreamland. "Why were those books in the kitchen?"

Sebastian gave him a look of wide-eyed innocence. It was too overdone to be convincing. "What books?"

And just like that, it was easier for James to ignore the mushy things Sebastian made him feel. How could someone so infuriating also make James's heart pound with longing? "You know what books. *The Magical Tales*. Why are you moving them around the house?"

Sebastian gave a lazy one-armed shrug. He grabbed the bread off his plate. "I don't know. Seems like a weird thing for me to do."

James frowned. "So why do it? Is it so I'd notice?"

Sebastian laughed.

"What? Stop messing around."

"I'm not." Sebastian scooped a large forkful of eggs into his mouth and took a bite of his bread.

"Really? You're not trying to drive me mad? This isn't you playing games?" James was frustrated now. Maybe he could goad Sebastian into explaining himself. "Then what is it, some sort of —I don't know—secret book code?" James sneered.

Sebastian put his bread down and stared at James with the same unnerving intensity from the day before. Did that mean James was right? The books were some sort of message, *seriously*? Why not just admit it now that James had guessed? Or was it all meant to drive him up the wall, the message being: *I'm fucking with you.*

"Sebastian." James gripped his coffee tight, resisting the urge to grab Sebastian and shake the answers out of him or maybe kiss him until his frustration abated. "Are the books a code? What are you trying to tell me?"

Sebastian blinked, the intensity leaving his stare. He turned back to his food. James wondered if it was all nonsense. He let out an unmistakable sigh of annoyance so Sebastian knew exactly how he felt and went to stand by the French doors, staring out into the yard.

As he sipped his coffee, a familiar van pulled up to the Storm House gate. James was relieved to see Hazel and Eli jump out. "Looks like my rescue has arrived."

"Wonderful." Sebastian's tone dripped with sarcasm. "So happy for you."

Was it just James, or did he sound bitter? It was like Sebastian didn't want James to go. That shouldn't give James a small thrill. Not after Sebastian had tricked him into getting stuck here and refused to tell him anything. James shouldn't want to be around a man who liked toying with him.

James was so screwed. This whole situation was a mess.

Outside, Eli was pointing through the gate at James's truck.

James turned back to Sebastian. "I'm going to go let them in. Can I get the key?"

Sebastian shook his head. "I'm coming with you." He set his plate and coffee aside, the eggs already gone. "Let me get dressed."

By "get dressed," he only meant pulling his purple robe over his sweats and T-shirt. Once he was ready, Sebastian grabbed his bread and coffee and led the way out of the room. James followed, full of mixed feelings, none of which he was happy about.

The two of them made their way down the driveway to find Eli on top of the wall.

"You Gray boys really can't keep away from me, can you?" Sebastian teased.

"James!" Eli shouted from his perch on the wall. "We couldn't get a hold of you! What's wrong with your phone? Did you not go home last night?"

"I've been calling all morning," Hazel added from the other side of the gate.

"James spent the night." Sebastian's tone heavily implied that something intimate had happened between them.

"Because my truck died," James corrected.

"Right." Hazel narrowed her eyes at him, like she believed Sebastian's implication was more likely.

Eli looked put out. "I've been worried all morning. You could have been off dying somewhere while I was over at Parker's and had no idea."

Sebastian munched his bread, looking between them all like this was great entertainment.

"Sorry, Eli." James felt terrible for causing his brother stress. "My phone died too." He turned to Sebastian. "Can you let them in?"

"Oh, right." Sebastian put the last bit of bread into his mouth, holding it between his teeth as he delved a hand into his robe pocket.

"Can you call a tow for me?" James asked Hazel as his brother hopped off the wall onto the Storm House lawn.

She shook her head. "We don't have time for that now. We have to get back to town."

"Why?" James asked.

"Shades smashed all the lights in the center of town. We've got a lot of work to do."

CHAPTER TWELVE

No one knew exactly what had happened in town last night, other than that sometime after midnight, a swarm of shades descended on the town center. All of the surrounding businesses had been empty, except the B&B around the corner from the ice cream shop. The guests and owner had been woken by the commotion, but by then, almost all the lights had gone out and no one wanted to venture outside.

James and Hazel spent the whole day putting up new lights with the help of Parker and the mayor, Eleanor Ashley. The three of them often helped the mayor with supernatural concerns. James had no interest in joining the local government, but he still wanted to give back to the town as much as he could, even when the jobs weren't strictly electrical business. Hazel and Parker were the same.

Even with the extra help, reinstalling all the lights was too big of a job to complete before nightfall. Gray Electrical didn't even have enough stock to finish reinstalling everything. But it wasn't the end of the world. Some light was better than none until they could finish things off.

"What if they come back tonight?" James asked the others as

they watched the sun go down from the diner. Eli was there too and had been supplying them with hot coffee all day.

Eleanor, a woman in her mid-forties with a pixy cut, grimaced out the window. "You're right. They very well could come back. We might need to ward the lights."

"I can cast a couple of wards tonight." Parker rubbed his stubble-lined jaw as he weighed this up. "But I don't think I have enough energy left for more than that."

"I'd appreciate it." The mayor nodded at him gratefully. "If you could do one on either side of the street, that would be best."

"But why are shades suddenly attacking lights when they've never done anything like this before?" Hazel tore open a sugar packet like it had offended her, letting the contents fall into her mug. She tended to get frustrated when she was tired, something James could understand. They'd all had a long day.

"I don't know." Eleanor leaned back in the booth with a tired sigh, her gaze focused on Hazel. "The ice cream shop incident could have been a fluke on its own, but what happened last night feels like another new shift in shade behavior. I'll check the town records in case there's been anything like this before. See if there's anything helpful."

Not that he wanted to add to the mayor's problems, but James figured he needed to tell her about the shades attacking him beneath Storm House. He relayed the story briefly. Eleanor didn't look particularly pleased to hear it.

"It wasn't quite like what happened to Eli," James assured her. "I don't know if they intended serious harm, but a second unprovoked incident isn't great."

"No." The furrow in the mayor's brow deepened. "Their aggression seems to be escalating all around. It might pay for me to call a few people. See if any other towns like ours are experiencing strange shade activity."

James wasn't sure what was more worrying: their problem

being unique and completely unprecedented or a part of something changing on a much larger scale.

"You'll keep us updated?" Parker asked.

"Of course." Eleanor nodded before getting up from the booth. "And let me know if you three need anything more for the lights."

THE NEXT MORNING, James was worn out before he got to work. There were too many questions on his mind, swirling endlessly and distracting him from simple tasks, like not burning his toast.

He managed to call a tow truck in Apple Valley to retrieve his vehicle and drop it off at Gray Electrical to be refilled. The person on the other end of the line promised he'd have it back by midday. James was glad he'd thought to push his truck down the driveway and out the gate before leaving Sebastian's yesterday so the tow company wouldn't have to deal with Storm House.

James walked to work. It wasn't far. He lived on the southern end of town and enjoyed making his way through the familiar streets. The fall colors were in full swing, and he was pleased to note that none of the new lights in the town center had been smashed the previous night.

Hazel was already at work when James arrived. He went straight for the coffee and grabbed one of the larger mugs, wondering why the shades had been so destructive the other night and not last night. Not that he was complaining about last night's inactivity.

James took his coffee to his desk and began putting through an order for more shade-lights. "Something weird happened out at Storm House the night before last. Maybe even around the same time the shades were destroying things in town."

Hazel paused as she fixed herself a second coffee. "What do you mean?"

James explained how shades had swarmed Sebastian in the middle of the night and how the house seemed to be some sort of energy sink. "I have no idea what's going on out there."

He frowned at his coffee, unable to shake a renewed worry for Sebastian. What if something had happened again last night while Sebastian was alone? There wasn't even a way for James to call and check on him.

Half of James was annoyed by his concern. Sebastian wasn't being honest and was toying with him to some extent. He didn't want to worry about someone who was playing games, but at the same time, he still suspected something could be going on with Sebastian's mental state. He didn't know how much that might be influencing his behavior.

James couldn't stop thinking about the books. Were they nothing, or was it similar to the way Sebastian had waited for James to figure out the energy-draining issue? He'd given James that creepy stare in both instances.

Hazel returned to her desk, taking a seat with her fresh coffee. "Is there any point rewiring the house if the property will just suck up the energy?"

"I don't know." James set his mug down, feeling every bit of his exhaustion. "I've got to figure out what's causing it first."

Hazel wrinkled her nose. "Why's that your job?"

"I said I'd help."

"But it doesn't sound like Sebastian is helping himself. It's his problem, not yours. I know you can't resist taking care of everyone, but if someone's going to return your kindness by messing you around, they don't deserve it."

James shifted in his seat. "I don't think it's that simple."

Hazel eyed him more closely. "Why?"

James hadn't told her everything. He hadn't mentioned how

he felt about Sebastian or how he wondered if some of Sebastian's actions could be due to social phobia or some other mental health condition. He didn't know how to explain to Hazel the bone-deep feeling he had that there was more to the situation than he understood. Somehow, understanding Sebastian felt key to all of it.

James fixed Hazel with a stern look. "People who are easy to deal with aren't the only ones who deserve help."

She put her coffee down. "That wasn't what I meant. I just don't want someone taking advantage of your good nature."

"Good nature," he scoffed. People acted like the favors he did for others were a big deal when they weren't. It was basic courtesy, and yes, he was going beyond that for Sebastian, but he didn't think Sebastian was taking advantage.

James supposed he could explain to Hazel that he cared for Sebastian, that liking him was part of the reason he didn't want to let this go. But he didn't. He wanted to keep that detail to himself since he was still determined to fight off his feelings as much as possible.

He was already too attached. He didn't need to make it worse.

They left the conversation there and got to work. James was restless all morning. He wanted to check that nothing had happened with the shades at Storm House and hated that Sebastian had no way to call for help if he needed it.

The more James brooded over everything to do with Sebastian, the more the books seemed like something. There had to be a reason they kept appearing in places he couldn't help noticing them.

He was thinking in circles, which was frustrating. James couldn't figure out the significance of the books. Maybe there was none. He wasn't sure if the only reason he wanted there to be more to it was to prove Sebastian wasn't messing with him for no reason.

By lunch, James couldn't take it. Maybe he was overthinking. What could the books possibly mean and why the hell wouldn't Sebastian just tell him? But Sebastian had always done things his own unfathomable way. What if the books *were* some kind of code? Using a code seemed ridiculous, but so was the rest of the situation.

James walked to the library instead of eating lunch with Hazel. He didn't remember *The Magical Tales* in much detail and wondered if taking a closer look at them would help.

The library was an old whitewashed building next to the town hall on the opposite side of the circle from Moonlight Diner. Mila Lopez, the librarian, was at her desk just inside the entrance. She was in her early sixties and had run the library most of James's life.

Her silver hair was in its familiar bun, glasses perched on the end of her nose. She beamed at him as he entered. "James."

"Ms. Lopez, how are you?" He always felt like a kid when he saw her. The same went for any of his old elementary school teachers who still lived in town.

She took off her reading glasses, letting them hang from the beaded chain around her neck. "I'm well. Can't say I'm happy with all the trouble in town though."

"Neither am I." James hesitated, not wanting to get sucked into a long chat about shades right then. "Do you have copies of *The Magical Tales* I could look at?"

Mila's eyes widened. "That's an odd choice, but sure. They're back here." She got up and led him to the children's section.

They walked through the quiet library, no one else in sight.

"Do you remember Sebastian Storm?" James asked as Mila pulled two books from a shelf.

"Of course." She gave him a look like he should have known better than to ask. Mila knew everyone. "He was such a sweet boy."

"Was he?"

Mila's look turned stern as she handed James the books. "It shouldn't come as a surprise. But then, no one seemed very interested in getting to know Sebastian. Kids can be so cruel sometimes. I'd have thought you'd have realized by now—with all the wisdom from your advanced years—there was nothing too unusual about Sebastian. He was just lonely."

James didn't know what to say. He felt scolded, and like he probably deserved it. But he hadn't been cruel to Sebastian growing up, and he didn't think any of the other kids had been either. Maybe he was wrong. It wasn't like he knew everything about everyone, or maybe excluding Sebastian was the kind of cruelty Mila meant.

"There wasn't any particular reason he and I weren't friends." James couldn't help sounding defensive. "There were plenty of kids I didn't hang out with."

"True." Mila gave James an assessing sweep of her eyes. "It's not up to you to look out for everyone. That's not what I'm saying. It's just interesting when everyone seems to avoid the same person. I always wondered if it was hard for Sebastian, only living here off and on. It wasn't the same for him as it was for the kids who really grew up here. He spent a lot of time with me in the library during the summer. His uncle didn't drive, so I'd go pick him up and bring him to town."

"Really?" James set the books on a nearby table.

Mila nodded, a sad smile turning her lips. "I grew up with Stephen, of course. He had a bit of a funny turn around the time I moved back to Moonlight Falls to look after the library, and we were never close after that. Not like we had been when we were young. But I was happy to help look after Sebastian." She turned away, unnecessarily straightening a few books on the shelf.

It seemed strange that the librarian would have been looking after Sebastian at all. Though Mila seemed almost wistful, like maybe Stephen had been important to her, so maybe her involvement in Sebastian's life hadn't been anything out of the ordinary.

Before James could come up with a reply, Mila continued, "I was surprised when Sebastian came back. Well, it's never a total surprise when one of us comes home, but I hadn't expected him back so soon."

"Do you know why he came back?"

Mila frowned. "Stephen was sick. Sebastian was taking care of him. I didn't see him much during that time. No one even told me Stephen had passed away until months after."

"I'm sorry." James could see how much this still hurt her by the way her features tightened to temper her expression.

Mila gave a tiny shake of her head, picked up her glasses, and put them on, only to look over the top of them. "Nothing to be sorry for. I shouldn't have expected anything from a man I hadn't been friends with since high school. Or from his family. Even if he did take me to prom." She rolled her eyes, but James didn't quite buy into her dismissal.

"Sebastian should have told you Stephen passed away."

"He probably wasn't thinking about his old babysitter in his own grief. Which is fair enough. Though it would be nice if he'd come by and see me now."

"He doesn't come into town, so I don't think it's personal," James offered.

Mila's brow furrowed. "No, you're right. It must run in the family."

"What must?" James asked, confused.

"Whatever makes the Storms fold in on themselves and hide from everyone. I tried to get Stephen to see someone years ago. I told him there's nothing wrong with seeking help, but he was very touchy about mental health. Said he was fine and didn't have to interact with people if he didn't want to." Mila removed her glasses and let them hang around her neck once more. "I stopped bringing it up. He was right, really. It wasn't my business. He was good to Sebastian, and there wasn't any serious cause for concern. I just couldn't let go of who he used to be, I suppose."

An uneasy feeling crept up on James. "People change, but it sounds more complicated than that."

"Maybe. It hardly matters now, does it?" She flicked her wrist like she was shooing the past away. "Why the sudden interest in *The Magical Tales?*"

"I'm not sure." James took a seat at the table and cracked open the first book. "I don't remember them that well. Did Sebastian like these books when he was young?"

Mila gave him a funny look. "I don't think so."

She left him to it.

James was less sure about the books being some sort of clue after their conversation. He should have been researching dead zones and energy draining, not trying to decipher Sebastian's behavior. But he couldn't let the books go. Sebastian's intense stare haunted his thoughts.

This version of *The Magical Tales* was split into two volumes, not seven like Sebastian's copies. His would have two stories per book, while these had seven each. James scanned the table of contents. The titles in the first volume didn't prove illuminating.

There was a story about children lost in the woods, finding their way home via magic. Another story was about a prince of light conquering shades that—as James remembered—was very heavy-handed with its metaphors and not a good depiction of the realities of shades. There was a story about a girl put to sleep for a thousand years for reasons James couldn't recall, and one about how skipping school would turn you to stone. They were all like that. Morality tales as Sebastian had called them.

None of the stories had to do with energy draining, but they had been written before electricity was invented. Still, nothing seemed remotely related to Storm House or its mysteries.

James tried to look at things from a different perspective.

Sebastian hadn't had all the volumes. Maybe that meant something.

The last story on the first table of contents—which would have been missing from Sebastian's collection as it would have been in his fourth volume—was about a talking frog. That could hardly be relevant.

James opened the second book, feeling like he was looking for an explanation that didn't exist. The first story listed was *Little William's Voice*. It would also have been in Sebastian's missing volume. Seeing the title, James was reminded how he'd liked this story even less than the others when he was a kid. It was about a boy whose tongue had been bound for lying, making it impossible for him to speak. James had always thought the punishment was unreasonably cruel and had avoided the unpleasant tale after hearing it only once.

He scanned the rest of the titles, but none led to a lightbulb moment. Maybe skimming the stories would help. He started with *Little William's Voice* since he remembered it the least.

Reading the story now, James found he agreed with his younger self. It was awful. The poor kid in the tale couldn't even use written words to communicate after the tongue-binding spell had been cast on him. He was forced to try and act out what he wanted to say and trick people into figuring out what was wrong with him.

James stopped, putting the book down. Sebastian had basically tricked him into figuring out the house was sucking up any and all power. Was he physically unable to tell James the problem? Had someone bound him to secrecy? The spell in the tale had prevented the boy from talking at all, but binding secrets was a more common use for that kind of dark magic in the real world.

If James was right, then someone had performed a blood-and-bone ritual on Sebastian. He thought of the teeth they'd found in the house. The Storms dabbled in that sort of magic, or at least some of them had. It wasn't outrageous to think Sebastian had been forced to keep a secret, even if that sort of dark magic was illegal and rarely seen these days.

What else was Sebastian being forced to hide? Did he know why the house was sucking up energy? He must. This had to be it. Being bound to silence explained so much of Sebastian's behavior. His intense stares, his whooping celebration when James's truck didn't start. It could even be the reason he couldn't explain going outside in the middle of the night.

James jumped up from his chair. He had to talk to Sebastian. But—if James was right—that wouldn't be possible without first breaking the secret-binding spell. Sebastian would most likely be prevented from saying someone had bound his tongue in the first place. Just like the boy in the story, he probably couldn't directly communicate that anything was wrong.

His heart pounded as he returned *The Magical Tales* to the shelf and walked to the second floor of the library, where the magical texts were kept.

Any blood-and-bone magic that took away autonomy or free will was illegal. There would be no books explaining how to bind a secret, but hopefully, there would be information on releasing someone from that kind of magic.

James knew he could report what he suspected and get help that way, but he hesitated. He didn't want to call in outsiders. At least not yet. Investigating any illegal magic cast on Sebastian would take time, and Sebastian might not want too many people involved. He seemed to have chosen James to help, and James wasn't going to let him down.

This job really wasn't for an electrician, but Sebastian must have selected him for a reason.

He pulled magical theory books from the shelves and began reading about counter magic and reversing blood-and-bone spells. At last, he found a section on releasing secrets bound in blood. James checked the internet as well, cross-referencing different unbinding spells, and noting anything that might be useful on a scrap of paper.

Once he was confident he had what he needed, James put all the books away, except for the one that specifically talked about countering blood-binding. He shot off a text to Hazel saying he was going to Storm House and hurried to check out the book.

CHAPTER THIRTEEN

James pulled up to the Storm House gate. Unsurprisingly, it was locked. He tucked his notes into the book and opted to leave his phone in the truck. There was no point taking it when the battery would just drain away.

He climbed over the wall.

Storm House looked the same as it always did. James couldn't help glancing toward the paddock, at the path where he'd found Sebastian in the middle of the night. Nothing was there now. Relief flooded James as if he'd been worried he'd find Sebastian there again, left out in the cold with no one to help him.

The house's sinister presence felt like it had kicked things up a notch. Figuring out Sebastian had most likely been magically silenced made James's anxiety almost unbearable. His stomach hurt. He never would have guessed something like this was going on.

As he climbed the steps to the front porch, the cow came around the side of the house and started eating the grass beside him. It didn't seem at all concerned with his presence. James walked past it and knocked on the door.

There was no immediate answer. Impatient, James knocked again.

The door swung open, revealing Sebastian dressed exactly as he had been when James left yesterday morning. A few scratches were visible on the backs of his hands and on his neck. He looked perfectly fine otherwise.

"James Gray." Sebastian eyed him as if he weren't surprised. His lips twitched, a smile briefly shaping his face.

"Sebastian." James felt frantic. He pushed past him into the house, needing to get away from the property's haunting effects. His anxiety calmed once he was over the threshold, but only slightly.

"What have you got there?" Sebastian pointed to the book.

James clutched the leatherbound volume desperately with both hands. "Has someone bound your tongue? Is someone forcing you to keep secrets? Secrets about Storm House?"

Sebastian's casual demeanor disappeared. He seemed frozen, his eyes wide, then his face split into a beautiful grin. He reached for James, gripping him by both shoulders. "I could fucking kiss you, you perfect, perfect man."

James blinked. His voice didn't seem to be working. Did that mean he was right? Sebastian was probably prevented by the spell from confirming directly, so this might be as good of a *yes* as he was going to get.

"So your tongue is bound?" James couldn't help asking again. If Sebastian wasn't under the influence of a spell, surely he'd say so.

One of Sebastian's hands found its way to the back of James's neck. He hummed as his fingers caressed James's skin. "May I kiss you? I'm so happy right now."

Kissing had nothing to do with the questions James was asking, but he found he couldn't deny Sebastian anything just then. He wanted to help Sebastian, take care of him, and express all the feelings he'd been trying to push away.

"Okay." The word came out breathy, chills running down James's spine.

Sebastian didn't hesitate. He leaned in and pressed a closed-lip kiss to James's mouth. It was quick, a brief moment of firm pressure before Sebastian pulled back. He took hold of the sides of James's face with both his hands and leaned down, locking their eyes. "I knew you were clever."

"Um, thanks." James wasn't exactly sure what was happening. The kiss had been much more chaste than he'd hoped it would be. Was this just Sebastian trying to communicate to James that he was right about the secret-binding spell? Did Sebastian's whole seduction plan have nothing to do with liking him? Was it only tied up in getting James's attention when he couldn't ask directly for what he needed?

He didn't want that to be the case when the images that had filled his mind for days were so pretty and comforting. His eyes dropped to Sebastian's lips, longing for another kiss.

His desire must have been evident in the way he was staring. Sebastian made a soft, pleased sound and pulled him close, one of his hands threading through James's hair, and James angled his face upward, his lips parting involuntarily.

Their lips met again, and this time, Sebastian didn't pull away. His mouth moved in an exploratory kiss, careful but confident, and James eagerly matched every touch.

Sebastian took the kiss deeper, working James's mouth open so they could taste each other. James's pulse pounded in his ears. His arms were trapped between them, holding the book, but he wanted to wrap them around Sebastian. He wanted to touch and be touched, have this kiss go on forever.

Sebastian's kisses became more consuming. James had heard kissing described as hungry but had never felt anything like that until now.

When Sebastian let out a soft moan, James thought he might

die. Hot desire rocketed through him. It was the most beautiful sound he'd ever heard.

But Sebastian pulled back, letting go of James's face. He was sporting one of those sly smiles James was never sure how to interpret. "So what's the book for?"

James was dazed. The kiss had him reeling. The crush he'd been trying to deny had solidified and was growing in intensity. He wanted to get to know Sebastian, to talk to him without the spell holding him back. He wanted to spend more evenings together having home-cooked meals in the cheery pink kitchen, to see what Sebastian was like when he wasn't trying to get James to decipher Storm House's secrets.

Did Sebastian share any of those desires? It didn't seem like the kiss had fazed him. If anything, he appeared smug, satisfied, and maybe like he had James right where he wanted him.

James looked down at the book. He needed to focus. They could figure out their feelings later. "It's on counter magic. If you've been bound to secrecy against your will, we have to break the spell."

Sebastian crossed his arms. He didn't speak, only stared. Now this behavior made sense. Sebastian most likely couldn't talk about anything to do with the spell and didn't seem able to acknowledge it unless you counted that significant look in his eye. Or the kiss.

James was going to have to figure out how to undo the spell on his own. He was nervous about doing that kind of magic but determined to help Sebastian. "I've never done magic like this before." James pulled the scrap of paper out of the book. "I mean, obviously. It's *blood magic.*" He hesitated, watching Sebastian closely. "We could report this. Get professional help instead."

Sebastian took the paper from James. "I trust you," he said like it was the only thing that mattered.

James found some comfort it that. He was more confident undoing the secret-binding spell than he was snooping around

Storm House and the grounds, looking for the reason it was draining the power out of everything. At least he had instructions for the counter spell. He understood the principles behind it and had always been good at magic when he had clear guidance.

"We'll need your blood." James reminded Sebastian, but he didn't look the least bit alarmed by the news. "I've written down the symbols required. They should release any secrets bound within you when written in your blood."

Sebastian took a moment to study James's notes. He didn't look up or acknowledge James at all.

Even if James was sure he could pull off the spell from a technical point of view, he was still uneasy. "I know you can't answer me directly, but if I'm getting this totally wrong, maybe you could crumple the paper, run screaming, or something. Let me know if you don't want to do this."

Sebastian laughed, and James cracked a nervous smile. "I'm not running away from you."

James had to assume that meant Sebastian was on board with the plan, but there was one more thing. "I may need to channel you to have enough energy to complete the spell," James admitted.

He'd looked up information on channeling magic after reading warnings about the energy required for blood-magic rituals. Channeling itself was blood magic and could be dangerous if you took too much of the other person's power. Sebastian might not have realized James would need to do this and might not be willing to go there.

"Your magic is stronger than mine." Sebastian handed back the papers. "But I don't want you hurting yourself trying to do too much, and I really do trust you more than anyone I've met in my entire life."

That decided it as far as James was concerned, even if he had no idea why Sebastian felt that way. They hardly knew each other, even if he wanted to be someone Sebastian could lean on.

Thinking he could actually be that person made him glow with warm satisfaction.

"Okay, let's do this." James walked toward the kitchen, trying not to be squeamish about needing a bowl to collect Sebastian's blood. Halfway down the hall, James realized Sebastian wasn't following. He turned back. "You coming?"

Sebastian hadn't moved from the entry. "I'm having trouble actually."

Trouble what? Following him down the hall?

James took a step toward Sebastian, who immediately stepped back. Sebastian's eyes widened in surprise. James took another few steps, but Sebastian continued to back away. James reached out a hand. Sebastian jerked out of reach, his expression turning frustrated, as if he didn't want to avoid James but wasn't in complete control of his actions.

An unpleasant chill ran down James's spine. "It's the magic, isn't it?"

Sebastian grimaced, backing away. "Nothing is easy, is it?" He made a frustrated sound, expression turning wild and almost angry. "I—I won't just lie there and let you do what you want with me."

James froze. This complicated things. It seemed like the secret-binding spell was fighting to preserve itself. It must be extremely strong to not only control Sebastian's ability to reveal information but also prevent him from passively accepting help.

Sebastian slowly moved away until he was across the entryway from James. "Did I ever tell you I've got a kinky side?"

"*What?*" James had no idea where that had come from. The random comment felt like a slap in the face, one that made his cheeks hot.

"I've got handcuffs in my room." Sebastian began backing down the hall toward the sunroom. Soon, he'd be out of sight.

But James was distracted by thoughts of Sebastian cuffed to a bed, or even more appealing, the thought of himself restrained and at Sebastian's mercy. He shook off the idea and took a step after Sebastian. "Wait."

Sebastian ran.

Fuck, James was an idiot. Sebastian was trying to tell him he'd have to restrain him to undo the binding spell, but he couldn't state it plainly, just like everything else. And here James was lost in fantasyland.

He chased after Sebastian. "Wait, come back."

Sebastian didn't stop. Was James seriously going to have to hunt him down? He sped up as Sebastian rounded the corner, cutting back toward the kitchen.

"Come on, James. I'm not even the athlete here," Sebastian called as he headed toward the ballroom.

"Fuck. This is ridiculous." James gained on Sebastian, reaching for him. He almost caught Sebastian's robe before he made it to the ballroom.

Sebastian slammed the door in James's face. The lock clicked.

"This makes me feel like I'm doing something against your will," James called through the door.

After a pause, Sebastian responded, "Be smart, James."

The ambiguity in the statement didn't make James feel great. Was he seriously going to do blood magic on someone without their explicit consent, after they'd tried to run away? It felt so fucking wrong. But James was positive the spell was keeping Sebastian from agreeing to have it removed. He said he trusted James. He had to do this. There was no backing out now.

James stalked to the kitchen, grabbed what he needed, and proceeded to Sebastian's room.

He found the handcuffs at the bottom of the second bedside-table drawer. James felt distinctly uncomfortable going through its contents. What he and Sebastian were about to do wasn't sexual. He wasn't ready to know exactly how many dildos the man owned. That sort of thing was private.

James grumbled his way back down the stairs and along the

hall. He found the ballroom door still locked. James set his supplies on the floor—except the pink fuzzy handcuffs—and called out, "Sebastian!"

There was no answer. James couldn't believe things had led him here. He gritted his teeth and took several steps back, then charged the door, slamming his shoulder into it. The old wooden frame cracked and the door burst open, sending James careening into the room.

He looked around, ignoring the way his shoulder ached. Sebastian had shed his robe. The purple fabric lay in a heap in the middle of the large room. That was too bad. The flowy garment would have made it easier to grab him.

Sebastian was over by the window, standing behind the piano. "You here to hunt me down?" he taunted, sounding way too gleeful. Almost like he was loving every bit of this.

James supposed it was better than fear. If Sebastian had looked scared, he'd doubt he was doing the right thing and might have been unable to follow through. As it was, James wasn't thrilled about having to forcibly capture Sebastian, even if Sebastian seemed happy about the turn of events.

Maybe he could lull the spell into a false sense of security instead.

"We don't have to do this," James said cautiously, pausing where he stood. "Just come over and talk to me."

"See, I know you're lying," Sebastian called across the room.

Dammit. James inched forward. "I'm afraid of accidentally hurting you."

Sebastian laughed. "You worry too much."

"I know, but I can't help it. It's just how I am." James started moving to his right, not heading directly toward the piano, hoping he could get a better shot at running at Sebastian if he came in from an angle.

Sebastian didn't take his eyes off James. "There's no need to worry. I promise. You can rest assured that being chased down by you was one of my teenage fantasies."

"No, it wasn't," James snapped, even as his face heated. Sebastian was being absurd.

"Don't try to tell me what I used to dream about. Though this would be much more fun if we were in a pool. I wouldn't stand a chance at outswimming you."

James did not need to be thinking about capturing a squirming Sebastian clad in nothing but swim trunks. He inched closer, opening the handcuffs so they'd be ready. "I think this might be easier if we stopped talking."

Sebastian inched around the piano, away from James. "At least admit you're having fun."

"This is serious." James tried to sound convincing. "But I'm glad you're enjoying yourself." And he was glad. He wanted to make Sebastian happy, give him the things he desired even if they confused the hell out of James.

"I am enjoying myself. This might be the best night of my life," Sebastian said without sarcasm, grinning like a mad man.

"It's the afternoon." James tried to grumble, but it came out more like a laugh.

Sebastian rolled his eyes. "So? Stop trying to kill the mood, James. Have fun with me."

James lunged. He was close to the piano but not close enough. Sebastian bolted in the opposite direction. He almost collided with the window as he tried to keep an eye on James but corrected just in time and headed back toward the center of the room.

With a burst of speed, James grabbed for Sebastian, but Sebastian dodged him easily. James swore.

Sebastian cackled gleefully.

James had to catch him before he escaped the ballroom. Chasing him all over the house would be a nightmare. Sebastian wasn't that far ahead. He could almost reach him.

Sebastian stumbled, his feet caught up in his discarded robe. He didn't fall, but it was enough for James to gain on him. He grabbed Sebastian around the waist. Sebastian squealed, and they fell to the side, landing hard on the floor. James let out a grunt of pain.

"Stop moving," he growled in Sebastian's ear.

"Come on. You can do better than this. Restrain me," Sebastian taunted as he tried to wiggle out of James's hold.

James let out a frustrated growl. They struggled, but Sebastian failed to slip free. James finally got enough leverage to roll on top of Sebastian, sitting on his thighs and holding his arms tight against his body. "Got you."

They stared at each other, both breathing hard.

Sebastian's cheeks were pink. His tongue darted out to wet his lips. "Not quite. I'll escape as soon as you move."

James stared at Sebastian's lips. He couldn't believe any of this was actually happening and was even more surprised to find he wasn't hating it. Sebastian's playful mood made it hard to remember this wasn't some sexy game. But James had a knife out in the hall. There was nothing playful about that, and Sebastian was right. He'd slip away before James could even get the spell started.

James held Sebastian tight as he considered his next move. Looking into each other's eyes wasn't helping anything, and neither was thinking about the kiss they'd shared. James shook off his thoughts and made a snap decision, jumping up. It took a half-second for Sebastian to realize what was happening, and in that time, James grabbed a hold of the man's legs, lifting them into the air. Sebastian struggled but couldn't get free. James dragged him by the ankles over to the piano. He was going to cuff Sebastian to it.

When James had Sebastian as close to the piano legs as possible, he pounced, sitting on Sebastian's chest. His captive squeaked and his arms flailed as he tried to fight James off.

James got a handcuff around Sebastian's right wrist. They were stronger than the fuzzy padding made them look. James shoved Sebastian's arm above his head and slung the handcuff chain around the piano leg. He was panting, his face close to Sebastian's, whose eyes were bright with what looked like desire.

This whole thing was a mind fuck. James wanted to kiss Sebastian as he struggled beneath him, and James was sure Sebastian wanted it too. He'd never had someone look at him like they wanted him as badly as Sebastian seemed to right now.

James got a hold of Sebastian's hand and pulled it up to meet the other, closing it in the second cuff. Sebastian yanked his arms, but the cuffs held strong. The piano leg was thick and not in danger of moving anywhere.

"You got me." Sebastian sounded faintly surprised. "I'm totally going to have bruises tomorrow." He didn't appear upset by the idea.

James tried to catch his breath. "I feel like a fucking predator right now."

"It's kind of hot."

"Stop that." James barked, quickly shifting to his knees so he wasn't sitting on Sebastian, just hovering over him—straddling him—which wasn't much better. "Those kinds of comments aren't helping."

"No?" Sebastian arched his body, pressing back into James. "I'm having fun, and I think you are too." His gaze was much too knowing, causing James to blush. "Just so you know, you can do whatever you want to me now that I'm trapped here. You have my permission."

James's thoughts ran wild. His adrenaline was already pumping from the chase, and he couldn't deny there was something exciting about all this nonsense.

If he could do whatever he wanted with Sebastian, what would he do? James couldn't decide where he'd start, which was for the best. Sebastian was only trying to give him permission to do the spell. Right?

Okay, the look in Sebastian's eye said he meant other more explicit things too, but James couldn't think about that right now. Blood magic wasn't a joke.

"I'm going to have to take off your shirt." James swallowed. He wasn't helping matters, but he had to draw symbols on Sebastian's chest. That was the only reason he wanted Sebastian's shirt off.

"Lucky me." Sebastian squirmed, but not as if he were trying to get away. It was an obscenely seductive motion.

James tried not to lean into Sebastian's movements, even though the urge to ravage him was overwhelming. James took a breath, trying to calm himself. He'd never been so caught up in someone before. It felt dangerous. James should have told Sebastian to stop trying to seduce him days ago. But that wasn't what James wanted.

He forced himself to concentrate on the problem at hand and managed it by sheer power of stubborn will. He got off Sebastian and stood, stepping back. "I need to go get the supplies. Stay here."

Sebastian gave him a wicked smile. "Yes, sir."

James was in over his head with this man. He turned and hurried to the hall. At least the sight of the knife sobered him. This wasn't a fucking game.

Back in the ballroom, James set everything on the floor beside the piano. He looked down at Sebastian, who'd stopped struggling but still seemed to be breathing harder than normal, almost like he was panting in arousal or anticipation.

"Strip me," Sebastian ordered, the command sending a jolt through James. "And please, do whatever you want with me."

"Stop saying that," James muttered without conviction.

He briefly considered granting Sebastian's request and sucking him off before doing the ritual. Shit, it was tempting, but he wanted to be able to talk to Sebastian without magic in the way before doing something like that. He knelt and grabbed the hem of Sebastian's shirt. "How am I going to get this off? I don't want to leave it tangled around your head."

"Get creative." Sebastian made it sound like a challenge. He seemed completely comfortable being at James's mercy, the excitement in his eyes impossible to ignore.

James liked that. It meant, among other things, that Sebastian's trust in him was real.

He knelt and picked up the knife, then pulled the shirt away from Sebastian's body before slicing the hem. He set the knife to the side and ripped the shirt the rest of the way open.

Sebastian gasped, his bare chest heaving. His cheeks flushed and his lips parted as he stared up at James.

Even though he'd seen Sebastian's chest before, James took a moment to appreciate the freckles cascading along his collarbone and how his dusky pink nipples pebbled in response to his stare.

James's whole body was on fire. He wanted to bend and press his lips to Sebastian's skin. He wanted to lick him up and down until he was writhing. But that wasn't what they were doing. That wasn't why they were here.

"I need to link us before I begin the unbinding spell," James said. "I won't know for sure if I'll need the extra energy until I start the unbinding, but it will be too late to stop and link then."

"Okay. Got it. You're in charge," Sebastian said, a little breathless.

The linking spell allowing James to channel Sebastian was relatively simple for something that could be so dangerous, and now that it came down to it, James was nervous. For the obvious risk-of-harm related reasons, but also because blood magic felt intimate. Too intimate. He was doing this with someone he had feelings for. In a situation they both found arousing. James felt exposed, like he and Sebastian were about to share something deeply personal.

James took off his jacket and pulled his shirt over his head.

Sebastian's eyes raked over him. "It's not fair that my hands are bound."

James had to agree. He wanted Sebastian's hands on him too. "Concentrate," he grumbled as if he didn't care.

Sebastian pouted, sticking out his bottom lip. "I am."

He might be, but James suspected he was concentrating on all the wrong things.

James pricked the index finger of his nondominant hand with the knife. He waited for a large drop of blood to well up, then pressed his bleeding finger to Sebastian's chest, approximately where his heart would be, completing the first step in binding them together. Sebastian sucked in a breath at the touch, some of the overt playfulness disappearing from his features.

James's pulse pounded as he marked himself with his own blood in the same way. "I'm going to have to cut you now. So I can mix our blood and complete the link between us." He looked down at Sebastian, searching his face for any hint he'd changed his mind.

"I know. Don't worry about it," Sebastian said with full confidence. "Just make sure I won't need stitches."

"I'll be careful. I looked it up. I'll use magic to draw blood out of a small cut, then again to stop the bleeding. I'll take what I need to free you from the secret-binding now. That way, we only have to do this part once."

Sebastian nodded.

James placed the bowl under Sebastian's arm and checked his notes. He made a shallow cut on his forearm while reciting a spell to bleed Sebastian safely. Magic drew out more blood than a small wound in this location would normally produce. It dripped steadily into the bowl.

Sebastian's breathing was shallow, puffs of air hitting James's chest as he leaned over him.

James took his eyes off the cut to check Sebastian's face. "Are you okay?"

He gave a tiny smile. "Perfect."

James stopped the bleeding with a second spell. He'd taken less blood than a routine blood test would have. The magic use made him momentarily woozy, but he recovered after a few deep breaths.

Trying not to think too much about it, James moved on to the next step of the linking spell and dipped a finger into the bowl. He pressed the bloody pad of his finger to the smear of blood already on his chest, mixing the two together. James repeated the process on Sebastian, then moved so he was straddling Sebastian's hips, leaning over him so their chests aligned. All that was left to do was the incantation, and he'd have access to Sebastian's magic.

They looked at each other for a moment. James wasn't sure exactly what he was feeling. It wasn't as simple as affection or desire, but now wasn't the time to stop and analyze it.

James pried his gaze away from Sebastian's to double-check his notes, then began reciting the linking spell.

As the spell connected them, a surge of power seemed to rip James open and expose all his fear and uncertainty, not just about the ritual but everything in his life. Was that supposed to happen? He had a moment of panic.

His emotions were quickly overwhelmed by a desperate need. James didn't think it was coming from him, but it felt oddly familiar, so he wasn't sure. He hadn't expected any of this. Was this neediness Sebastian's emotion? If so, this process was even more intimate than James had thought, more intimate than he'd ever been with anyone. Raw emotion wasn't meant to be shared, yet the link between them seemed to be doing just that.

Before he could dwell on it, the clash of feelings was overtaken by the buzz of magical energy. It came as a relief, and James welcomed the distraction, hoping to forget the first part had ever happened.

James had never felt magic like this before. It was as if he was being consumed by the connection growing between him and Sebastian. "I thought you said you had less power than me," he gasped.

Sebastian blinked at him. "I do."

That didn't make sense. The energy James felt seemed enormous, almost unfathomable. It was nothing like when James scoped out the power left in a battery. He swore he could feel life in the magic. He could feel Sebastian. How wild was that? Maybe being linked to another person was what was so unfathomable, the vast power not about magical strength but about human life.

"Okay," James said, mostly to himself. He was panting, but not from magical overexertion. His mind was overwhelmed. All his fear was gone, but its absence wasn't as calming as it should have been.

"M-maybe we need to give it a minute." Sebastian's voice shook even though he didn't look frightened. "To s-settle down."

"This is so—" James let his eyes close. "Yeah, let's get used to it before starting the next spell."

James let his head drop until his forehead rested against Sebastian's. Their breath mingled. The magic winding between them slowly became less overpowering, almost like it was solidifying, the sensation turning warm and welcoming.

Sebastian shifted, the handcuffs clinking. He turned his face, rubbing his nose against James's. They were a hair's breadth away from kissing. James could feel Sebastian's chest rising and falling beneath him as he breathed. The motion was inviting, as if the idea of sharing breath was a precursor to sharing other things, moving together in other ways.

James's cock swelled. All he had to do was drop his hips, let his weight rest against Sebastian, and they could see what all those other shared movements would feel like. Shared blood, shared breath, shared pleasure.

"Magic shouldn't be this erotic," James whispered as Sebastian continued to nuzzle their noses together, making soft little sounds. It was like the spell had removed the filter that would normally have stopped him from saying the thought aloud, but at the moment, he didn't care.

"Why shouldn't it?" Sebastian's voice came out husky. "It's so good, James. This feels so good."

James turned his head to close that last little bit of space between them and let his lips brush over Sebastian's. He was rewarded with a painfully needy sound.

"I want to know everything about you," James breathed as he trailed his lips along Sebastian's jaw to his neck. "I want all your secrets, Sebastian."

He felt Sebastian swallow. "Everything?"

James had to be losing his mind. He'd normally never say anything like that. He didn't mean just the secrets Sebastian had been bound to keep. James wanted all of Sebastian's intimate secrets too. He wanted to know all the sounds Sebastian made in the throes of pleasure. He wanted to know how to undo Sebastian as completely as Sebastian had undone him.

"Yes, everything," James promised.

But to have that, they needed to finish the ritual. Pulling back, he eyed the smear of their mixed blood on Sebastian's chest. The sight shouldn't have filled him with a fresh wave of affection, but it did. "Are you ready for the next part?"

Sebastian had a dazed look but nodded without hesitation.

James checked his notes, concentrating on the paper until he was able to push his lusty feelings away. He dipped his finger in the bowl of blood, preparing to draw on Sebastian's skin. The first symbol went on his forehead. James carefully brushed Sebastian's hair out of the way with his unbloody hand before tracing a red circle.

Sebastian watched as James moved on to the symbols on his chest. Desperation lined his face, and Sebastian made a raw, helpless sound as James began to recite the unbinding spell.

James pushed on.

The bloody symbols began to glow as James poured power into the ritual. He was glad he and Sebastian were linked. If he didn't have the extra energy, he was sure he'd have drained himself.

His arms shook from holding himself up, so he leaned back, resting all his weight on Sebastian's lap. Sweat prickled James's brow. He was almost through the incantation, the glowing blood shining brighter. Sebastian stared at James, wide-eyed and even more desperate than before.

James dipped his finger in the last of the blood to draw the final symbol to release Sebastian. As he painted the design, energy poured out of James so quickly that it stole his breath.

Sebastian cried out, writhing beneath him before going completely still. Light flared, turning all the symbols white, and then snuffed out.

James was lightheaded. He sucked in air until his mind cleared and he could see straight. Sebastian seemed alert, eyes wide, as he went boneless beneath James.

The spell was over. They'd done it.

James fought the urge to flop onto Sebastian's chest and fall asleep. "How do you feel?"

"I don't know." Sebastian looked down at himself as best he could in his current position. "It felt like someone ripped my fucking soul out."

"Sorry." James reached out and stroked Sebastian's cheek before he could stop himself.

Sebastian leaned into the touch. "It's okay. I think it worked." He closed his eyes as he nuzzled James's palm. "You were right. Someone bound me to secrecy, but it isn't just about what's going on with the energy here. It's not about the draining power. That's only a symptom." Sebastian's eyes snapped open like he'd surprised himself. "Oh my god, I just said that. Aloud. That's more than I've been able to tell anyone in years."

Years? How long had he been forced to keep secrets? James had so many questions. "Let me get these cuffs off." He fumbled in his jeans pocket for the key.

As soon as Sebastian's hands were free, he sat bolt upright and grabbed James on either side of his face. The sudden movement caused James to rock backward in Sebastian's lap. He almost fell over but steadied himself in time, his hands on Sebastian's hips.

Sebastian dug his fingers into James's hair, but the touch wasn't anything like their sensual exchanges from earlier. "I'm trapped," he rasped in a voice that sounded completely unlike the Sebastian James knew. "I'm trapped, James. You have to help me."

James's heart hammered. "What do you mean?"

"I'm trapped here. At the house. On this property!" Sebastian's voice rose to a shout. It felt like he was going to pull James's hair out. "You've got to get me the fuck out of here!"

CHAPTER FOURTEEN

"W‍hat do you mean you're trapped at the house?"

Sebastian shook James. "What do you think I mean? I can't leave. I'm not some antisocial recluse avoiding everyone in Moonlight Falls by choice. I wasn't only bound to secrecy. I'm tied to this damn place—trapped by magic, cursed—and unable to tell anyone what's really going on."

James's stomach dropped. He suddenly felt cold. "So this isn't about the energy draining at all? You need me to free you? From Storm House?"

"Yes!" Sebastian's eyes were wild. He looked completely unhinged, covered in blood and shaking, his breathing getting shallow like he was starting to panic.

"Okay." James covered Sebastian's hands, where they still had a death grip on his hair. "We'll get you out. Unbinding your tongue worked. Things are better than they were this morning. You won't be stuck here now that I know you need to be freed."

Sebastian blinked, his eyes going shiny. "You're right. Oh hell, I can't believe this worked." He let out a shaky laugh and let go of James's hair.

James didn't release Sebastian's hands, bringing them to rest in his lap. "I can't believe those damn *tales* really were a coded message. I said that just to annoy you."

"Clever, right?" Sebastian smiled, filling James with relief even though the situation was much worse than he'd ever have guessed. He couldn't imagine what it would have been like for Sebastian to be trapped out here and unable to tell anyone.

"Let's get this blood cleaned off. Then I have about a million questions for you."

"There's a bathroom down the hall," Sebastian said, but he didn't seem to want to let James go. His grip on James's fingers tightened.

They stayed on the ground for a minute longer. Sebastian's hold on James was more desperate than sensual, but that was okay. James waited until Sebastian was ready to release him. He'd have sat there the rest of the day if that was what Sebastian needed.

When they got up, James almost fell back down, a dizzy spell hitting him hard.

"That was a lot of magic." James steadied himself and grabbed his shirt and jacket.

Sebastian peeled off the remainder of his ruined shirt and dropped it to the floor. "I'm feeling it too. We'll raid the pantry while I tell you everything."

They slowly made their way to the bathroom across the hall from the kitchen and cleaned up in the sink. Wiping off the mixed blood from above their hearts broke the link between their magic, sending a shiver through them both.

At least unlinking was less intense than linking. They didn't need more heightened emotions right now.

Sebastian picked up James's jacket. "Can I borrow this?"

James pulled his shirt over his head. "Sure."

Sebastian slipped the jacket on. It was too large in the shoulders for his slight frame. He pulled it tight around himself as he often did with his robe, but the sleeves rode up, too short on

Sebastian's longer arms. It fit terribly, but James found the sight of Sebastian in his clothes more appealing than anything he'd ever seen.

In the kitchen, they piled food on the table. Apples, bread, butter, a tin of fresh-looking cookies, a bag of tortilla chips, and an unopened jar of salsa. They ate for a good ten minutes straight without pausing for more than a breath here and there.

"How long have you been trapped here?" James asked once his brain felt less foggy.

"Six years. Ever since I've been back. Well—" Sebastian paused to drink some water. "Not from the second I came back. From when my uncle died."

James had a very bad feeling about this. Mila said Stephen had hidden himself away and brushed off her offers of assistance. Was he no more of a voluntary recluse than Sebastian? "He was trapped here too?"

"Yeah, he was." Sebastian gazed morosely at a cookie, lost in thought. It was a defeated sort of sadness, unlike his frantic demeanor from the ballroom. "I didn't know it at the time." Sebastian's voice wavered, and he cleared his throat. "Uncle Stephen was trapped here my whole life. Since before I was born. The whole time I knew him, I thought he was just this antisocial, paranoid man who couldn't let go of the past, and none of that was true."

"He didn't tell you?"

"He couldn't." Sebastian tossed his cookie back into the tin. "He was bound to secrecy via blood magic, just like me. This curse and the secrecy spell go hand in hand. I only found out when I inherited it from him."

"What do you mean?" James leaned forward, his appetite forgotten.

"I had no idea when I came home." Sebastian looked desperate for James to understand. "Stephen was dying, and I just wanted to help take care of him. But he knew the curse would pass to me when he died. He knew my whole life that I'd eventually be a prisoner here like he was. He never tried to tell me. No one did. That was the whole point."

Sebastian let out a humorless laugh. "He didn't try to say anything until right before he died. That's when he explained it all, but it was too late for me to escape the property. The magic already had hold of me. As his life faded, it latched onto mine."

"The whole point? I— Sebastian, why would he have known you were going to inherit a curse and not try to tell you?"

Sebastian ran his hands through his hair. "I'm not explaining it well. The curse didn't start with Stephen. It started with Sullivan and Nelson Storm, my great-great-grandmother Selma's sons."

James's brow furrowed. "The grandma with the teeth?"

"That's her." Sebastian looked pissed off rather than sad now. "Sullivan and Nelson built this house, and while they were at it, they messed with things you aren't supposed to touch. There's a vein of power running through the property. Two of them, actually. They intersect in the woods. That's why they bought this land in particular. They messed with the veins and threw off the balance of energy transferring between here and Beyond. It was a big fuck up. Like almost blew up the whole town kind of fuck up. But Grandma Selma fixed it."

James didn't like the sound of any of this. "How?"

"To prevent the veins of power from exploding, there needed to be a constant energy debt paid. She bound Sullivan to the land so his life force would stabilize the veins."

James's eyes widened. "What about the other brother?"

"He ran off as soon as things went to shit. As far as I know, he never came back. Left Sullivan and Grandma to deal with everything."

James ran a hand through his hair, trying to peace it all together. "But that was ages ago."

"Yeah, nineteen forty. The catch is Grandma's fix didn't solve the problem. It just patched it. As soon as Sullivan's life wasn't there to hold things together, the veins would explode, so Grandma made sure her spell would transfer with her son's death to his son, who was only six years old at the time this all happened."

"She doomed her descendants to be trapped here?" James asked in disbelief. It sounded harsh, even if the alternative was some big explosion. Surely, there was another way to prevent disaster.

"They didn't know exactly what would happen to the veins if they exploded or how far the destruction would reach, so I think they felt it was a necessary sacrifice. And everything I've come across makes it seem like Selma wasn't sorry about punishing her sons for their mistake. They shouldn't have messed with the veins in the first place."

"Damn." It was a harsh punishment. James couldn't fault the woman for saving Moonlight Falls and the other residents, but still.

"I'm the fourth down the line to take on the curse." There was venom in Sebastian's tone, like he hated his ancestors, and James couldn't blame him. "Sullivan and his son, Simon, supposedly didn't mind being here and took it as a duty to protect Moonlight Falls from destruction. They had their families with them—wives and kids—and thought of themselves as guardians of magical power, looking after the balance between here and Beyond.

"Whether that's true or just what Simon told Uncle Stephen as he died and passed on the curse, who knows. Stephen clearly bought into it and accepted the curse as his duty. He couldn't tell me I'd be the next to bear the family burden directly—he couldn't even say the Storms were cursed—but he didn't even try to hint at it. Not like I did with you. He never implied anything was going on here, nothing big or sinister. And like"—Sebastian shoved his chair back and crossed his arms—"it's not as if I'd have run away and let the town explode, bringing unknown magical consequences to fruition, if I'd known. I'm not that selfish. But I could have been better prepared when I came home to take care of Stephen. I don't know why none of them ever tried to find a better solution to the problem. I don't get why they all accepted that we had to be trapped here forever."

Unless it was because there was no other solution.

James was overwhelmed and tried to push that hopeless thought away. This was so much more than he thought he'd be dealing with. He wasn't even remotely equipped to handle this. At least he had Eli. He'd know where to start. He studied veins of power and would know much more about what an energy imbalance like this meant. They'd sort it out. They had to. It was the only option.

"Is that why the energy is all wrong here? Why it feels haunted?" James asked.

Sebastian nodded. "I can't feel it because I'm essentially part of the property. I used to get all the creepy feelings when I was younger. But as soon as the curse claimed me, the unsettling sensations all went away."

James rubbed his chin. "Fuck. This is some serious shit, Sebastian."

"Tell me about it. I've been trying to covertly communicate with the outside world for six years, but no one sticks around long enough for any of my random actions to make sense. I used to try and stalk the mail man, wait for him to show up down by the gate, and try to get him to come in and talk to me for more than a minute. I think he thought I was a serial killer, trying to lure him into some sick trap."

It was heartbreaking. James didn't know how anyone could take the isolation. No phone, no computer or radio, no connection to the outside world except the newspaper and mail.

"How old were you when you got trapped here?"

"Twenty." Sebastian sounded every bit as bitter as you'd expect. "Didn't even get to finish college. And I'd just started dating this girl, Emily, before I came home for Stephen. We kept in touch while I was able to go into town and use my phone. You know, before it was too late. But I was still oblivious to what was coming. I had to break up with her via written letter, pretend I was choosing to push her away. And I didn't even get to say goodbye to my other college friends since I didn't have their home addresses."

"I'm so sorry." James had to resist the urge to rush around the table and crush Sebastian into a never-ending hug.

"It's not your fault." Sebastian made a visible effort to rally. He grinned mischievously. "I'd love to know what Emily thought of my letter. She probably took me for the biggest dickhead ever, saying there was no need to discuss the breakup over the phone, let alone in person." He laughed.

James smiled grimly at Sebastian's ability to find any of this amusing. "When you're out of here, you can ask her what she thought. Tell her what really happened. Reconnect with your friends."

Sebastian huffed. "Don't think that'll be on my to-do list, to be honest. Everyone I ghosted six years ago has moved on and forgotten me."

"Oh, maybe." James was saddened by Sebastian's dismissal, but thoughts of reconnecting with people might be premature. "So what do we do now?" he asked, hoping like hell Sebastian had a plan.

From the look of panic that flashed across his face, James wasn't sure he did. "I still can't believe you figured out my tongue was tied so quickly."

"It would have been faster if you had shoved Little William's story under my nose."

"I tried that." Sebastian grabbed a chip, dunked it in the salsa, and ate it. "I got the book out of the library upstairs, intending to wave the story at the next delivery person to come by, but I ended up burning it instead."

"Why?"

"The magic. Like how it made me run from you. It wouldn't let me do anything to communicate what was happening so directly. So it made me get rid of the book."

At least they were past that now. James was relieved he'd figured it out. It seemed like his tendency to over-worry had resulted in something positive for once. "So you don't know how to break the curse? How to get out of here without blowing up Moonlight Falls?"

"Not exactly," Sebastian admitted.

James tried to not panic under the weight of Sebastian's request to free him. "I'm going to have to ask for help on this."

"Go for it. Tell whoever you want. I just want to get out of here." He fixed James with a serious stare.

James stood from the table. "We'll find a way, I promise. But I should go talk to some people. Eli, for a start, and do some research. And if that doesn't work, we need to report this."

Sebastian nodded. "I'm not against telling everyone exactly what's happening out here. Report it now. I would have done it myself if I could have."

"True, of course." That was a weight off James's mind. This mess needed a professional solution, magical practitioners whose job it was to help people deal with this sort of thing. "I'll head back to town and get started. Make some calls."

Sebastian stood in a rush. "Now?" His brow creased with worry. James had never seen him look so anxious.

He paused. "We shouldn't delay. You've been here long enough."

"No, I just—" Sebastian pulled James's jacket tighter against his bare chest. "You'll be back soon, right? I don't like being left out here. I don't want you to go." Sebastian looked down, avoiding James's eye. "Please don't leave me here," he said in a small voice.

James moved closer, putting a hand on Sebastian's shoulder.

He had no idea how to respond to the anguished request. Sebastian had to be traumatized by all the years of involuntary solitude and in desperate need of company. How many times had he longed to ask someone not to leave him, only to be stopped by the secret-binding? James wanted to stay and comfort him, wrap him up and never let go, but he needed to go get help.

After a heavy pause, Sebastian turned away, his face going red. "Sorry."

James squeezed his shoulder. "Don't be. I'd stay—"

"No," Sebastian interrupted. "You're right. I've waited long enough." He rolled his eyes unconvincingly.

James didn't let go of Sebastian's shoulder. "I promise I'll be back as soon as I can tomorrow."

"Yeah, got it. It's fine." Sebastian shook him off. "I can deal with it. I'm just bored out of my mind." It couldn't just be boredom, but if Sebastian wanted to take back his moment of vulnerability, that was okay.

Sebastian walked James to the gate. It was late afternoon, and Hazel wouldn't be pleased he'd left her on her own for so long with only a measly text as an explanation. At least she would understand when he told her about Storm House. She wasn't going to believe this shit.

James waited as Sebastian unlocked the gate, deciding not to ask for his jacket back. "I'll come by at lunch tomorrow—at the very latest—and let you know what everyone says. I'd come in the morning, but I've got to keep working on the lights in town, and I don't know if I'll have anything figured out before then."

"Sounds like a plan." Sebastian was acting like he didn't care, but James hoped knowing when to expect him would help him cope with the isolation.

James headed for his truck, a million things circling inside his mind. Something hit him out of nowhere, pain shooting through his face as his nose crunched.

CHAPTER FIFTEEN

JAMES FELT like he'd walked into a brick wall. "Ow, fuck." He cupped his nose as blood flowed freely down his face. "What was that?" He glanced over his shoulder.

Sebastian had gone pale, like he'd seen a ghost. Had it been a shade? It wasn't dark, but there were plenty of long shadows falling across the road.

"What did I just run into?" James spun in a circle, searching. Both sides of the iron gate were well out of his way. He moved forward, needing to get a tissue out of his truck so he didn't bleed all over his shirt.

He banged into it again. Except there was nothing there. "What the fuck?" He stuck out his hand, and it collided with what felt like a wall but looked like nothing.

Ice ran down James's spine. He abandoned his bloody nose, feeling the solid air with both hands. He was standing right in the gateway, but an invisible force kept him from stepping beyond the property line.

Full-on panic hit James like a tidal wave. *No.* He couldn't be trapped. It wasn't possible. There had to be a way through.

He fell to his hands and knees, feeling near the ground and all the way across the open gateway. The barrier went right into the dirt and melded seamlessly with the stone pillars framing the gate. He pushed everywhere he could reach. The barrier didn't give in the slightest.

James jumped up and climbed the wall. He got one hand on the top ledge, but as he reached over with his other, he hit the invisible barrier, preventing him from reaching the other side.

He jumped down and spun to face Sebastian, who was still standing frozen. "Am I *trapped* here?" He didn't want to believe it. Couldn't believe it.

Sebastian was even paler than before. "I—I don't know how—"

"What do you mean you don't know? Why can't I get out? I thought the unbinding spell worked. You're free to tell your secrets. We didn't even mess with the curse. How could this— how—I can't be trapped!" James's chest tightened, his next words coming out in a growl. "What did you do?"

"*Me?*" Sebastian spat back, anger temporarily replacing his fear. "Why do you think I did anything?"

James pointed wildly at the impenetrable gateway. "Because this is exactly what you did with my truck. You tricked me then, got me stranded here, and you've tricked me now."

"I'm not tricking you, James. I swear." Sebastian took a step toward him. "Yes, I knew exactly what would happen with letting your truck die, but I only did that to try and show you what was going on. *This* wasn't supposed to happen! I don't even know how it happened. All you did was release the secret bound in my blood. The curse trapping me here is so much more complicated than that!"

"I don't believe you." Primal fear had taken over James. He'd never quite trusted Sebastian and couldn't see past that doubt. All James could think was that Sebastian had been here for *six years*. His uncle had died here after being trapped for decades. That couldn't happen to James as well. "Let me out," he croaked. "I said I'd help. Just let me out."

"I can't," Sebastian pleaded. "I don't know how this happened. Please believe me, James. I wasn't trying to trap you. Why the hell would I do that?"

James felt unlike himself. As if everything he knew had twisted until nothing made sense. He pointed a bloody finger at Sebastian, his hand shaking. His nose dripped, getting blood all over his shirt. "You didn't want me to leave."

"Excuse me for being pathetically lonely, but that doesn't mean I want you stuck here with me." Sebastian let out a pained sob. "I don't want more people *here*. I want to get the fuck out! You can't get me out if you're stuck here. This isn't what I wanted! It ruins everything!" Sebastian's words got increasingly frantic. He fell to his knees, his breaths coming short and fast, like he was hyperventilating. "*Fuck!*" he screamed so loud the birds on the lawn took flight.

Sebastian began to sob, big, choking, uncontrollable sounds tearing from his lungs.

James was numb with shock, his fear so acute he'd short-circuited and couldn't feel anymore. If Sebastian wasn't lying and hadn't planned this, they were both completely screwed. How had they messed up so badly? This couldn't be happening.

That was when James realized he couldn't feel the haunting effects of the property. His emotions might be dulled in his current state, but even as he'd walked down the driveway, he hadn't felt it. He just hadn't registered the change before, with everything else on his mind.

Not feeling the skin-crawling wrongness of the place meant the curse had him, Storm House had claimed him, and he wasn't getting out any more than Sebastian was. Of course Sebastian hadn't wanted that to happen, but it being an accident didn't feel any better.

The ice encasing James thawed and his feelings crept back. None of them were good.

He wiped his face with the bottom of his shirt. At least his nose had stopped bleeding. He knelt on the gravel next to Sebastian, who was still sobbing like the person who'd meant the most to him in the world had died. James hadn't realized crying could be quite this loud.

He pulled Sebastian into his arms.

All his reasons for not trusting Sebastian stemmed from the way the secret-binding had made Sebastian behave. James couldn't hold that against him. Sebastian had never been messing with him. Trapping James wasn't logical if Sebastian was trying to break free, and James had no doubt he wanted to escape more than anything.

James had accused Sebastian in a blind panic and already regretted it, and he felt more and more guilty the longer Sebastian cried. James started to worry Sebastian was having a serious breakdown.

"Six years," Sebastian rasped between sobs. "It took me six years to get one person to realize something was wrong. I'm never going to get out of here."

"Hey." James placed a finger under Sebastian's chin and tilted his head up. "You're still better off than before. People will know something is wrong when I don't come home. They won't be able to explain away my absence, saying I'm avoiding the world by choice. No one will believe I've randomly decided to live at Storm House. We can still figure this out. Still tell people what's going on."

Sebastian's expression was grim. "I hope so."

"What do you mean?"

He chewed his bottom lip. "There's a chance finding out the secret triggers silence. So you might not be able to tell anyone. See, my mom knew about the curse. She was here with Stephen when their father died, and they found out together. Stephen told me her tongue was bound after she found out, so I shouldn't be mad she kept things from me."

James was surprised Sebastian hadn't mentioned this sooner. "But you were acting like I could tell anyone. Ask for help. Report the curse."

"Well, Mom never broke the secret-binding, did she? So, of course, she was kept silent. And she's a Storm. The binding spell is in our blood, along with the curse. I thought freeing the secret would mean there was no way you could be silenced for finding out. The spell would be broken. Plus, you aren't a Storm. Your blood has never been touched by the binding. But you got trapped after learning the secret, so I clearly have no idea how these spells actually behave in relation to one another and could've been wrong when I thought that breaking the binding meant you couldn't be silenced."

James's head swam. It was all so cyclical. "So the curse and the secret-binding might be interconnected, magically? They react to each other?"

Sebastian sagged against James. "Seems like it. I always thought of them as two separate spells cast on Storm blood. However, it's looking like breaking the binding triggered the curse, regardless of you not being a Storm. That's the only way you could have possibly gotten trapped. But, James, I swear I never suspected it was possible before now." He looked at James desperately, a hand tightening on James's wrist.

"I believe you," James assured him, and Sebastian relaxed. "I'm sorry I reacted like that. I should have stopped and thought."

"That's okay. I get it." Sebastian let out a tired sigh. "Now that this has happened, the curse capturing anyone who breaks the secret-binding and learns the truth sounds like something Grandma Selma would do. If she thought it was the only way to stop us escaping and leaving things to explode."

The speculation made sense in hindsight, sitting here on the gravel driveway trapped behind an invisible barrier, but James understood that Sebastian wouldn't have seen this coming, especially when he thought the spells could only affect his family members.

"There's no information on exactly how Selma cast the curse," Sebastian admitted. "Not about how she constructed the spell or what fail-safes she might have woven in. I never thought there was more than the secret-binding. Even connecting the two to react to each other is some seriously complex spellwork."

James was tired. So tired he thought he might never fully recover. "I guess it doesn't really matter." He was resigned to his fate in a way that surprised him. "It doesn't matter exactly how the curse got me, only that it did."

"If I had any idea that you getting sucked in was a possibility, I never would have let you break the silencing spell." Sebastian grabbed James's hand and squeezed. James assured him he understood, but Sebastian went on. "I mean, my mom found out and walked away from the property, so that meant all I had to do was break the secret free from my blood and tell someone who cared. Then we could try and break the curse."

James couldn't bring himself to ask why Sebastian's mom didn't care. The situation was heartbreaking enough already.

They were silent for a long time. The birds landed back on the grass, picking at worms and other bugs. James watched them hop around until the sky went orange and the shadows lengthened.

"We should go inside." Sebastian stood, stretching like he was stiff. He closed his eyes for a moment, then went to lock the gate.

CHAPTER SIXTEEN

T HEY CLEANED up the kitchen in silence, putting away the remaining snacks.

Sebastian inspected James's nose and gave him a cold, wet cloth to ice his face as best he could without any actual ice, then insisted James take something to help with the pain and swelling. The nose wasn't broken, but still, Sebastian fussed.

"What would you like for dinner?" Sebastian leaned against the counter, hands folded behind his back as he eyed James, watching like he expected his nose to suddenly start bleeding again.

James turned and gazed out the window. Sebastian's attention was making him squirm. "Don't feel like you have to cook for me or anything. Just do whatever you were planning to if I wasn't here."

It was fully dark now. Unlike the other night, James hadn't yet spotted any shades drifting around. He'd count it as a blessing.

"I can't exactly keep going as if you aren't here. We're"—Sebastian paused—"roommates now."

The statement elicited a strange wave of emotions within James. He was crushed by the turn of events, yet part of him was glad it was Sebastian he was stuck with. It didn't make sense to be happy about the chance to spend more time with Sebastian. He was the reason James was trapped in the first place, even if he hadn't done it on purpose, and it wasn't like he wanted to spend *all* his time with the guy.

"Roommates," he echoed. It was too bland a word to describe their situation.

They ended up having peanut butter on toast—well, pan-fried bread since there was no toaster—and calling it a night.

Sebastian brought firewood up to the spare room and lit a fire in the hearth. The mood was somber. James wished they could go back to joking around, Sebastian scandalizing him with suggestive comments and trying to get him into bed, like the last time he'd stayed over. All that felt like a lifetime ago.

Sebastian stood from the fireplace. "Want me to get you something to wear that isn't bloody?"

James blinked at Sebastian, feeling dazed. It was probably exhaustion from all the magic use, but the situation certainly wasn't helping him stay out of his own head. "Sure," he agreed and watched Sebastian leave.

James sat on the bed, staring blankly at the flames growing in the small fireplace.

Sebastian returned with a pile of things, which he dumped on the bed. "My stuff will be too small for you, so these are some of Stephen's old things."

James wasn't sure what he thought about wearing Sebastian's dead uncle's clothes. "Thanks." Everything looked dated, from the nineties or so.

Sebastian rested a hand on James's shoulder. "I'll get us out of here. I know I asked for your help, but this is on me. I'm not going to give up while you're stuck with me. Okay?"

"We'll figure it out together," James countered. "I just need to sleep. I'll be less mopey tomorrow, promise."

Sebastian let out a harsh laugh. "Mope all you want. I spiraled for months when I was first stuck here." With that, Sebastian left him, closing the door.

The silence was crushing.

JAMES WAS ROUSED from sleep by Sebastian knocking on his door. "James, James." He poked his head in. "Get up. I think your brother is here."

James rubbed sleep from his eyes. He needed approximately one million more hours of rest before he was ready to function. He slipped his shoes on and grabbed a robe from the pile of Stephen's old clothes to throw over the flannel pajamas he was wearing.

Sebastian led the way down the stairs and out the front door, oil lamp in hand. "I was watching out my window and saw headlights pull up. There are people poking around your truck."

James was still disoriented from sleep. "What time is it?"

"Just after eleven."

Someone here so soon was good. They hurried across the front porch and down the driveway. Sebastian was still in James's jacket with no shirt, like he hadn't gone to sleep yet.

"Hello? James?" Eli called from the other side of the gate. He turned to Parker. "Here they come."

"Eli." James's whole body flooded with relief at the sight of his brother and Parker shining shade-lights through the gate.

"Why didn't you come home or answer your phone?" Eli scolded as if he was the older one. "Are you trying to give me gray hair worrying where you are all the time?"

"No. There's nothing to worry about," James found himself saying. He shopped short. That wasn't what he'd meant to say. He'd been planning something along the lines of *Help me!*

Parker shone a flashlight at Sebastian, then at James. *"Jesus,* what happened to your face?"

A bruise must have started forming. James's nose and left eye ached dully. "I walked into a wall." He wanted to say more but couldn't.

There was a strained silence. James wished he could see Parker more clearly. He was in shadow, the light he was holding making it impossible to see his expression.

"Seriously?" Parker asked. "You expect me to believe you're that clumsy?"

James wanted to say it was an invisible wall and that he was trapped. Instead his words twisted, his mind forced to come up with a believable lie to divert Parker's suspicion. "No, you're right. It's just that Sebastian and I were playing a little game. I was hunting him down, and it got—um…" James tried to stop talking. "Just don't worry about my nose. Nothing I didn't sign up for, if you know what I mean."

Why was any of this coming out of his mouth?

"Right." Parker sounded stunned. "If that's what you're into."

Before James could begin to say anything else, Eli cut in, his frustration clear. "Why didn't you tell anyone you weren't coming home?"

"Because I'm a grown man," James grumbled as if he were mad at Eli for asking. He was horrified with how rude the comment was. He'd never talked to his brother in that tone before.

"Yeah," Eli said slowly. "But you can still text to say not to expect you. I always let you know when I'm not gonna be home."

"Sorry." James glanced at Sebastian, who was watching them all blank-faced. "I'm just spending the night with Sebastian. There's nothing to worry about. Go home."

Parker shone the light between him and Sebastian again, seeming to linger on Sebastian, maybe noting he was wearing James's jacket and no shirt.

James wanted to tell them what had happened that afternoon more than anything, yet he stood silent. His tongue was tied as firmly as Sebastian's must have been all these years. Sebastian didn't seem any better off than James, or he would have been begging Parker and Eli for help.

"Really, you guys can go," James insisted. The experience of saying things he didn't mean to was surreal, almost like there was something inside him with its own agenda, filtering his thoughts before they reached his mouth. It might be better to keep his trap shut and not speak at all.

"I can't believe we came all the way out here for this." Eli sounded hurt by James's dismissal. "Are you sure you're okay?"

"I'm fine," James repeated, lying through his teeth more convincingly than he ever had of his own free will.

"Okay." Parker clapped a hand on Eli's shoulder. "But do us a favor. Next time you're staying over playing bedroom games with a friend, let your brother know you won't be home. You, of all people, should understand how he'd worry."

They turned and climbed into Parker's car. The tires crunched loose gravel as they pulled back onto the road, leaving Storm House behind.

CHAPTER SEVENTEEN

James was roused a second time by someone knocking on his door.

"Wake up, James. It's sunny outside," a cheerful Sebastian called from the hall.

James groaned. "Coming. Just give me a minute."

The grandfather clock outside his room said it was almost noon. James couldn't remember the last time he'd slept that late. Not that it mattered. He had nowhere to be, or more accurately, had no way of getting to where he needed to be.

He found a bottle of painkillers and a glass of water waiting for him in the hall bathroom. The bruising on his face looked worse than it felt. He had a black eye and nice greenish-purple mottling over the bridge of his nose, which matched the bruises on his shoulder and hip from when he'd tackled Sebastian to the ballroom floor.

James took the medicine and a quick shower before going to confront Stephen's clothes. Eventually, he found Sebastian in the kitchen.

Sebastian's lips twitched at the sight of James. He quickly

turned away to pull a quiche from the oven. "You look good retro."

James was wearing a button-down teal-and-white bowling shirt that he had mixed feeling about. He looked down at himself. "You didn't give me any T-shirts to choose from."

Sebastian set the quiche to cool on a butcher's block and began heating water for coffee, keeping his face turned away from James. He made a snorting sound, suspiciously close to a laugh, before collecting himself. "Stephen wasn't a T-shirt guy, even when he was younger. I think he was in a bowling league before he got trapped here."

James grabbed two mugs out of the cupboard. "I should have asked Eli for some clothes last night. Though I suppose the spell wouldn't have let me." He didn't actually care about looking silly. If it made Sebastian smile, James would take it. What he wasn't keen on was wearing hand-me-down underwear, and there were only so many days he could keep reusing his current pair.

"I can order you some things. Just let me know what you want." Sebastian scooped sugar and powdered creamer into his mug, eyes darting to James, then away.

The kettle whistled.

James helped himself to the powdered creamer. "Order things how?" It wasn't as if mail-order catalogs still existed, and stores didn't generally respond to handwritten letters, as far as he was aware.

Sebastian poured hot water over the coffee grounds in the French press. "My lawyer orders anything I need. I just have to send him a letter detailing what I want, and he has it delivered to the house. The Storms have had a trust managed by a firm down in Sacramento since forever."

"So you're going to ask a lawyer to buy me underwear?" James found the idea incredibly embarrassing.

"He's used to it. Underwear isn't the most scandalous thing I've asked him to buy." Sebastian raised his brows and leveled a pointed look at James. "It's not like he isn't paid for his time. It's part of the arrangement—most expensive personal shopper ever." Sebastian began serving up the quiche as if that settled things.

"How will I pay you back?" James had the grim realization that if they never got out of here, he'd never be able to work again.

Sebastian waved him off. "Don't worry about it."

Yeah, that wasn't going to happen. James's primary occupation was worrying. "How do you even have money?" The rude question slipped out before he remembered to be tactful, the need for details outweighing everything else.

Sebastian was acting like clothing and feeding James, possibly indefinitely, wasn't a big deal. Sure, Sebastian grew his own produce, but he had other food and general supplies delivered. He must be paying for it—along with water, gas, and property taxes—somehow. James would worry about all of this, as well as being a burden, if he didn't know how any of it was covered.

Sebastian looked up from cutting the quiche. "The trust has a pretty healthy investment portfolio." He didn't sound bothered by James's nosiness. "Grandma Selma set it up a few years before she died, so she wasn't all about screwing over her descendants. She knew whoever was stuck here wouldn't be able to work outside of taking care of the property but also couldn't be completely self-sufficient."

James wanted to ask where the money to fund the trust had come from and how it hadn't run out. But it was none of his business, so he made himself stop prying. Besides, with a house like this, the Storms had probably been rich to begin with.

"Let's take breakfast outside," Sebastian said once the coffee was poured.

James had no objections now that being outside didn't make his skin crawl. Sebastian led him through the mudroom—where the abandoned circuit board still lay on the floor—past the raised vegetable beds and greenhouse and through the fruit trees.

A picnic table sat next to the apricot trees in a patch of sun. It really was a beautiful day. The morning would have been cold, maybe even frosty, but by now, it was clear and perfectly still.

They set their plates and coffee mugs on the table and enjoyed breakfast in silence. There was a barn off to their right, close to the stone wall edging the property. James wasn't surprised to find it painted dark green.

Sitting out here was more relaxing than it had any right to be, given James was a prisoner of the damned property. He had to admit, without the haunting effects, the place wasn't bad.

As they lingered over their coffee, the cow wandered up, eating the grass beneath the trees.

"What's the deal?" James pointed to the cow. "Fresh milk?"

Sebastian wrinkled his nose. "Miss Moo is not a milking cow."

James choked on his last sip of coffee. "I'm sorry. What did you call her?"

Sebastian's cheeks turned pink, and he glared at James. "Miss Moo is a perfectly good name for a cow."

James suppressed the urge to laugh. "Okay. But why do you have a cow?"

"To eat the grass," Sebastian said like this was obvious. "I can only take so much of the push mower. Plus, she's a nice pet."

"I'm surprised you don't have a cat or a dog or something." Now that he thought about it, James figured a dog would have helped the place feel less lonely.

Sebastian stared off toward the barn. "I considered getting a dog but worried how I'd cope when they died." His words came out brittle, breaking James's heart.

"The cow is a good compromise," he offered, hoping it was the right thing to say.

Sebastian looked back at Miss Moo and shrugged. "I didn't get her as a pet, strictly speaking. Like the chickens, she had another purpose."

"Keeping your lawns under control?" James hadn't realized

there were chickens. He should have guessed the eggs were coming from somewhere. Store-bought ones had to be refrigerated after all.

Sebastian considered the cow more closely. "Yeah, the grass. But I actually had this wild idea I could use Miss Moo to free myself from the curse."

James sat up straight. "How?"

Sebastian leaned his arms on the table, resting his chin on his hands. "I was hoping to transfer the curse to her—it's not like she'd care about not leaving the property—but I knew my magic wasn't strong enough to pull it off. I never ended up trying, in case I drained myself to death."

The thought of Sebastian dying during a spell gone wrong jolted through James like he'd been physically struck. He couldn't bear the thought. "In that case, it's a good thing you didn't try." He took a breath and looked at the cow. "But now that I'm here, we have more power. Do you know how to transfer the curse? Is that even possible?"

A flicker of hope settled some of James's discomfort but not all of it. He hated thinking of Sebastian dying in some hypothetical scenario where he'd tried the spell on his own. As often happened to James, his concern wouldn't go away now that the possibility had entered his mind. It didn't matter that he was worrying about something that hadn't happened and wouldn't happen. His brain treated it like any other worry that plagued him. Having something to latch onto and potentially solve the problem was one of the only things that kept his fear under control.

Sebastian's expression turned dark in response to James's question. "I know the curse can be transferred. I've seen it done." He didn't immediately elaborate.

"Well, don't kill me with anticipation," James grumbled.

Sebastian laughed, his face transforming as he focused on James, but his subdued demeanor returned quickly. "The Storm curse claims the firstborn child of whoever it's currently latched onto unless that person has no kids like Uncle Stephen, then it moves to the sibling's children. The curse should have gone to my older sister, Kira."

James frowned. "Why didn't it?"

Sebastian made a sound like he was exhausted by life. "Kira was two years old when the curse passed to Uncle Stephen. Stephen was single and had never planned to have children of his own, not to mention he was suddenly stuck on the property and unable to meet someone to have a kid with, even if he'd wanted. Mom knew her daughter was doomed to be next in line and became determined to save her from Storm House."

James really did not like where this was going.

Sebastian continued, "Mom apparently searched the house looking for information on the curse. She read through all the papers and notebooks until she found a note from Selma. In the event that the person cursed had no children and there were no other living Storms left, she had given us instructions on how to transfer the curse to someone else. Stephen said he wouldn't do it. He wouldn't damn some unsuspecting person to our family's burden. Mom just wanted the curse off Kira and didn't care where it went after her brother died. So she came up with a plan."

Sebastian went quiet, picking at the wood of the picnic table. "She got Stephen to agree that if she had another kid, they'd transfer the curse from Kira to them. That way, it was still in the family." He paused, still picking. "And I didn't know any of this shit until Stephen was dying. But it explains so much." His words faded, swallowed by something James couldn't fathom.

He got up and rounded the table, coming to sit beside Sebastian. After a long moment, Sebastian shifted until their shoulders touched.

"My mom decided to have a spare baby to save her daughter. She was a single mom to Kira from the start and always told me my dad didn't know about me. They hadn't been together long, and it wasn't the same man who'd fathered my sister. Growing up, my mom was so distant toward me, and I never understood why. She'd always say I had to spend time with Uncle Stephen during the summer to have a 'man's influence.' She told me that's why I had to move here permanently during high school. I tried to explain to her that was bullshit on about a million levels. All I ever needed was my mom. But anyway. It makes more sense now that I know about the curse. She didn't want to get attached. I think she wanted to dump me off with Stephen as soon as I was born, but he refused. He told me he'd changed his mind about transferring the curse. How was one child getting it any better than the other? He and my mom apparently fought about it for years."

The quiche wasn't sitting well in James's stomach. "Jesus. I'm sorry, Sebastian."

He shrugged, their shoulders rubbing together. "I only brought it up because they didn't transfer the curse until I was twelve and Kira was fifteen. I remember the ritual pretty well. They didn't tell me or Kira what they were doing, of course. They said it was about enhancing family magic, but it was a flimsy lie."

"Do you think we can repeat the ritual? Remembering something from fourteen years ago would be pretty hard, at least with the kind of detail we'd need to pull this off." James wasn't sure about the idea at all. "I mean, look at the mess we made of unbinding your tongue."

"We need to consider it much more closely than we did our last foray into blood-and-bone magic, that's for sure." Sebastian grimaced. "But let's not write it off yet. I have no other ideas, and if we have enough power between us, it might be our only hope to get free."

"Any spell like that is way beyond my skill set." James wanted to be clear. "I only did the unbinding ritual because I had instructions from that book, which I double-checked with sources online. Do you still have Selma's notes on how to do it?"

"I haven't been able to find them," Sebastian admitted. "But they have to be here. Besides, I wrote down the whole ritual after it happened. I could tell something dodgy was going on, and I wanted to try and figure out what we'd really been doing in the woods that night. So even without Selma's notes, we have a lot to go on."

James wasn't convinced. The account of a twelve-year-old was far from foolproof. But like Sebastian said, it might be their only hope.

SEBASTIAN GAZED up at the apricot tree nearest them. "Want to help me pick these? I should have started on it days ago."

James glanced at the tree. "Shouldn't we try to find Selma's notes first?"

Sebastian rose from the table and walked off toward the barn. "I've already spent countless hours looking for them. It could be a while before they turn up if they ever do. I don't want the fruit to go to waste."

James trailed after him. "But putting off searching isn't going to help us get out of here."

Sebastian opened the barn door and faced him. "Look, James, I've been at this a while, and what I've learned is you have to live your life and take care of yourself first. Yes, we could spend the next few hours or the next week looking for the notes. But what if we never find them? What if we can't do the spell, even with instructions? *And*, on top of that, all the apricots have spoiled. Let's look for the papers tonight and enjoy the sun while it's out."

James got where Sebastian was coming from but found it hard to suppress his urgent need to escape Storm House. Being trapped was all new to him. His gut told him he needed to be doing something about it, that he shouldn't rest until he escaped.

But Sebastian was probably right. Burning themselves out on what might be a long and fruitless search wouldn't be good for morale in the long run. James needed to adjust his expectations and come to terms with the possibility he'd be here for a long time, even if that scared him.

James gestured inside the barn, committed to trying. "You're right. Let's pick some fruit." After all, there were worse things to be doing than soaking up some sun with Sebastian.

They grabbed wicker baskets and a long stick-like tool with clippers on the end.

Back at the trees, Sebastian separated the baskets. "Put all the really ripe ones in here so we can eat them first and chuck anything gross on the ground for the birds."

"Sure." James eyed the first tree. Its branches were heavily laden.

The long clippers had an open sack and pulley string attached. James watched Sebastian use it to gather the fruit from the top of the tree. His restless urge to return to the house and look for the notes faded. He could officially watch Sebastian do anything, especially stretching his long arms above his head while the hem of his T-shirt rode up. The sliver of exposed skin was tempting, especially knowing what Sebastian looked like bare-chested.

Sebastian caught him staring and winked. James shook himself and started picking apricots.

James had never been one for gardening. Doing yard work for his grandma, and now for himself, had always been a chore he'd grumbled about. He didn't expect to like picking fruit at the best of times, and certainly not when he was ignoring monumental problems.

He enjoyed himself anyway. The sun was warm, and Sebastian hummed while he worked. The whole thing was enjoyable, from eating sweet apricots and watching birds to Sebastian accidentally dropping fruit on James's head and dissolving into a fit of giggles at the look on his face. James was beginning to see why people went apple picking as a date.

Once six baskets of apricots were settled in the kitchen, Sebastian dragged James along to the vegetable garden. He had a pumpkin patch, and for some reason, that amused James to no end.

"You'll be thankful when you're eating pumpkin bread." Sebastian shoved James's shoulder. "Not to mention my pumpkin soup."

They weeded the garden, and James didn't mind the work one bit. Sebastian cut flowers from the greenhouse to replace the ones in his kitchen and explained his yearly planting routine, showing obvious pride in his work. He wasn't just growing food so he had something to eat. He seemed to love the plants too.

Sebastian was bright-eyed, like he was excited to be sharing all the details of his garden with James, who was more than happy to soak it all up. He asked Sebastian countless questions, suddenly more interested in plants than he'd ever been before.

James was disappointed when the sun started to dip in the sky, taking its warmth with it. They'd have to go in before it got dark to avoid the shades, and knowing that, James was glad they hadn't spent the day haplessly looking for eighty-year-old papers.

Sebastian looked up and swiped hair out of his face, leaving a streak of dirt on his forehead. "What was that sound?"

James was about to ask what he was talking about when a distant voice cut across the soft bird chatter. "Must be someone out front."

They walked around the house. The gate was still locked—Sebastian pretty much never unlocked it unless he was expecting a delivery—and looking through the bars was Hazel.

"What the hell, James?" she called as they approached. "You just ditching work now?"

"I—" James had no idea what to say. He wanted to tell the truth, but it died on his lips.

"You look awful." Hazel's eyes went wide as she got a better look at him. "Is your nose broken?"

James gently prodded his bruised face. He'd forgotten he looked like shit. "I ran into a wall," he said, hoping to avoid repeating the story he'd told Parker.

"Come on, seriously?" Hazel crossed her arms and waited for James to explain himself. She knew he wasn't clumsy. When he didn't speak, she lost patience. "Why didn't you come to work. Or even call me?"

"I—remember I told you about Storm House." James tried to give her a significant look. "I'm just staying here with Sebastian for a while."

Hazel turned her glare on Sebastian. "Parker told me you two were having a sleepover, but I don't see what that has to do with you not going to work."

"A sleepover? Am I five?" James asked, indignant.

Hazel narrowed her eyes. "An adult sleepover, you know, the kind with orgasms. And while I'm happy you're giving your romantic life some attention for once, you need to keep it out of business hours. I had to get Eleanor to help me with the lights this morning. It wasn't until I tracked down Eli and Parker at lunch that I found out you might be here. I've been swamped all day and had no clue what was going on."

"Sorry." James tried to ignore the twisting in his gut. He knew Hazel had been worried about him, even if she chose to cover that with annoyance. He couldn't think of a way to communicate that he didn't want to skip work. Every explanation died before he could get it out. How had Sebastian gotten around the binding at all? James had no idea how to use his words to convey a double meaning.

"Don't be sorry." Hazel deflated, maybe picking up on some of James's internal struggle. "Just come help me with the last of the lights, and we'll forget about it."

James's heart sank. "I don't want to go into town."

Hazel gaped at him, renewed hurt lining her eyes. "Why not?"

James looked at Sebastian. "I need to stay here."

"Need to?" Hazel looked irate for a second, then paused. "Wait. Is this about the energy draining? Have you figured it out? Because you could have told me if you were staying here to work on that."

"No." The lie made James want to scream. "It's not about the energy draining. I just want to be with Sebastian. I like him, okay?" He clamped his mouth shut. The damn spell was a real pain in the ass. He didn't need it to reveal his private feelings on top of everything else. It was bad enough everyone thought he and Sebastian were sleeping together. He didn't need them knowing there were feelings involved, at least on his side.

"That's great that you like him, James." Hazel gazed at him with surprising softness. "But since when do you let that take over your whole life?"

"It's not," James shot back. "I never do what I want. Never take any risks, never date. Why are you making a big thing out of me finally going for it? I'm allowed to change, and if I want to be here with Sebastian, please respect that." Anger was clear in James's tone, but he wasn't mad at Hazel. He was furious at the binding spell for using kernels of truth in its lies.

Hazel's mouth tightened into a line as she turned to Sebastian. "What have you done? Tell him it's okay to go home."

Sebastian was the picture of innocence with wide, slightly confused eyes. "James can do what he wants."

"Of course he can, but this isn't how the James I know acts. Don't pretend any of this is his normal." Hazel pushed on the bars of the gate. "Open this damn thing. Why are you barring me out?"

Sebastian let Hazel in. She walked right up to James. "So you aren't coming back to town to help close up *your* shop for the day or going home to your brother tonight? The brother you were dying to have return to Moonlight Falls so you could spend more time with him."

James backed away. It was good she was suspicious. He just didn't know how to get Hazel to make the leap to thinking he was trapped and not in control of his own voice. He tried not to speak but couldn't control it. "Why can't I have some time to myself?" he snapped at his oldest friend.

"You can. Take a vacation. You deserve one. But don't act like having a busted face and suddenly refusing to leave this one"—she jabbed a finger toward Sebastian—"isn't cause for concern."

"What? Do you think Sebastian hurt me?" James was shocked.

"None of this is like you. I don't know what to think. If Eli shacked up with some guy, turned up all bruised, and refused to come home, tell me you wouldn't be freaking out."

Sebastian's cheeks reddened, his eyes narrowing to slits, but he didn't deny Hazel's accusation.

"I didn't shack up with—with anyone," James said weakly. "Sebastian didn't—I explained it to Parker. It was a game—"

"Game?" Hazel cut him off. "If you've hurt him, Sebastian, goddammit, you are going to be sorry."

"He didn't." James tried to give Hazel the significant stare Sebastian had used on him, but he wasn't sure if he'd pulled it off. He wanted Hazel to know something wasn't right but not think Sebastian was abusive. He repeated the story he'd given Parker, saying more clearly this time that he liked things to get rough during sex, even though it wasn't true.

Hazel's brows pulled together as she studied James. "Okay. Not something I ever would have suspected about you, but to each their own." She crossed her arms. "So when are you coming back to work? Tomorrow? The next day? I'm not trying to manage your personal life. I just need you to communicate so I'm not worrying you're off dead somewhere."

"I'm not coming back to work," James said through gritted teeth. "Just leave me alone."

"I can't believe you." Hazel turned abruptly and stormed off to her van. "You're my best friend. You should be talking to me, not —whatever this is."

She got in her car and drove off. The sight of her rounding the nearest bend and disappearing made James's throat tighten.

"That was a good start," Sebastian said as if the exchange had been mildly interesting and nothing more.

James spun to face him.

Sebastian put up his hands in surrender. "Good that she suspects something isn't right, and after just one day. It's quicker than I thought. Then again, a dependable guy like you doesn't just ghost on his responsibilities. Excellent job telling her about the power draining beforehand. We need people on the outside trying to figure out why you won't come home. We need them wondering what's going on here."

It was all true, not that it stopped James from wanting to pull out his hair. "She's never going to guess the real reason I'm staying here."

"No." Sebastian pursed his lips. "But she'll be back. So will Eli. Next time, we need to get them in the house. Pull out *The Magical Tales*. Maybe put them on the entryway floor, trip over them even, or see if we can bring them outside without the spells stopping us. If you figured it out, they will too."

James wasn't so sure. His need to understand Sebastian, which was impacted by his growing attraction, had been critical to deciphering the books. It wasn't just having the volumes shoved under his nose.

Sebastian's hand closed around James's forearm. "Even if they don't figure out our tongues are bound, we still have a plan. And maybe if you're stuck here long enough, Parker will try and drag you away by force."

James frowned. "How will that help?"

"I imagine if someone tries to drag one of us over the property line, it won't work. We'd hit the wall and reveal that we're trapped behind an invisible barrier."

"I don't know if Parker would do that. He thinks I'm here voluntarily. He'll respect my decision to abandon my life, even if he disagrees." James suspected he'd lose all his friends if this went on long enough. They'd all write him off as a selfish asshole with the kind of convincing lies he was telling.

"Should we play into the you're-my-prisoner angle or imply you're getting sucked into an abusive relationship?" Sebastian asked, completely serious. "You can backpedal on the consensual rough play line easily enough. Then maybe they'll try and rescue you."

James's mouth fell open. "No. I don't want anyone to think you're an abuser. That's horrible."

Sebastian rolled his eyes. "They can think whatever the fuck they want about me. As long as we get out of here, I don't care. I'll do almost anything to get free, James. There's nothing I won't give up and very few lines I won't cross."

CHAPTER EIGHTEEN

After a dinner of leftover quiche and salad, they went to look for Selma's notes on transferring the curse.

"This is the library." Sebastian opened a door upstairs, at the end of the hall, past the study where they'd found the house plans.

"Holy fucking hell," James muttered into the cavernous dark space.

The library looked as large as the ballroom, which was situated beneath it. There were no windows on the outer walls, just shelves of books, floor to ceiling. Narrow skylights set along the sloping roof allowed moonlight to filter in, illuminating countless dust particles floating in the air. A shade peered down at them from behind the nearest section of glass.

The center of the room housed rows of waist-high bookshelves. A desk faced the doorway, with a leather couch and matching armchair tucked behind it. Unlit oil lamps were scattered on every available table.

Sebastian entered the room, his own oil lamp held aloft. "You'll never run out of things to read, that's for sure."

James spun in a circle. "Have these books all been here since the place was built?" The ones nearest them had cracked leather spines and looked at least eighty years old.

"Not all of them. Everyone adds to the collection." Sebastian led the way toward the back of the room. "There's a whole section of magazines that's pretty interesting. Everything from National Geographic to vintage porn."

"Right," James muttered, too distracted to care about explicit library content. "If your mom slipped Selma's transfer spell into a book, it's going to take ages to find."

"It's not in a book." Sebastian set his lamp down on a row of filing cabinets that made up an aisle in the middle of the room. "I've checked them."

James surveyed the vast room. "All of them?"

"Don't sound so skeptical. I went on a tear after getting trapped. Barely slept or ate. I was so determined to find a way out of here. I've flipped through each book. Shook them all out. Paid close attention to any of the ones about magic. Even checked the newspapers." He opened a drawer and pulled out a folder to show James clippings from the *Moonlight Falls Tribune* in 1996, the year after James was born. The cabinets must have been full of old articles, going back who knew how many years.

The top article was about an incident between a shade and a tourist. The local paper closed down in the early 2000s, so it was odd seeing Moonlight Falls events in print. James scanned the article. It was a familiar story: someone from out of town wanting to poke around supernatural creatures and getting scared when they poked back.

"Are there lots of articles like this?" James picked up the news clipping.

"About shades?" Sebastian raised his brows as if to say, *come on*. "I mean, it's the *Moonlight Falls Tribune*. They probably printed more words about shades than world news and politics combined. Why?"

"Shades have been acting up in town." James described the

busted lights. "We were wondering if anything like it had happened before."

Sebastian took the article from James and glanced at it more closely. "There's plenty like this tourist mishap, but attacking lights—I don't remember seeing anything like that. You're welcome to search for yourself."

James was about to say he would, then remembered he couldn't get to town to share any useful stories he might find. Surely, the mayor had access to all this information, and she'd have firsthand memories of the eighties and nineties. The public library probably had an even better archive of Moonlight Falls's history. Besides, James had to focus on the more pressing problem of escaping this place.

"If you're sure Selma's instructions aren't in the library, why are we here?"

Sebastian put the folder away and opened a different drawer. "I just wanted to show you. Let you know you can come in here whenever. Grab something to read. I also wanted to give you an idea of how long I've spent looking for Selma's note." He selected a slightly newer-looking folder and set it on top of the cabinet. "Look, Stephen saved your article."

James scowled at the smiling picture of himself he was so sick of seeing. His face heated. "Why would he save a fluff piece like that?"

Sebastian snickered. "So touchy." He poked James in the side, and James shifted away. "Everyone stuck here has taken it upon themselves to keep a record of the town's history. Stephen started getting the *Apple Valley News* delivered once the *Tribune* was gone and kept everything they printed about Moonlight Falls or the people who lived here."

James closed the folder and returned it to the drawer. "Do you collect articles too?"

Sebastian raised a lazy shoulder. "Yeah. Might as well. Makes reading the paper feel purposeful. I think it's so whoever is stuck here next has access to as much local information as possible."

James tried not to think about someone being stuck here after he and Sebastian were gone. He didn't want the curse to outlive them and claim another life. There had to be a way to break it without catastrophic consequences. "Do you really think transferring the curse to a cow will work?"

"We won't know till we try." Sebastian picked up his lamp and headed back toward the room's entrance. "The energy imbalance requires life energy to stabilize. I don't see why it has to be a human life. From a magical perspective, life energy isn't fundamentally different between different species. Life is life as far as energy theory goes. You can look it up. There are plenty of books here on the topic. I figured the amount of energy in any large animal would be enough for the curse."

"*Hm.*" James shut the library door behind them. "So where are we looking for the instructions then?"

"Mom's old room. Then, Selma's room. I'd come to terms with not having enough magic to transfer the curse before I searched either room and didn't look as thoroughly as I did with the library or the study, which we can check again if both bedrooms are dead ends."

"Should we check Selma's room first?" James asked as they walked around the landing. More shades peered down at them from the skylights over the stairs. "Isn't it more likely they're in there?"

"I don't think so. We know the instructions were discovered and moved in the mid-nineties when Stephen and Mom found out about the curse and were probably put away somewhere in 2009 after the curse was transferred to me. The instructions aren't going to be where Selma left them, and no one really goes into her old room. It hasn't had any new occupants since she died, like the other bedrooms have. I doubt my mom would have hidden the note in there, and I've checked all the obvious spots you'd think to put something back so it could be found again."

James had to admit he wasn't keen to poke around Selma's things after the teeth incident in the study, so he wasn't going to argue too hard, but one thing Sebastian had said struck him. "You don't think your mom hid the instructions? Just put them somewhere or misplaced them?"

Sebastian paused, turning to face him. "No, I don't think she hid or destroyed them. They're important for future Storms to have in case our family line dies out and we have to kidnap some poor soul to transfer the curse to like Selma worried we might." Sebastian scrunched his face like he'd smelled something awful. "Maybe the mailman was right to be scared of me. Not that I'd ever intentionally damn someone to this curse, but snatching a visitor to the property would be the only way to get someone unsuspecting to transfer the curse to."

James shivered at the thought. Being kidnapped by the creepy man living at Storm House was the kind of urban legend kids told each other when he was young. At least it seemed like no one in the family other than Selma was willing to do something that sinister.

Next to James's room was another green door leading to Sebastian's mom's old bedroom. Unlike Sebastian's teenage room, which he'd said had previously been Stephen's room, Samantha Storm's room hadn't been cleared out. It was an eighties time capsule, from the shoes by the door to the posters on the walls and magazines on the desk.

James was surprised Samantha hadn't done anything to the room in the years after leaving high school. She'd come back to Storm House since the eighties. Why not update the room or take her belongings with her? Though, the closer he looked, the more he could see why things were left behind. One of the shoes had a busted heel. The closet was empty except for what looked like a prom dress. "Did your mom stay in this room when you all visited Stephen?"

Sebastian nodded. "Yeah, not that she stayed over often. Mom usually dropped me off for the summer and drove out of town the same day. But she slept here the night they did the transfer spell. It was the last time she stayed at Storm House." He set the lamp on the desk and lit a candelabra on the bedside table before crouching to pull a shoebox from under the bed.

James hovered in the doorway.

"What have I told you about privacy?" Sebastian grumbled, reaching farther under the bed.

"Not to respect it."

Sebastian righted himself. His lips twisted. "Correct."

James pushed away his discomfort and began going through Samantha's things. The desk was full of papers but nothing useful. Unfolding notes from the woman's high school crushes made him frown.

"There's a reason I told you not to respect my privacy, you know." Sebastian wiped his dusty hands off on his pants. "I was trying to get you to snoop around the study and my old bedroom, hoping you'd read something tipping you off to what was going on here."

"Oh." James cringed. That made a lot of sense. "Sorry."

Sebastian shrugged. "Don't worry about it. You got there anyway."

They turned back to their searching. James opened another love note. "Couldn't we ask your mom where she left the instructions?"

"Tried that." Sebastian shoved a shoebox—which had contained nothing but well-worn shoes—back under the bed. "She didn't write me back. Any of the times."

James was shocked. "Have you seen her since being stuck here?"

"Nope." Sebastian's response came out clipped, not inviting further discussion.

James crushed the love letter in his hand. How could Sebastian's mom ignore his letters and not visit? She was the only person who knew what her son was going through. It was cruel any way he looked at it.

"Forget about it, James," Sebastian warned.

That wasn't possible, but James tried to act like he'd moved on.

His parents' deaths had devastated him when he was younger. Their loss still made him ache sometimes, and he'd thought it couldn't get worse than losing your parents as a child. He'd been wrong.

THEY HAD no luck that night but went to bed confident the instructions weren't in Samantha's old room. They'd left no dark corner uninspected.

James woke up relieved they weren't returning to the search immediately. He had a better idea of how daunting the task was and was increasingly afraid their efforts would be in vain. Samantha and Stephen Storm might not have meant to hide the instructions, but misplaced items could easily be lost forever.

James dressed in one of Stephen's baggy knit sweaters to stave off the chill that had settled over Storm House. The previous day's fine weather was gone, and Sebastian still hadn't given James his jacket back. Not that he'd asked.

He ran into his fellow prisoner a few minutes later in the downstairs hallway.

"Morning." Sebastian gave James a familiar sly smile. "You slept in again."

"It's not that late." James fidgeted. His jeans were less than comfortable after skipping the borrowed underwear. "It's not even ten."

"Suppose late is a relative term. I was just going to clean up the ballroom." Sebastian gestured down the hall. "I'm regretting leaving all those towels sitting around in the bathroom. The bloodstains will never come out now."

James followed Sebastian toward the ballroom. "You've been up doing laundry already?" James realized everything would have to be hand-washed and cringed inwardly.

Sebastian looked over his shoulder. "Doing laundry, and I've fed the chickens."

It was enough to make James feel lazy. He'd have to offer to pitch in more.

They paused in the ballroom doorway, the busted frame painfully obvious.

"Sorry." James rubbed the back of his neck. "I can fix that for you."

Sebastian patted his arm. "Thanks." He strode off to the middle of the room and picked up his purple robe, shrugging it on over his T-shirt and jeans.

The knife and bowl stained with dried blood were still by the piano, and the handcuffs were discarded near the leg Sebastian had been bound to. The whole ritual felt like a fever dream.

"I can't believe any of this actually happened." James picked up the cuffs.

Sebastian retrieved the other items. "Don't pretend you didn't enjoy it."

James's face went hot. He looked away. "Sure, we both did. Until we found out how badly it went."

Sebastian tutted. "So negative. It was still one of the most thrilling nights of my life."

James stole a glance at Sebastian but couldn't tell if he was being serious or not.

"You can keep those." Sebastian pointed at the cuffs. "I'm

throwing this bowl out. Really wish you hadn't picked a wooden one. I guess I can keep the knife if I sterilize it." He began walking out of the room.

James hurried after him, brandishing the cuffs. "I don't want to keep these. They're yours."

Sebastian didn't turn around. "I've never used them before. They were a joke gift from my last birthday with actual friends."

"And you brought handcuffs home with you when your uncle was sick?"

"No. My mom had movers pack up my dorm room and ship all my stuff back after I got trapped." He turned abruptly, looking down at James as they almost collided. "Keep them. You seemed to know how to use them." He winked and turned away, continuing down the hall and disappearing into the kitchen, leaving James alone.

He swiped a hand over his face. His stubble was longer than he usually let it grow, and it itched. The cuffs felt heavy in his palm. Sebastian seemed to be taunting him. Did he want James to use the cuffs on him again? Did James have any interest in the idea?

Images ran through his head, and the sudden perkiness of his cock suggested he did, even if restraints weren't his usual thing. He wasn't that bold. James would have rather left the cuffs with Sebastian and let him decide if he wanted the two of them to play around.

James decided to forget about it. He could deal with the problem of what he and Sebastian wanted from each other later.

With the handcuffs stored safely out of the way in his room, James made his way to the kitchen, where Sebastian was pulling muffins out of the oven. It was beginning to look like he baked something every day. The whole room smelled wonderfully like cinnamon. There wasn't a dirty dish in sight or even flour on the countertop. Sebastian had cooked and cleaned up after himself, in addition to the other chores he'd mentioned, all before James had started his day.

"What have you got there?" James inched closer, his stomach grumbling in response to the tempting smell.

"Apple muffins." Sebastian set them on the butcher block.

"They look great."

"Thanks." Sebastian fiddled with the oven mitt in his hands. "How do you feel about making some jam today?"

"Overjoyed," James deadpanned.

"Jackass." Sebastian swatted him with the oven mitt.

James couldn't resist grinning. "I guess we won't be gardening in the drizzle."

Sebastian waved dismissively out the window. "We could. It's not raining that hard, but I need to get these apricots under control. You can keep searching for Selma's instructions instead if you want."

James was disappointed by the suggestion. The search was beginning to stress him out. "Not really. I'd prefer to make jam."

"Oh, how quickly you've fallen." Sebastian reached out and caressed James's stubble-lined cheek, his smile turning wicked.

James swallowed. "I see the flirting is back."

Sebastian patted his cheek and turned away. "Is that a complaint?"

"No," James said carefully, trying to ignore the pleasurable flutter in his chest. "Just an observation."

After James ate breakfast, he helped Sebastian sort and wash the fruit. They needed apricots that were ripe but not too ripe and also some that were slightly underripe. Sebastian explained this was key to getting both a good flavor and a firm set to the jam. James took his word for it.

Once the fruit was selected, Sebastian weighed it on a kitchen scale and then weighed an equal measure of sugar. It turned out that making jam was pretty simple. The only other ingredients were lemon juice from some of Sebastian's fresh lemons and some water. But before they threw it all together, Sebastian brought out a box full of jars.

"Want to help wash?" he asked, setting the box by the sink.

James rolled up his sleeves. "Sure, that's a task I've actually got under control."

"Great." Sebastian helped himself to the remaining coffee in the French press. "If I never wash another dish, it will be too soon."

James would gladly wash all the dishes for Sebastian, even though he wasn't fond of the chore. At least he'd been spoiled with a dishwasher the past six years.

As he cleaned the jam jars, James marveled at how good it felt doing homey tasks with Sebastian. He'd never thought doing dishes would make him wistful, but it made him want a partner to share all of life's little things with.

Sebastian checked the fire in the stove, explaining how they had to sterilize the jars. James never would have imagined this scene when he'd first walked up to Sebastian's door. Sebastian was relaxed, full of easy smiles and dimples, and worlds away from the erratic man who'd snapped at James for not knowing why the lights didn't work.

They laughed as they quartered the fruit and discarded the pits. James wasn't even sure what about. He just kept catching Sebastian's smile like it was contagious, light, joyous emotions bubbling out of him.

Sebastian teased James for abandoning his perma-frown, and James couldn't find it in himself to be grumpy about it. He liked amusing Sebastian and gave him plenty to shake his head at with his ignorance of making anything from scratch. James couldn't seem to get over the amount of sugar they were using.

"It's key to a long shelf life," Sebastian said as he poured four pounds of sugar into the simmering fruit.

"Sure." James understood the concept. He'd just never really thought about it before. "But what are you going to do with fourteen jars of jam? It's a lifetime supply, and you'll have more fruit next year."

Sebastian snorted, amused as he stirred the sugar through the mixture. "I swear, you'll find anything alarming, James."

"I just like to have answers," he grumbled as if he weren't holding back a face-splitting grin.

"This isn't even all the jam we need to make. Once more of the fruit ripens, we've got another batch. Not to mention what's still on the trees." He glanced at James for a reaction, and James dutifully widened his eyes. Sebastian shook his head. "I give the jam away. I mean, I keep a jar or two for myself each year, but the rest goes to Beth to sell in her souvenir shop. Tourists love bespoke stuff like this from small towns. California's spookiest jam, grown and handcrafted on a shade-infested property." Sebastian waved his arms around in a stereotypical depiction of a ghost, making a *woo* sound.

James snorted. "Is that really how Beth markets it?"

"Yep. The label she puts on it has eyes on the back to make it look like an orange ghost is trapped inside the jar, peering out." Sebastian dug around in one of the cupboards until he found an empty jar and tossed it to James. Sure enough, a logo bearing the town's name and the phrase "California's Spookiest Jam" was plastered to the front, with narrow black eyes on the back.

They took turns stirring the bubbling jam mixture and skimming the top. The kitchen warmed steadily from the oven and sweet, steaming jam, causing James to pull off his sweater and Sebastian to discard his robe.

"Right, I think we're good," Sebastian said when his wind-up egg timer sounded. "Go get the plate from the mud room."

"Why is there a plate in the mud room?"

"It's supposed to be cold." Sebastian pushed James toward the back door like he wasn't moving quickly enough. "Couldn't exactly put it in the fridge, could I?"

James did as he was told, the feeling of Sebastian's hands lingering on his shoulders.

Plate retrieved, Sebastian spooned a glob of jam onto it and waited for it to cool, then ran his finger through it. "Perfect." He licked his finger clean.

James tracked the progress of Sebastian's tongue. He was positive Sebastian didn't need to lick his top lip that thoroughly. He didn't call him on it though.

The jam stayed in two separate blobs on the plate, meaning it was ready to set. They retrieved the jars from the oven and ladled out the jam, careful not to fill them too far but also careful not to underfill them. James found it fiddly and didn't want any of the jars he did to burst or spoil, but figured if he copied Sebastian close enough, it would be fine.

Sebastian reached out to grab James's wrist. "Careful, don't spill."

"I wasn't," James said as if Sebastian hadn't just saved him from making a mess of his last jar.

Sebastian patted his forearm. "No, of course not."

James's cheeks flushed. He liked it when Sebastian touched him. Sebastian must have noticed because he started touching him more frequently the longer they were in the kitchen. He guided James around the room with pushes and pulls, leaning into him when James amused him and swatting at him playfully.

By the time the jam jars were done boiling to create the necessary seal and set aside to cool, James found himself boxed in against the counter and not sure how he'd gotten into the position. Not that he was complaining.

Sebastian was an inch away from pressing his body against James. He reached behind him, grabbed something, and leaned in until his breath tickled James's ear. "Are you enjoying yourself?"

James had his hands clamped firmly on the counter, unsure whether he could move even if he wanted to. "Yes."

Sebastian leaned back enough to look down at James. He raised a jam-covered finger between them. "Taste?"

James's pulse pounded. "From your finger?"

"Only if you want." Sebastian gave his best wicked smile.

James couldn't resist, not when Sebastian's hands felt so good casually brushing against him. He leaned forward, taking Sebastian's finger into his mouth, and sucked the sweetness off.

Sebastian slowly pulled his finger out. He placed his other hand on James's hip. "You like that?"

"Yes." James was surprised by how desperate the word sounded. His eyes seemed to be glued to Sebastian's. It felt like a loss when Sebastian's attention flicked away.

Sebastian's gaze settled back where James needed it, finger covered with a fresh offering of jam. "Have some more." Sebastian pressed his body flush against James, not waiting for James to take his finger into his mouth. Instead he smeared the jam over James's lips and licked his finger clean.

James's mouth parted involuntarily. Sebastian angled his head down and licked the jam from James's lips. James groaned as Sebastian's tongue caressed him, dipping into his mouth and chasing all the sugary goodness away.

Sebastian hummed in pleasure. "So sweet."

James wanted to laugh at the ridiculous line, but he made a desperate sound. He took hold of Sebastian's waist and brought their mouths together in an apricot-flavored kiss. Soft lips and hungry movements opened James up, and all he wanted was more.

Sebastian didn't hesitate to take what James was offering. A hand found its way to the back of James's head, holding him in place, as Sebastian's tongue took James for everything he was worth. James liked this kiss even more than their previous ones. He couldn't get enough of the possessive way Sebastian touched him.

Sebastian rubbed against him shamelessly, showing James

how hard he was. James panted into his mouth. He was just as hard and needier than he'd ever been.

Sebastian pulled James's bottom lip between his teeth, biting softly. It made James dizzy. Sebastian didn't linger. He moved his kisses along James's jaw and down his neck before sinking to his knees. He took hold of James's hips and looked up. "May I?" His lips twisted, a sly smile saying he had no doubt what James's answer would be.

James should have hesitated. Should have remembered why he was resisting this, but he couldn't. There was no reason to deny his attraction to Sebastian. He was already attached, already in trouble with how much he'd fallen for him. He might as well enjoy it.

"Yes, please," James managed to say. He ran a hand through Sebastian's loose curls. "I'm negative across the board and haven't been with anyone since my last test."

"Same." Sebastian bit his lip. His fingers flexed on James's hips. "A doctor comes out to give me a physical every year, do all the tests, and I'm sure you've deduced that I haven't been with anyone in years."

James continued to play with Sebastian's hair. "It's been a while for me too."

Sebastian cocked a brow as if to ask *really?*

James swallowed. Maybe he shouldn't have said anything, but it was true. "Please, Sebastian."

"Yeah." Sebastian's eyes flashed with a devilish glint. "I want this so fucking bad."

His attention shifted from James's face, sliding back down his body. He unfastened James's jeans, freeing his cock. "No underwear." His eyes darted upward like James had surprised him. Then he leaned forward to press a kiss below James's belly button, following the hair trailing downward.

James's pants were tugged down to his knees. Sebastian's hands ran up his exposed thighs. James's whole body tingled with anticipation, every touch sending shivers through him. Knowing what was coming unraveled him, his breathing harsher than it should be.

Sebastian took hold of the base of James's cock and licked his tip, swirling his tongue around and around. James bit his lip to keep from making a truly embarrassing sound. He gripped the counter with one hand to steady himself, leaving the other tangled in Sebastian's hair.

James feared Sebastian would tease him mercilessly, make him squirm and beg. James would have begged without complaint, anything to get more of the man kneeling before him. He would have let Sebastian have him any way he wanted, endured any amount of teasing or denial if it pleased Sebastian.

James sucked in a surprised gasp as Sebastian swallowed his cock all the way in one eager motion, no begging required. James's cock hit the back of Sebastian's throat, and Sebastian gagged before pulling back.

"Take your time." James ran his fingers through Sebastian's hair.

Sebastian shot a challenging look at him and hollowed his cheeks. James's hand tightened on Sebastian's silky curls, and his knees threatened to give out on him.

"Fuck, that feels good."

Sebastian moaned, bobbing his head with the kind of enthusiasm James had forgotten was possible.

"So good," James murmured. "Oh yeah, just like that."

Sebastian soaked up all his words like he couldn't get enough, making needy sounds and doubling down on his efforts whenever James told him what he liked. And he liked all of it.

"You look so hot on your knees, Sebastian. So pretty. *Oh fuck,* I'm going to be thinking about this forever."

Sebastian looked up. There was something almost vulnerable in the way his brows pulled together, his eyes bright and full of unrestrained lust. He didn't seem able to look away as he continued to suck, bobbing his head, lips stretched so beautifully.

That look was it for James. "Gonna come, Sebastian. Too good," he groaned as his hips twitched. Sebastian sucked harder, still looking up at him, and James's pleasure tore out of him.

Sebastian didn't release him, even after he'd swallowed everything James had to give. He continued sucking and licking until James whimpered, oversensitive and possibly about to fall over.

Sebastian pulled back. His ragged breathing was as loud as the thudding pulse in James's ears. Sebastian kept his eyes cast downward, in stark contrast to how he couldn't look away from James only moments ago.

James ran his fingers through Sebastian's hair until Sebastian leaned in to rest his face against James's thigh. The contact felt good, a closeness James yearned for. After a long moment, he pulled Sebastian up.

Sebastian hunched forward, tucking his head into James's neck and wrapping his arms around his waist. James's chest tightened at the intimacy of the embrace, and he pulled Sebastian close.

"Your turn," James murmured, trailing a hand up and down Sebastian's back, caressing the beautiful lines of his body.

"You don't have to," Sebastian whispered against James's neck.

"I know, but I want to."

Sebastian pulled back, his cheeks red.

James pulled up his pants and tucked himself away, keeping his focus on Sebastian. "How does that sound?"

Sebastian rolled his eyes, maybe in an effort to pretend he wasn't blushing harder. "Sounds good to me."

James turned them around, pushing Sebastian against the counter, and dropped to his knees. He undid Sebastian's jeans, finding his underwear wet with precum, the large, dark spot giving away how turned on Sebastian had been while sucking him off. "Hell, that's hot."

Sebastian bit his lip, eyes wide. The look on his face suggested he was embarrassed to be seen like this. It made James want to give Sebastian everything, spoil him, show him it was okay to be this open with him.

He ran a hand over the dampened fabric, feeling the hardness beneath.

Sebastian squirmed at the touch, and his legs trembled. "James, please." The words came out raw, desperate.

James pulled Sebastian's underwear down, revealing the most beautiful, swollen pink cock he'd ever seen. Sebastian leaked for him, precum beading at his slit and running over his glistening head. James gave Sebastian a firm stroke, eliciting a groan from Sebastian that made it seem like the simple tug had given him everything he needed. James loved that sound. He wanted to hear it again, every day, always.

He leaned in to lick Sebastian's cockhead, lapping up his arousal. Both of Sebastian's hands found James's hair and took hold. More moisture leaked onto James's lips as another moan left Sebastian's. No longer able to resist, James took Sebastian into his mouth, sucking firmly. He wanted to drown in Sebastian's pleasure, fill himself up with it, suck and taste until he couldn't breathe.

"*Oh god, oh god,*" Sebastian whimpered above him. "*James!*"

Sebastian's cock pulsed against his tongue, cum flooding his mouth sooner than he'd expected. James pushed past his momentary surprise and worked Sebastian through his orgasm, sucking hard as cum dribbled down his chin.

He pulled off and wiped his mouth, bumping his sore nose, which he'd been able to ignore more easily up until now.

"Here." Sebastian handed him a dish towel to wipe up. As soon as James grabbed it, Sebastian began readjusting his clothes.

James rose and tossed the cloth into a hamper in the mud room. When he turned back, Sebastian was facing away, inspecting the jam jars.

"God, that was good." James didn't hold back his satisfaction. He wanted Sebastian to know how much he'd liked getting him off.

"Yeah." Sebastian laughed, but the sound warbled at the end. It was nothing like his usual carefree giggle.

James placed a hand on the small of Sebastian's back. "Come here." He turned Sebastian around and pulled him into a kiss. Sebastian went willingly, but James felt him trembling.

Sebastian loved to tease and scandalize James, but now that they'd finally acted on his explicit suggestions, he seemed fragile. Sebastian had been alone for a long time, and it made sense if sex was different for him now than it had been the last time he'd had it. His shy reaction and softly returned kisses suggested he was overwhelmed or caught off guard. James wanted to show his acceptance of whatever Sebastian might be feeling, even if they didn't talk about it.

They kissed and held each other in the sweet-scented kitchen, and James forgot he was there for any other reason than the ache in his heart.

CHAPTER NINETEEN

They searched Selma's room that night.

"Here, take this extra lamp." Sebastian handed it to James as he lit another and set it on a side table. "I want lots of light for this room."

The bedroom was large, almost as big as Sebastian's. They'd opened the curtains to let in what moonlight they could and had several candles burning, but the shadows and the dated decor gave the room an undeniably ghostly look. The gauzy curtains hanging from the large four-poster bed didn't help, and neither did the cloth doll bound in ropes sitting on the desk.

"What the hell is that?" James asked, not wanting to get closer to the doll. It had no face, just something that looked a lot like blood smeared across its chest.

"That's Nelson." Sebastian grimaced at the doll before turning away to set a lamp on the other side of the room, near the spiral stairs leading to the tower above them. "He ran off, like I said, but Selma must have had his blood. She used the doll to bind him to his brother Sullivan."

James wrinkled his nose. "Why?"

Sebastian made an unsure sound. "Sullivan's journal said it was to prevent Nelson from escaping the consequences of his actions. He got away in time to avoid being trapped like his brother, but Selma linked them via the doll. The journal made it sound like Sullivan could channel his brother and steal his power or force him to feed the curse through the link, leaving Sullivan free to use his magic at full strength. It didn't say the bit about the curse in so many words, but reading between the lines after knowing what was going on made it clear."

"No wonder he never came back." James thought the whole family sounded horrible, except Sebastian and Stephen. And okay, Stephen's father, who James hadn't heard much about, but those first generations seemed nasty.

On that bright note, they began opening drawers. Sebastian took things out of the desk while James dove into the wardrobe.

"Wait." James paused as the rest of what Sebastian had said caught up with him. "The curse makes it harder for you to do magic?"

"Yeah, my ability is weaker than it was before I got trapped. Not that I was ever that strong. Since my life is feeding the veins, I don't have the same amount of magical energy I used to." Sebastian sounded less annoyed than James might have thought. Living in a place without electricity would be easier with full access to your magic, but Sebastian had probably come to terms with the way things were. There was no reason for James to press the point or make a big deal of it.

"Why didn't they install any electricity upstairs?" he asked instead as he checked all the pockets of the vintage trousers he'd found in the wardrobe. The instructions probably weren't in an eighty-year-old pocket, but they were checking every possibility during this search, no matter how unlikely.

Sebastian scanned the sheets of paper he'd pulled from the desk. "The manor was still under construction when Sullivan and

Nelson ruined everything. After the curse settled things and saved everyone from disaster, they realized the property was draining energy and stopped installing any kind of power. They tested what had been installed, but drawing from the electrical grid caused a black-out for the whole region."

"Damn." James began putting the trousers away.

Sebastian set a few of the papers aside. "There are several articles about the *mysterious* outage in the library. Only the Storms know what really happened."

They searched the room methodically, emptying each drawer and shelf one by one, checking each item, and trying not to choke on the dust. By midnight, they were sure the instructions weren't there.

"Anything up here?" James asked, peering up the metal spiraling staircase into the dark.

Sebastian brushed his hair from his face, looking tired. "Just a telescope and a single chair. There's a nice view, but I'd recommend going up during the day. Otherwise, you'll just get a bunch of shades looking in. Bastards are always blocking the telescope, so you can't even look at the stars."

They blew out the candles, extinguished the lamps, and closed up the room. The landing, with its high ceilings and skylights, felt open and welcoming in comparison.

Outside James's room, there was an awkward pause, both of them standing frozen in hesitation. Unsurprisingly, Sebastian found his confidence first. "Want to keep me company tonight?" He waggled his eyebrows ridiculously, causing James to choke on a laugh. You'd never have known how vulnerable he'd seemed that afternoon.

The awkwardness between them disappeared.

"Lead the way." James tried not to smile too hard. Big silly grins weren't exactly sexy.

Sebastian sauntered down the hall to his room, James close behind. Sebastian had already lit his fire, so his room was pleasantly warm. The soft orange glow suited him, bringing out the light and dark ginger tones in his hair. He pulled his shirt over his head in one graceful motion, revealing soft, freckled skin and a bruise on his hip.

James ran a delicate finger along it. "Sorry."

"Don't be. I don't mind aching, remembering you tackling me to the ground." Sebastian lifted the edge of James's sweater, revealing his own fading bruise. "I want to feel you even when you're not touching me."

James's breath caught. Even though Sebastian had seemed affected after what happened in the kitchen, his reaction hadn't necessarily been about James in particular. Did this mean Sebastian spent a lot of time thinking about the two of them touching? Had he been thinking about the incident in the ballroom since it had happened? If he had, maybe Sebastian's attraction to James went deeper than physical desire.

James wanted Sebastian to think about him. Imagine if he filled Sebastian's daydreams the way Sebastian occupied his.

Sebastian took advantage of James's stunned state and pulled his sweater over his head, followed by his shirt. Goosebumps erupted over James's newly exposed skin. Sebastian ran his palms up James's chest, coming to rest on his pecs. "I promise, this time, I won't come the second you touch my dick." He sounded dismissive, almost exasperated with himself, but a deep blush stained his cheeks.

James ran his fingers over the heated flesh. He didn't want Sebastian to be embarrassed. James had loved how excited he'd been, even the way he'd taken James by surprise, filling his mouth before he was ready. Knowing Sebastian responded to him so easily made James feel wanted.

"You can come whenever you want," he promised.

Something like relief loosened the strain around Sebastian's eyes, and he pulled James into a kiss.

They kept it light as Sebastian guided James back toward the bed. When they hit the mattress, Sebastian pushed, and James let himself flop back onto the lush bedspread. Sebastian reached for James's fly and had his jeans off a moment later.

"James Gray, naked in my bed," Sebastian taunted, throwing the jeans aside and looking at James like all his dirty dreams had come true.

James's whole body heated. He had to resist covering his stiffening cock.

Unable to lie there and take Sebastian's appreciative look for long, he sat up, perched on the edge of the mattress, and undid Sebastian's pants. Sebastian pulled them off and turned around, shooting a sultry look over his shoulder, peeking out from behind tousled hair. He hooked his thumbs into the waistband of his boxer briefs and pulled them down slowly, bending over in the process and putting his ass on display.

James forgot to breathe.

When his ass was fully exposed, Sebastian paused, leaving his underwear pulled taut, cupped beneath his perfect ass cheeks. No one had ever presented themselves so shamelessly to James. He fucking loved it and couldn't get enough of how much Sebastian seemed to love it too.

Sebastian looked over his shoulder with his bottom lip between his teeth, his lashes lowered in a lusty haze.

James reached out and squeezed the pert ass in his face, causing Sebastian to let out a satisfied *uh*. He palmed each of Sebastian's cheeks, spreading them until the tight pucker of his hole was exposed. He could have looked at the view forever, basking in the deep-seated desire coursing through him.

Sebastian braced himself, hands on his thighs. "Fuck me, James," he panted.

"Exactly what I was thinking." James let go of Sebastian's ass and tugged his underwear the rest of the way down, eager to get him fully naked.

Sebastian kicked the boxer briefs away before turning into James's arms. They crashed together in a frantic, messy kiss. Sebastian's cock pressed into James's stomach, leaking on him already. James reached between them to stroke it, running his thumb though the beaded precum.

"Fuck, why does that feel so good?" Sebastian whined.

James squeezed and stroked. "Complaining?"

"Never." Sebastian climbed onto James's lap, straddling him. "But don't push my self-control too far. I don't want to come until you're inside me."

James swore. He didn't think he'd ever get used to the things Sebastian said. Even when they were naked and all over each other, Sebastian's words sent a jolt of shock through him.

He obeyed Sebastian's request, releasing his cock in favor of feeling up the rest of him. Sebastian kissed him like he was drowning and it was the only way to get air. James couldn't get enough of Sebastian's round ass, squeezing and pulling Sebastian tighter against him.

Sebastian's outrageous flirting and bold moves gave James confidence. He didn't hold back or worry if he was making a lust-addled fool of himself. He just did whatever his desire demanded, whatever he thought Sebastian craved.

James ran his fingers up and down Sebastian's crease. When he ran the pad of his finger over Sebastian's hole, Sebastian released a groan into James's mouth. James massaged the sensitive flesh, his cock straining as Sebastian rocked into him, painting his stomach with precum.

"You got condoms?" James managed to ask when his brain could spare a thought.

"Yeah," Sebastian replied, sounding breathy and indignant at once. "It'd have been no good trying to seduce you if I wasn't prepared for it to work."

Sebastian's advances definitely had a calculated element—

especially back when James first started coming to Storm House —but James liked knowing the two of them in bed together wasn't a whim. Sebastian wanted this and had planned for it. He wanted to remember James's touch and hadn't held back in going for everything he desired. He'd seduced James, and James had fallen for it because he wanted it all just as much.

James was a goner for the man in his lap. He hadn't ever wanted anyone this bad. The longing was starting to hurt, pulling at his heart and cock until he couldn't function. James hadn't had a lot of sex and had never felt like he was missing out, but sex with Sebastian was another story. It was like uncovering a new layer to life, one he could never unsee or live without now that he'd been given a taste.

Sebastian climbed off James's lap and rummaged in his bedside-table drawer. James thought of all the dildos in there, some of which were in creative shapes James had never imagined. An image of himself fucking a handcuffed Sebastian with one of the toys flashed across his mind. He'd have to file that idea away for later. Right now, he needed to know what it felt like to join their bodies. He wanted every bit of Sebastian to be his.

James crawled up the bed. Sebastian tossed him lube and a condom before sprawling beside him.

Sebastian propped his head up with a hand. "Do me, James. Before I die of need."

James bit back a smile. "We can't have that," he said with full sincerity.

Sebastian threw his head back and cackled. "How are you managing to be serious right now?"

"I'm not." James ran a hand down Sebastian's stomach to the trail of light hair leading away from his belly button. "Or I am. I'm very serious about pleasing you."

"Yeah?" Sebastian's muscles tensed, the single syllable undeniably needy.

James's gaze returned to Sebastian's face. Before he could

interpret his expression, Sebastian shifted, flipping over and positioning himself on his hands and knees.

"Then please me."

James smiled as Sebastian turned toward him with a sultry expression. He leaned down to give him a quick kiss, then settled behind him.

Sebastian's gorgeous ass was on full display, in the air and waiting for him. The sight was better than any daydream or fantasy he'd come up with. James caressed Sebastian's thighs, his cheeks, and the dimples in the small of his back before running his hand up and down Sebastian's arched spine.

Sebastian's breathing grew heavy. He let out a small moan as James kissed the dimples above his ass. There was a cluster of freckles on his left ass cheek. James kissed that too.

"Can I taste you?" James asked into the soft skin.

"W-what?" Sebastian stammered.

James pulled back, resting his hands on Sebastian's backside. His face was flaming, and he was glad Sebastian couldn't see it. "Would you like it if I rimmed you?" James almost died as the words left his mouth. He didn't say explicit things like this often but found himself consumed with the desire to put his lips all over Sebastian's body.

"I've never had—I mean—of course I'd like it."

James bent and trailed kisses from those gorgeous dimples down to Sebastian's crease. "I haven't done this before either," he admitted. "Tell me if it's no good."

"Okay," Sebastian said, barely above a whisper.

James parted Sebastian's cheeks and ran his tongue up Sebastian's crack. He felt Sebastian twitch as his tongue made contact with the puckered flesh of his hole. The response gave James a thrill, and he went in with another swipe of his tongue, this time with more confidence. James licked up and down and swirled his tongue around Sebastian's hole, pressing his face between Sebastian's cheeks until his nose protested.

"*Yeah*. That's good," Sebastian breathed. "Don't stop."

James smiled, nuzzling Sebastian's hole before placing an open-mouthed kiss against it. His whole world was smooth skin and the musky scent of sex. James licked and sucked at Sebastian until he was soft and slick with James's spit.

"So good, oh shit. Fuck me, James," Sebastian whined.

James could have eaten Sebastian's ass until they both came, but he wasn't about to deny such a desperate request. He opened the lube and let it warm on his fingers as he continued lapping at Sebastian's hole. Just a little more. He needed it. His dick ached between his legs. It wouldn't take much to get himself off. One tug from his hand would do it.

But Sebastian wanted to come with James filling him up, and James was going to make that happen. He pressed his tongue past the ring of softened muscle and Sebastian pushed back with a low groan. James lost himself in the way Sebastian moved against his mouth until he feared he'd come untouched before his cock got anywhere near Sebastian.

James made himself stop, giving Sebastian one last lick. He replaced his mouth with his finger and pressed forward, meeting little resistance before Sebastian gave way, allowing James entrance.

"More, James," Sebastian whined.

James let out a satisfied huff. "Getting impatient?"

"Yes, fuck. Don't want to wait any longer." Sebastian pressed back, trying to fuck himself on James's finger. "Need it."

All of Sebastian's pleasure hit James straight in the center of his chest. His cock took notice too, but there was something about pleasing Sebastian, knowing he felt good in James's arms, that made his soul ache.

"I'll give you what you need, Sebastian. Don't worry."

The promise drew another moan out of Sebastian. James finished prepping him without lingering, adding a second finger, then a third. He was just as eager as the man writhing beneath him.

Once Sebastian was ready, he got the condom on and slicked himself with lube. Anticipation pounded through James's veins and his pulse quickened. He lined himself up, pushing gently against Sebastian's hole.

"Please," Sebastian begged.

James loved being the cause of Sebastian's desperation. He wanted to play with Sebastian, see how wild he could drive him. Tease him until he screamed. But not tonight. Right now, he longed to give Sebastian everything, reward his openness, and fuck him exactly how he wanted.

He pushed forward in one steady stroke, not stopping until his hips pressed flush against Sebastian's ass. Sebastian moaned, whimpering when James's cock was fully seated inside him. James panted with effort, dizzy with the feeling of Sebastian's body accepting him. He took a moment to let Sebastian adjust, running a hand up his spine. James closed his eyes with the effort it took to restrain himself. Sebastian holding his cock inside him felt so good he worried he'd come the next time he moved.

Sebastian thrust his hips back. "Please, James."

"Feels good?" James asked as he pulled back, sliding partway out before thrusting steadily back in.

"Yes." Sebastian moved with him, his hands fisting the bedspread. "Harder," he groaned. "Fuck me hard, James. *Please.*" He glanced back over his shoulder and caught James's eye, hitting him with a look so desperate and pleading that James gasped at the sight.

"Anything, Sebastian," he groaned, and Sebastian's eyes fluttered closed, a complete look of pleasure lighting his face. "Anything you need."

James took hold of Sebastian's hips and thrust.

Sebastian groaned as his body was jolted forward. "*Yes.*"

James pulled back and slammed home hard, causing Sebastian

to shout in pleasurable surprise, his eyes flying open as he looked over his shoulder once more. James tightened his hold and pounded into Sebastian, his world narrowing to the feeling of Sebastian's tightness squeezing his cock and the sounds falling from Sebastian's lips.

James faltered as he almost came but managed to hold off. Adjusting his angle, he picked up his pace, fucking Sebastian relentlessly into the mattress.

"Oh god, yeah." Sebastian bucked his hips. "Fuck me."

James worked his hips, hitting Sebastian's prostate if the wild sounds Sebastian was making were anything to go by. He reached for Sebastian's cock, his own orgasm threatening. He smeared Sebastian's precum down his shaft and jacked him hard.

Sebastian came with a shout, cum covering James's hand as Sebastian's tight muscles clenched around his cock. James filled the condom, his orgasm drawn out, the most exposing moans falling from his lips. He was left panting, dizzy with release, and collapsed against Sebastian's back.

The two of them lay together, sweaty and breathing hard. James kissed Sebastian's neck. "Did you enjoy that?" he murmured in his ear.

Sebastian huffed. "You know I did."

"Just want to make sure."

Sebastian turned his head to the side so he could look at James. "It was perfect."

James's chest constricted. "Good. I agree." He kissed Sebastian, then pushed himself up. He pulled out carefully and forced himself to walk to the bathroom to toss the condom away.

To his surprise, Sebastian followed.

They cleaned up in silence. James felt adrift in a way he wasn't familiar with. He'd never felt so connected to another person but didn't know what to say or if he should even say anything. Just as he started to worry he was making the afterglow awkward for them both, Sebastian swatted James with a hand towel, snapping it against his ass and surprising a shout out of him. Sebastian smiled deviously.

"You're a nightmare," James grumbled, rubbing his stinging backside.

"Whatever, you fucking love it," Sebastian shot back.

He really did.

CHAPTER TWENTY

JAMES STAYED in Sebastian's bed that night. He figured he'd sleep soundly until at least nine after the long day and the best sex he'd ever had, but something woke him while it was still dark.

He blinked up at the ceiling. The fire's glow had died down, allowing deeper shadows to overtake the room. He smiled. How could he be in such a dire situation and still grin like a fool? Well, Sebastian, that was how.

He'd had a crush on Sebastian before, had been seduced by the mystery of the man and enticed by the temptation he offered, but the Sebastian he'd gotten to know was someone he could fall in love with. The more he learned about Sebastian, the harder he fell for him. James couldn't pretend his feelings were surface-level attraction, not when he loved spending time with Sebastian in the kitchen or garden as much as he enjoyed their time in bed.

James wouldn't have been open to tumbling down such a love-sick path under normal circumstances. He had reasons for avoiding these kinds of attachments, but stuck at Storm House, it felt like he and Sebastian existed in a bubble where the rest of his troubles didn't matter. He didn't have to worry about Sebastian leaving. He didn't have to worry about their lives not fitting together or growing apart and losing another person he loved.

If they never escaped Storm House, they would always have each other, and while James didn't want to be trapped, he was glad it canceled out some of his fears of abandonment and made Sebastian easier to reach for.

Maybe James was being reckless, and this would all blow up in his face. There were still a million ways he could get hurt, but it was hard to care while lying naked in bed with Sebastian. He refused to regret letting his feelings grow, no matter what happened.

Beside him, Sebastian stirred. "James?" His name came out in a barely audible whisper, delicate, and not just through an effort to be quiet, almost like Sebastian hoped it would go unheard but couldn't help calling out.

"I'm here," James murmured back, rolling onto his side to see Sebastian looking at the ceiling.

His gaze flicked to James and then away. "Sorry, didn't mean to wake you."

"It's okay." James scooted closer, reaching out and putting an arm around Sebastian.

Sebastian stiffened on contact, then melted into James's embrace, snuggling tighter against him. James pulled Sebastian in, positioning him as the little spoon.

Neither of them said anything. James could have asked Sebastian if he was okay, but honestly, how could he be? Sebastian had been alone for years. He had to be touch starved. Hell, he had to be starved for any affection or companionship. There was no way what was happening between them wasn't overwhelming for Sebastian on some level.

It was overwhelming for James, and he hadn't been cut off from the world. Even if he thought he understood, he didn't want to push Sebastian to talk. They had a lot to deal with, and James needed to allow Sebastian space, even if he suspected Sebastian's whisper in the dark might have been a request for comfort.

James could give comfort just like this. He held Sebastian close, kissed his neck below his ear, and ran his hands up and down Sebastian's arms. James could make Sebastian feel cared for and treasured even if he wasn't ready to voice his growing feelings.

"I like this," Sebastian whispered after a while, again sounding soft and worlds away from the cocky man who'd declared he'd seduce James as if it were a sport.

"I like it too," James whispered back, and they fell asleep tangled together.

THEY WOKE up to pouring rain and clouds dark enough for shades to be peering in the bathroom window after the sun had risen.

"We won't be in the garden today," Sebastian said as they shaved together at the sink.

James rinsed his borrowed razor. "I wish they'd stop looking in on us. Makes me wonder what they're thinking."

The shade at the window swooped to the skylight to get a different perspective on the scene in the bathroom. It tapped the glass.

"I think they're just bitter they can't get inside." Sebastian patted his face dry. He stretched, naked aside from the towel slung low on his hips. "Oh yeah, I can feel it."

"Feel what?" James eyed him through the mirror, knowing he was doomed when an evil look blossomed on Sebastian's fine-featured face.

"How well you fucked me last night."

"Ah." James cleared his throat and looked down, rinsing his already clean razor and trying to hide his satisfied smile.

Sebastian slapped his ass, the sound muffled by the towel James wore. "Hurry up, we need to feed the chickens. You've made their breakfast late and should probably apologize."

James borrowed underwear from Sebastian, and they got dressed. He'd have grabbed a T-shirt too, but the skin-tight look wasn't his thing, so he ducked back to his room for a dated button-up.

In the hall, Sebastian took James's face in his hands and kissed him. He ran a delicate finger over James's bruised nose. "Does it still hurt?"

"Not so much." His black eye was looking better too.

"Good." Sebastian trailed a finger along James's brow. "We'll have to be more careful with you." Sebastian released him and turned toward the stairs, leaving James to follow, his heart aching at Sebastian's tenderness.

He wasn't quite comfortable with the feeling.

James looked after everyone. It was who he was. His urge to protect and care was especially strong with Sebastian, but he always resisted letting others take care of him in return. Accepting that kind of support only meant it hurt more when those people were taken from his life. James hadn't let himself lean on anyone since his grandmother had died, and he was fine taking care of himself. It wasn't something he was looking to change. He wanted to be there for Sebastian, not pass off his troubles to a man already suffering from years alone.

After feeding the chickens and opening the barn for Miss Moo, Sebastian started the fire in the kitchen. Apparently, it was time to make more bread, so he got going on that while James made coffee, the two of them seamlessly working around each other.

James couldn't help reaching out and touching Sebastian's lower back as he maneuvered behind him or brushing their arms together when they were near. Sebastian returned each brush of affection with one of his own, almost like he'd been waiting for James to give him permission to touch him more. It was different from the way Sebastian had steered James around the kitchen the day before. That had been playful but purposeful. This was indulgent. Small, barely-there connections rather than bold moves full of wicked promises.

It was something James could get used to.

Once the dough was set aside for its first round of proofing, Sebastian disappeared, returning with a battered notebook.

"Here." He handed it to James, who was sitting at the table with a second coffee and an apple. "It's my notes on the transfer spell. Start at the bookmark, but please don't read anything else in there, okay?"

"Of course." James set the book beside his coffee. "I had a journal too. I wouldn't want anyone looking at it."

Sebastian crossed his arms like he was uncomfortable but trying to hide it. "You had a journal?"

"I started it when my parents died." The grief counselor had suggested it. Writing out his thoughts had helped at the time, but James had no desire to ever look back at them.

Sebastian squeezed James's shoulder, a tender look softening his features. Then he turned away to stoke the fire. James cleared his throat, pushing away a strange wave of emotion with a hearty sip of coffee, and opened the notebook.

There was no date at the top of the passage. The messy writing went straight into an incantation with no context. Some of the words had been crossed out and replaced with others, like Sebastian hadn't been sure of the exact phrases used. Even so, it was more detailed than James had imagined.

The spell required blood from the cursed person and the one who was meant to take over. It wasn't phrased that way since Sebastian hadn't known what the spell was doing, but hindsight made it clear. Kira's blood had been taken first, then Sebastian's had been mixed with it as a spell was cast to shift magic from Kira's blood to her brother's. The mixed blood was then used to write symbols on Sebastian's forehead—which he'd drawn in the notebook—before a second incantation was used while bleeding Sebastian again to allow the transferred magic to enter his body.

At the conclusion of the incantation, Sebastian wrote there was a surge of power and a loud blast that knocked everyone to the ground and made his ears ring. James imagined the ordeal would have been horrifying for a twelve-year-old.

The last thing Sebastian had written was a question. *Why did they have to give some of Kira's magic to me but not the other way around? I never get anything she doesn't.*

James clenched a fist. Sebastian's mother had a lot to answer for regarding her son, but that wasn't for him to deal with, at least not before getting away from Storm House.

The account was good but not perfect. The wording wasn't inconsequential, and using the wrong phrases could screw the whole thing up. The power surge was concerning as well. It seemed dangerous. James wasn't sure if he'd agree to try the spell without Selma's proper instructions. Though he might if he got desperate enough.

He'd only been here a few days. What would he be willing to do when he'd been stuck at the house for a month? A year? He couldn't think about it. At the thought of his imprisonment never ending, anxiety like he hadn't felt since walking into the invisible barrier gripped his chest.

"It's hard to tell how much power we'll need for this," James said, pushing his fear away and getting himself under control.

Sebastian had been sipping his coffee at the counter, watching James as he read with more distance between them than they'd had all day. He set his cup aside. "I don't think Mom and Stephen had any more power than you and I do combined. Stephen's power was on par with mine, and Mom is good, but not off the charts or anything."

It sounded promising. At least both Storms hadn't been exceptionally powerful. James closed Sebastian's notebook. "I'd still like to double-check the amount of energy needed through theory, using the concepts the transfer is based around. Unless you don't have those kind of books here?"

"No, I do." Sebastian retrieved his notebook from the table. "Let's head up to the library. Then we might as well search the study."

It was a long day. James researched magical theory while Sebastian started searching the study. After a few hours of reading, James was confident they'd have the energy needed for the spell. It didn't require much more than the unbinding had. Someone with an ability like Parker's could have pulled it off on their own.

With that in mind, the energy surge Sebastian described in his journal didn't quite fit. A blast like that sounded like more power than the transfer spell used, so where had it come from, and why had it reacted explosively? At least it had done nothing more than knock everyone over. Maybe it hadn't been as intense as the young Sebastian's account made it seem.

James joined Sebastian in the study, where he received a briefing on what had already been searched. He settled into the desk chair as directed, trying to ignore the shade knocking on the window.

"I'm surprised Eli hasn't come back yet," James said after he'd relayed what he'd learned.

Sebastian didn't look up from the folders he was searching through. "Yeah, sometimes you think people will come back, and then they don't."

James's gut twisted. Whenever he thought he understood how lonely Sebastian must have been here, he was hit with something that made him realize he had no clue. He could have compassion for Sebastian's circumstances but would never know what it had been like, not even close.

James wondered if Sebastian would be as interested in him if he hadn't been the first person to spend time with Sebastian in six years. He wanted to say yes, of course, Sebastian liked him for who he was, for more than his body, but he wasn't sure. How different would things be if they weren't in an isolated situation? Would Sebastian have chosen to sleep with James if he had other options? Did he want James specifically, or was he just desperate for companionship? After so long, Sebastian seizing whatever came within reach was understandable, and James wouldn't hold it against him.

James might never know how the truth shook out and wasn't sure it mattered if they ended up trapped together forever. He'd only find out if they got free.

Would Sebastian want to stay with him in Moonlight Falls and be his boyfriend after they escaped? Or would he leave and not look back?

James hoped Sebastian wouldn't leave him behind. He found himself imagining what the two of them could have if they escaped the house and Sebastian freely chose him. The possibility filled James with enough longing to make his heart burst.

James forced himself to concentrate on the lawyer letters he was looking through. There was never any doubt he wanted to escape Storm House, but now that it felt like the life he'd always wanted—the life with a partner he'd feared reaching for but could never stop dreaming about—was laying just out of reach, he *had* to get out. He had to know if Sebastian would choose him when all this was behind them.

"Maybe Eli is giving you space," Sebastian said. James had thought they'd moved past his comment but was glad for the reassurance. "If he thinks you're just indulging in a new fling and having a little irresponsible rebellion, he might be trying to give you time to get it out of your system."

James frowned. He hated that Sebastian had referred to

himself as a fling. He was so much more than that to James. "None of that is something I would do. Eli should know that."

Sebastian shrugged.

After a while, Sebastian left the study to knead the dough and set it to rise one last time. He disappeared again later to put it in the oven and when it was done, returned with fresh slices for lunch.

Several hours after the bread was eaten, they deemed the study search complete, neither surprised to be emptyhanded.

"Should we look in here?" James gestured to the upstairs sitting room as they headed toward the stairs.

Sebastian had their empty lunch plates and was about to go down to the kitchen. "Might as well." He turned around and followed James through the archway, into the room.

The place was dusty. Everything looked incredibly dated, but not all from the same era. It was like the fifties had crashed into the eighties.

Sebastian set the plates on a mostly empty bookshelf. "I don't come in here much. I prefer the sunroom and the sitting area in my bedroom. This house is too damn big."

James wasn't arguing with that. "Have you searched here before?"

Sebastian picked up a stack of old magazines and began flipping through them. "Just a quick glance in the drawers and on the shelves. I'd given up by then."

They got to it, sneezing from the dust as they methodically picked through every single item in the room.

"I'm going to get some water," James said after a dust-induced coughing fit.

Sebastian waved in acknowledgment, not looking up from a notebook he'd found.

James took his time filling a water bottle in the kitchen, then chugged the contents before having another piece of bread.

Eventually, he went back upstairs, bottle refilled to share with Sebastian.

He re-entered the sitting room to find Sebastian standing in the middle of the room, tension pulling every muscle in his body taut as he read an old newspaper. The paper was yellow and discolored unevenly like it had been left folded for years. Sebastian's grip crumpled the edges beneath his fingers.

James took a step closer. "Find anything?"

Sebastian jumped at the question like he hadn't heard James's return. He gave James a wide-eyed stare before his attention drifted back to the newspaper, emotion flashing across his face too quick for James to decipher. "I found this tucked inside." He held out an aged piece of paper covered in tiny writing.

James rushed forward to grab it. A quick scan of the first scribbles was all he needed to see. "You found it!" Intense relief washed over him, making him lightheaded. James's mind raced as his confidence in their plan solidified.

"I can't believe it was here." Sebastian folded the newspaper closed and tucked it into a magazine rack next to the sofa. "It was just left inside the paper, sitting right there with all these nineties cooking magazines."

"What a weird place to put it." James glared at the magazine rack like it had planned this whole debacle itself.

Sebastian didn't comment. James thought he'd be annoyed at his relatives. Tucking the spell into a random newspaper was careless. The paper hadn't been clipped for articles, even though it was a copy of the *Apple Valley Times*, so it must not have been an important issue. What if it had been thrown out and the spell lost forever!

"When's the paper from?" James asked, reaching for it.

"A few days after Mom and Stephen did the ritual." Sebastian grabbed James's outstretched hand and pulled him close.

James found himself wrapped in a bone-crushing hug. He was bewildered but accepted the affection, embracing Sebastian in return and planting a kiss on his cheek. "This is so great. I can't believe we found it."

"Me either." Sebastian didn't let go. "We can do the spell. We could get out of here."

James pulled back enough to inspect Sebastian. His eyes were framed with fine, sad lines, his lips pressed tight, a slight frown tugging them downward. Maybe he was afraid to hope too much, or maybe it was overwhelming to be this close to a solution after so long.

"This is good," James said again, hoping to reassure Sebastian. "It's the best we could have hoped for." But he found himself longing for so much more, a life where Sebastian chose him, even when he was free and had the world at his fingertips.

James promised himself—if they got out of there—he wouldn't let his fear of losing loved ones come between him and Sebastian. He would take this chance Storm House had given him. He could face anything after this, especially if it gave him a future with a man as strong and wonderful as Sebastian.

CHAPTER TWENTY-ONE

They had everything they needed for the ritual. A knife, a metal —not wooden—bowl, Selma's instructions, and a cow.

Sebastian had the smaller items gathered on the table in the entryway next to *The Magical Tales*, which he'd discarded there after James had figured them out.

A single lamp cast a flickering glow on the scene. It was late, close to midnight. Selma's instructions said the transfer spell needed to be performed on the land directly above the intersecting veins of power and should be done at night to lessen the chance of passersby coming across the magic.

James wasn't going to argue about the location if it impacted the spell's function, but he had issues with the timing. They shouldn't be out at night when the shades were at their strongest. They'd be busy enough doing the transfer and didn't need distractions or complications.

Sebastian disagreed, explaining the need to avoid anyone passing by Storm House and encountering the spell wasn't about secrecy but safety. It was best to do the spell when no one was likely to be driving down the remote, winding section of North

Road, which cut close to the edge of the property where the veins intersected.

Sebastian pulled his robe tight around him. "I don't know if midnight is late enough. We need that dead time, closer to three in the morning. Just in case." The timing seemed to be stressing Sebastian out, but not in the shade-related way that had James concerned.

"If you say so." James was fine deferring to Sebastian on this since he'd been part of the ritual before. There was no need to add to the tension by arguing about the shades. Sebastian knew they could be a problem just as much as James did.

A light flashed across the entryway. In unison, they turned toward the front door, startled.

"What?" Sebastian muttered as he hurried to the window.

James followed, peering out into the darkness. "Someone's here," he said in disbelief as the car headlights illuminating the gate went out.

"Shit." Sebastian ran a hand through his hair. "See, they could have been driving by as we did the spell. What the hell is someone doing here this late?" He swung the front door open and marched across the porch like he was about to yell at the visitor to get off his lawn.

James grabbed the lamp and followed. A shade swooped in behind him. He turned and swung the light at it, and the thing backed off.

"Hello," Sebastian called into the dark.

Flashlights bobbed on the other side of the gate.

"It's just us," said Eli's familiar voice.

Sebastian unlocked the gate and yanked it open. "What are you doing here in the middle of the night?" He was furious, his words harsh and unforgiving.

"Thought we'd come by after work when we saw James wasn't home *again*," Parker replied from beside his boyfriend.

"Got your delivery," Eli added, pulling a box from his trunk and setting it inside the gate. "That way, I don't have to come back tomorrow." Parker retrieved a second box and set it by the first.

"But you never make deliveries this late," Sebastian protested, nearly shouting.

James didn't understand why he was so rattled. The last time Eli had come looking for him it had been late at night. It made sense when he was working the closing shift at the diner. Sebastian's agitation had to be due to the spell they were about to perform, but the instructions hadn't detailed any specific dangers to passersby who might detect the spell from the road, so James couldn't help wondering if Sebastian was overreacting.

"I just wanted to check my brother was still alive," Eli shot back, matching Sebastian's anger.

"I'm fine," James said, trying to interject some calm into the situation.

Sebastian all but cut him off, ignoring his words. "Don't come out here when you're not supposed to, Eli."

"Why?" Parker pointed his light directly in Sebastian's face. "What are you hiding?"

Sebastian flinched away from the glare but didn't say anything.

"I don't get what you're still doing out here," Eli said to James. "Why haven't you been home? You're screwing Hazel over, leaving her all the work at the shop. I thought you loved having Gray's reopened." When James didn't reply, Eli went on, anger rising. "I don't know how you can stand being out here. Driving this road, being in these trees, makes me think of nothing but Mom and Dad dying in this awful place."

With that punch to the gut, Eli climbed back into his car. Parker waited a second longer as if giving James time to respond. When he didn't, Parker turned toward the car.

"Stop coming here at night," Sebastian shouted as the doors

slammed shut. The car drove off and was soon out of sight around the bend.

"Is it that big of a deal?" James grumbled, his mind stuck on the pain in Eli's voice. He'd thought Eli had been doing better with his grief and the hatred he harbored for Moonlight Falls.

"Yes, it is," Sebastian snapped. "I won't do the spell if someone could get caught in it."

"Why?" James stared at him, unable to read his expression in the dark. "Would they get trapped by the curse?" There was nothing in the instructions to indicate that, but he couldn't think of anything else that would freak Sebastian out so much.

"No, they wouldn't. You'd have to be on the property for the curse to tie you to the land." Sebastian closed and locked the gate. "Messing with the veins is dangerous, even to transfer the curse. My family might have been knocked on our asses that night, but a lot worse could happen." He picked up one of the boxes like that was the end of it.

James grabbed the other without replying. He hadn't realized the power surge came from the veins and not the spell itself. How did Sebastian know a lot worse could happen? Was it something his uncle had told him?

As they returned to the house, James wished he hadn't been so distracted by Sebastian's agitation and had tried harder to talk to Eli. He hated the wretched feeling the encounter had left him with, but hopefully, it wouldn't matter after tonight. He'd be able to get back to his life and make up for his behavior.

Back inside, he and Sebastian took their time putting the delivered items away before making coffee. Sebastian's nerves were rubbing off on James. He couldn't sit still, and all the tension in the room was giving him a headache.

"Three should be good," Sebastian said like he was reassuring himself. "If those two just checked on us, no one else should be coming out. And the loggers won't be on the road before five."

James didn't argue.

When the pendulum clock in the hall struck three, Sebastian stood from the table and wordlessly led the way out of the kitchen. He slipped the instructions into his pocket and picked up the lamp, leaving the rest of the supplies for James to carry.

They made their way outside. A shade floated over to investigate as soon as they closed the front door. Sebastian shooed it away with a flapping sleeve of his robe. The shade hissed but didn't get aggressive.

The grounds were quiet. Even the rustle of branches in the wind and the sound of nightlife seemed absent. Sebastian roused Miss Moo in the barn and tied a rope to the bell slung around her neck, gently coaxing her outside. The cow followed along happily until they reached the edge of the forest. She planted her hoofs and wouldn't move a step farther.

"She knows there are shades in here," Sebastian explained. "But she shouldn't care. The bell on her neck is warded. Come on." He tugged on the rope.

James took a few steps down the path into the trees. "Should *we* care?"

"We don't have a choice." With one more tug, Sebastian got the cow moving.

The path wound through the trees. James couldn't see much beyond the illumination of the oil lamp. They didn't come across any shades, but James had a feeling they were lurking just out of sight. Watching.

They stopped in a dirt clearing. Redwood forests didn't have a lot of undergrowth, but in this spot, you could tell the lack of vegetation was unnatural. The earth had been turned over in the center like someone had been digging it up.

Sebastian guided the cow to stand on the disturbed earth. "We'll link our power like we've done before, then I'll follow the ritual and transfer your curse to Miss Moo."

Earlier, they'd discussed the fact that they couldn't transfer the curse from both of them to the cow. Energy theory didn't support that working. It was a life for a life, even though the curse usually only trapped one person at a time.

"You sure you want to free me?" James reached out and cupped Sebastian's elbow. "You've been here longer."

He shook his head. "This is my family's mess. I'm not leaving you here alone. This way, you can help me find a way to escape after you get out. Like I was originally hoping you would. Besides, we can just get a second cow and do this all over again. I won't have to wait long." He gave James a thin smile.

James nodded in acknowledgment. It was the best plan they had.

They shrugged off their shirts. This time, Sebastian picked up the knife. As he performed the linking spell, mixing their blood above their hearts, the sensation was nothing like it'd been in the ballroom. The absence of charged sexual desire left room for something else. The link between their magics hit James like a wave of warmth, the sensation of fear completely absent this time.

James grabbed hold of Sebastian, fingers digging into his waist. He trusted Sebastian to use his power well, not to drain him or overdo it. He was starting to trust Sebastian with a lot more than that, with more fragile things—like his heart. That had to be why the magical connection felt like baring a piece of his soul.

Sebastian leaned down and brushed a kiss against James's lips. "Let's get you out of here," he whispered.

How could James not trust a man willing to save him at his own expense? Sebastian cared about him.

James wanted to say he'd never leave Sebastian, but he didn't mean in relation to the house. He meant personally, as a partner. Not that they were even partners. It was a ridiculous thing to think, so he kept quiet, only nodding.

Hopefully, soon he'd get the chance to see what he and Sebastian could be together.

Sebastian gently took James's hand and cut his forearm. He recited Selma's spell, the words blurring into a haze of sound around James, making him lightheaded even though Sebastian wasn't taking much blood. James had to concentrate hard on not dropping the bowl he was holding as magic pulsed through him. That had to be good. It had to mean it was working.

Next, it was Miss Moo's turn. Sebastian used magic to numb a small area on her shoulder to keep her from feeling the cut and bolting. The cow's blood mixed with James's in the bowl. He could feel his magic being expended through the link he shared with Sebastian in a steady pull, and when Sebastian got to the last stage of the spell, James's heart rate sped up.

Sebastian painted symbols on the cow's face and bled her again so she would accept the magic of the curse. When the incantation was finished, both James and Sebastian stood frozen, waiting.

There was no surge of power. Miss Moo seemed bored and tried to pull away, back toward the direction of the barn.

"Did it work?" James whispered.

Sebastian looked between him and the cow. "I don't know."

James's heart sank. Something wasn't right. The magic that had been running through him was gone, leaving him with the sense of hanging in between. But before he could relay this to Sebastian, the ground shuddered beneath his feet.

CHAPTER TWENTY-TWO

Miss Moo made a sound of alarm. The earth rumbled again.

Sebastian's gaze darted around the clearing, dimly illuminated by the lamp on the ground. "That didn't happen last time."

A screech pierced the night air. They looked up to see dozens of pairs of onyx eyes peering down at them from the shadows. The cow tossed her head as if she could sense the shades. With another loud moo, she lurched away from Sebastian, pulling the rope from his grip, and ran off through the trees.

James slowly crouched to grab the oil lamp. Sebastian copied his steady movement, gathering their clothes and the ritual supplies.

"Sebastian." James reached out and took hold of his hand. "What happened the night I found you outside?"

Sebastian took a step toward the path, pulling James along. "I don't think the shades like it when you mess with the veins." His attention stayed glued to the eyes in the trees. "I came out here, hoping you'd follow. I made a bunch of noise on my way out. I was digging around in the dirt to try and draw your attention to the spot where the veins are, using a bit of magic to help soften the earth. I hoped you'd catch me or come investigating later."

They inched closer to the path, the shades slowly closing in on them, coming out of the shadows and down into the clearing.

"But you didn't, and the shades came down on me in the clearing," Sebastian continued.

"That was a risky thing to do," James whispered as if that would help avoid the shades' attention even though they were already staring.

"I didn't mean to drain myself," Sebastian argued. "I used too much magic digging and didn't expect so many shades. I conjured light so I could get away, but it was too much magic. They overwhelmed me when I ran out of power."

A shade darted forward and grabbed the clothes in Sebastian's hands. It bared its teeth, knobby fingers clutching Sebastian's robe.

"No." Sebastian dropped James's hand and tugged back. "That's mine, you little shit."

Another shade joined the first, helping its fellow pull on the purple fabric. The knife and the bowl clattered to the ground.

"James, help." Sebastian shot him a frustrated look as a third shade joined the tug-of-war.

"Just leave it," James hissed. Sebastian might be attached to his robe, but now was not the time to prioritize clothing.

A wisp of dark smoke appeared around Sebastian's throat, solidifying into a pair of clawed hands. James yelled, but the shade was already squeezing. Sebastian dropped the clothes, his hands shooting to the fingers tightening around his neck.

James lunged forward, grabbed the knife from the ground, and lashed out. He struck the shade in the shoulder. The beast dissipated in a puff of smokey shadow, only to reappear a few feet away. The ones in the air above them chattered excitedly, snapping teeth and hissing.

There were a hell of a lot more of them now. *Where had they all come from?*

As more shades materialized in the clearing, James whispered, "Run."

Sebastian didn't hesitate. He grabbed James's hand and took off through the trees, not bothering with the path.

The shades followed. Claws raked down James's bare back. He wasn't sure if he should risk summoning a light. His energy was low, and even though they were still linked, Sebastian had to be close to depleted. Overdoing a light summoning spell now could hurt them both.

So they ran through the woods without looking back. At last, they came across the path. The property was too damn big. If only the veins were closer to the house.

Sebastian swore as a shade grabbed his wrist, but he didn't stop running and managed to shake it off.

They cleared the trees. There was no sign of Miss Moo, so she'd probably gone to hide in the barn.

James chanced a look over his shoulder. The number of shades had doubled. He'd never seen so many in one place. There were even more than the night he'd found Sebastian in the dirt. "Just don't stop," he yelled, turning to face forward so he didn't trip.

"Wasn't going to," Sebastian shot back.

A group of shades tried to cut them off, separating from the pack and swooping around from the side. James swung his lamp at them. It was enough to confuse them and keep them from closing in completely. They made it to the porch, and Sebastian lunged for the door.

The shades scattered, making all kinds of noise as they flew around the house, careening in every direction and swarming the place as James and Sebastian tumbled across the threshold.

James looked up. The skylight was full of curious faces blinking down at them, teeth glinting, and more shades flying in the sky above.

"Damn pains in the ass," Sebastian wheezed, out of breath.

James glanced back out the door. "We still don't know if the spell worked."

"No." Sebastian wiped blood from a scratch on his arm. "We'll have to wait for sunrise to check."

THEY CLEANED up and checked each other's scratches. None were concerning. Even the ones on Sebastian's arm weren't deep. There was nothing to do but get out the antiseptic ointment and wait for the sun to rise.

As soon as it was light, they walked down the driveway together. Sebastian opened the gate, and James's stomach flipped. He wasn't confident the spell had worked but couldn't get the hopeful fluttering in his gut to calm.

He walked forward, his arms outstretched so he wouldn't smack his face. His hands shook. As he drew level with the stone pillars and ugly gargoyles guarding the property, excitement gripped him. *This was it.*

His hands smashed into the invisible barrier. Even though he'd anticipated it, he was hit with disbelief, the disappointment crushing in a way he couldn't have prepared himself for.

He pounded on the barrier. They'd done everything right. *Why hadn't it worked?*

Sebastian laid a gentle hand on his shoulder. "James."

He whirled around. "I don't understand. The theory checked out."

"I know. A cow's life should have been enough, but maybe it has to be human. Another fail-safe in the magic that wasn't detailed in the transfer instructions."

"No." James shook his head. "We can't transfer the curse to another *person* to free ourselves. Miss Moo was perfect. She was going to live on the property her whole life anyway."

Sebastian squeezed his shoulder. "I know."

But that meant they weren't getting out.

James tried to take a breath, except the air wouldn't come. He couldn't get free of this place. He was trapped with no hope of escape.

Almost everything important to James was out of reach. He'd let Eli walk away upset last night. He hadn't even tried to comfort him. He'd failed Eli, and he'd do nothing but fail his brother over and over for as long as he was trapped here. James might not be dead, but Eli was going to lose him. How long would he keep coming back when magic forced James to push Eli away?

Failing his brother was the one thing that was never supposed to happen. Everyone else in their family was dead. James had to be there for Eli. It wasn't negotiable. Only he couldn't be, not when he was imprisoned at Storm House.

"James." Sebastian turned him so they were facing each other. "James, deep breaths."

He couldn't. His chest burned. "Eli," he gasped.

What if something happened to his brother and James couldn't get to him. What if he needed help. It was James's worst fear.

He'd been powerless to save their parents and grandparents, but he'd told himself Eli would be different. Nothing would separate them and disaster wouldn't claim them, not after it had taken everyone else in their family. Except, that was nothing but an idle wish. Anything could happen to Eli, and there was nothing James could do.

There had always been a chance he wouldn't be able to get to Eli in time if a crisis befell them, that he'd lose his brother unexpectedly, but he'd told himself he'd make it. He'd protect Eli no matter what. Only none of it was true. It was a lie James had made himself believe in order to cope with his overwhelming worries. But stuck here, he was forced to see the lie for what it was, and it brought him no comfort.

James had never had the power to ensure he wouldn't lose Eli to disaster or an unexpected medical event. And now, if anything happened, he wouldn't even be able to say goodbye. Eli would think James had abandoned him. He'd be left all alone, and James couldn't breathe through the thought.

He was on his knees, but he was unsure when he'd stopped standing.

Sebastian murmured in his ear, telling him to copy his steady breaths. James gasped. He couldn't think past Eli dying out of his reach. Alone. He'd never be able to forgive himself if that happened.

James knew death was a part of life but had never been able to sit comfortably with it. It had hurt too much when his parents were ripped away from him. He feared news of another accident claiming someone he loved more than anything, and now, he couldn't even spend the time he had with the people who were still here.

Anything could happen, and James hated all the horrible possibilities that were out there. It was enough to leave him frozen and helpless under the weight of it all.

What if something happened to Sebastian? The thought ripped through James like a fatal knife wound. What if Sebastian got hurt and James couldn't save him? They couldn't even call for help.

James was overcome with helplessness, exactly as he had been when his parents died. His own life was out of his control. Everything that mattered to him could be ripped away, and there was nothing he could do about it.

James gripped Sebastian's hand hard. He closed his eyes and tried to concentrate on Sebastian's breathing. An eternity passed, and when he opened his eyes, he realized his cheeks were soaked with tears.

"James." Sebastian wiped some of his tears away. "James, I'm here. You're okay."

"No," James gasped. He wasn't okay. Sebastian might be here now, but what if something happened? Too many emotions were welling up inside him. His feelings for Sebastian were only starting to grow. He needed to see where they went so badly it burned. He couldn't stand the idea that it could all be taken away before they had a chance to love each other.

James tried to be rational, but it was no good. He was a ball of raw pain and longing and nothing more. He couldn't hold it all back like he normally did. His grumpy outlook on life usually kept the overwhelming stuff at bay. He used it as a barrier, holding everything at a distance, only letting himself be vaguely annoyed or frustrated. It helped him not feel the things he didn't want to. But he was worn down. He'd started letting hopes and dreams and love in, and his ability to cope couldn't combat that. He couldn't feel all this and pretend it didn't matter if he lost it.

"I know things aren't going how we thought." Sebastian stroked James's hair. "But you're okay. I promise. You'll be okay. I'll get you out of here."

James blinked back tears. They both knew there was no use promising that.

"I've got you." Sebastian's arm tightened around James. He looked up at the sky, blinking furiously, then fixed his gaze on James. "I'll take care of you. I'll do everything I can."

"But what if something happens to you?" James couldn't hold the desperate question in.

Sebastian's brow crinkled. "Why would something happen to me? I'll be here for you."

"But what if? We don't know what will happen." James had never been good at accepting things outside his control. He hated the helplessness, but being afraid didn't give him any more power. His fear hadn't stopped his grandfather from suddenly succumbing to a heart attack two years after his parents' deaths. It hadn't helped him cope when Eli had moved away to college. He knew he had to accept basic risks and uncertainty, and he'd tried, but he didn't know how to face any of it alone. Not in a way that didn't eventually leave him in a place like this, lying in a helpless puddle.

"I was trying to help you," James pleaded with Sebastian, not even sure what he was trying to say. "I can't lose you. I can't lose Eli. But I'm helpless to stop it if it happens. I can't face losing anyone, especially you. Not after everything."

His words tumbled out in an incoherent mess, telling Sebastian everything he was afraid of. Each chaotic thought that had just run through his mind came spilling out into the open. It terrified him, but he couldn't stop himself.

Sebastian listened without interrupting. He didn't argue or point out how irrational and ridiculous most of it was, how people faced these things every day and got on with it.

"I know that helpless feeling," Sebastian said when James had finished. Of course he did. Sebastian had control over almost nothing in his life. He lived by the whim of his ancestor's curse.

"You're so strong." James reached out to touch Sebastian's face. "You've done so well here on your own."

Sebastian laughed mirthlessly. "I really haven't. And if you think I'm strong facing this"—he gestured toward the house—"then so are you, dealing with what life has dealt you."

James wanted to disagree. People's parents died. His situation was hardly unique, but maybe he shouldn't discount his experience. It wasn't a competition between him and Sebastian for who'd had a harder time.

He shifted his weight, sitting up straighter. "Maybe you're right. Losing so many people has left me terrified of it happening again. I hate that I can't save anyone or stop bad things from happening. Not irrevocably."

Sebastian squeezed his hand. "I know I asked for your help, but you don't have to save me from this curse. You don't have to take care of or worry about me. I know you still will," he added, cutting off James's protest. "But I can do the same for you. We're both scared. We're both helpless in the face of what this curse is taking from us. But I'm here for you, James. You can be afraid with me. You don't have to keep it all bottled up. And even if that changes nothing about our situation, it feels like something." He looked down. "To me, anyway."

"Me too." James held back fresh tears, then shook himself and let them fall. "It is something, and it helps to know you understand."

"Good." Sebastian pulled James close, hugging him to his chest.

James needed Sebastian's support and acceptance more than he'd thought. Not being alone with his fears allowed him to breathe again.

THEY WENT to bed after that. Sebastian led James upstairs, stripped him to his underwear, and curled up with him under the covers, skin to skin.

James let himself be soothed. He didn't try to pull himself out of his low mood or try to tell himself not to think about everything bothering him. He didn't lie to himself. He let it all sit there in his head, and Sebastian held him through it.

Sebastian's arms were tight around James, their legs tangled together. There was nothing sexual about it. The embrace was a different kind of desperate than they'd been with one another before. Sebastian clung to him like he was afraid James would disappear if he let go, and for some reason, that made James feel better. Sebastian needed him as much as he needed Sebastian. Who knew if they'd ever choose each other out in the real world, but here, trapped in this messed-up situation, they were everything to each other, and James was glad it was Sebastian by his side and no one else.

He was still afraid of losing Sebastian to some freak accident, still devastated he might not be there for Eli when he needed it, but he tried to find peace with his inability to control these things.

At some point, they both fell asleep. Later in the day, Sebastian got up and went to the kitchen. He came back to the room with hot cider and a tray of food.

They ate in front of the fire, sitting on the carpet in their underwear. Sebastian watched James closely and reminded him to eat more and finish his cider. Once the food was done, Sebastian led him to the bathroom and turned on the shower.

"Want me to give you some privacy?" Sebastian asked, uncertainty leaving his voice hushed.

"No." James frowned at him like he should know better, and Sebastian cracked a smile.

"There's that prickly sweetness I like."

James wasn't sure what Sebastian meant but was too busy being pulled under the warm water to ask.

He was still raw, like his soul had been dragged over rough gravel, but he had room to let good things start seeping back in. It could be worse. Things weren't great, trapped here without a plan, but it wasn't all bad. Not when he had someone who understood him and took care of him. Someone who kissed him like he never wanted it to end.

Sebastian pressed James against the tiled wall, his tongue delving into James's mouth. He ran his hands over James, aligning their bodies so his hips pressed into James's stomach. "I want to make you feel good," he breathed in James's ear.

James ran his hands down Sebastian's back. "You do."

Sebastian took James's cock in his hand and stroked. "How's this?"

James moaned his approval.

Sebastian grabbed a bottle of lube he had hidden behind his shampoo. He squeezed a generous amount into his hand before returning it to James's waiting erection. "Are you going to let me take care of you?"

"Yes," James breathed, almost inaudible. He closed his eyes and swallowed. He would give Sebastian everything he had, let Sebastian be the one he leaned on, the one he trusted with all of him. He couldn't get through this without him.

"Good." Sebastian pressed his hard cock and James's together and stroked. "There you go, James." He trailed kisses along James's cheek to his mouth, and James shuddered at the perfect sweetness. "Yeah, just like that, babe," Sebastian crooned. "Let go for me."

With a whimper, James did as he was told. It felt good not to think or worry. To let Sebastian pleasure him and be the one holding him up.

Sebastian pressed his forehead against James's. Their breath mingled in a chorus of desperate pants. James sunk his fingers into Sebastian's wet curls and held on for dear life as Sebastian stroked their aligned cocks.

James came with a strangled moan. His cum spilled over Sebastian's dick, and soon, Sebastian was coming too, splattering against James's stomach.

The relaxed feeling that settled over James felt deep, like it was more than sexual satisfaction calming him. He leaned into Sebastian's arms and would have been fine with never moving again.

After, they curled up in bed.

"Do you like chocolate cake?" Sebastian asked.

James shifted to see him. "Who doesn't like chocolate cake?"

Sebastian raised a brow. "You must be feeling better if that incredulous tone is back." James frowned, and Sebastian booped him on the nose. "I'll make you a cake tomorrow."

And that's exactly what they did. They didn't discuss the spell, Miss Moo, or the shades. They assessed the apricots to see when would be best to make the next batch of jam. They made themselves sick on chocolate, eating gobs of icing and finishing off the carton of almond milk used for the cake in the form of hot cocoa so it wouldn't be left to spoil. They ate cake all day and picked vegetables in the garden to roast for dinner, then finished off the evening with a bottle of red wine and deep kisses in front of the fire.

It was almost perfect.

CHAPTER TWENTY-THREE

"We've got to figure out a way to tell Eli and Parker our tongues are tied," James said the next night over dinner.

Sebastian nodded. "I'm going to try and bring the books outside with me the next time they show up. They're our best bet. What do you think Parker would do if I just started throwing them at him?"

James laughed. "I don't know, but I'm on board for being cuffed to the front porch like your prisoner in order to temp them to rescue me if you are."

"See." Sebastian pointed a fork at him. "You get it now. Any means necessary. We can certainly give it a try."

James didn't ask what they'd do when people stopped coming to check on him. He supposed Eli or someone from the diner would come each month to make the food delivery, so at least there was that.

"Why do you think it didn't work?" James didn't need to specify what he meant. There was only one elephant in the room.

Sebastian slumped. "I don't know. I don't see why it has to be a human life for any reason other than Selma working that condition in unnecessarily."

"Maybe." James chewed his food thoughtfully. "But what if it's not about human life."

Sebastian narrowed his eyes. "Then what stopped it from working?"

"What if the curse requires a magical life. Cows don't have any magical ability."

"But the curse uses life energy to stabilize the veins," Sebastian insisted.

James put his fork down, sitting at attention. "Did you actually read that somewhere? Selma's instructions said nothing like that when talking about the transfer. Is there anything of Sullivan's around that explains exactly what tying a person to the land does?"

"No. They were careful not to leave behind anything helpful about how the curse worked. Stephen told me a life corrected the imbalance." He trailed off, lost in his thoughts. "But maybe you're right. Maybe it's magical life energy we need, not just any life energy. Like with the creepy Nelson doll. His magic must have been feeding the veins through the doll, not just his life. It was a magical link, after all, seeing as Sullivan could steal Nelson's magic for himself through it."

"Makes sense," James agreed.

Sebastian frowned. "But even if that's true, it doesn't help us. We aren't trapping another person. What other living thing has magical ability?"

James glanced out the window. "Shades."

"Good fucking luck catching one. I don't even know if they bleed."

James had to agree. "And I don't know if they're technically living since they come from Beyond. Not in the same way we are, at least."

They cleaned up the kitchen in silence. A loophole in the transfer spell would be nice, but Selma seemed devastatingly thorough. There might not be a way to make it work without involving an innocent person. Still, James wasn't ready to let it go. Waiting for someone to figure out their tongues were tied was too passive and left too much to chance.

When the kitchen was pristine, Sebastian suggested they take a bath. "We need to pamper," he explained.

James was game to follow along. Living with Sebastian made him happy when he could forget why he was here. He liked all the little things they did together. It was nothing like any of the relationships he'd had in the past. Not that they were in a relationship. They hadn't defined anything, but what was the need when they were the only people who existed in their isolated world?

Sebastian prepped the bath, adding oils and salts, as well as bubbles. They lit candles, forgoing the oil lamps, and it was the most romantic setting James had ever been in.

"What's that look for?" Sebastian asked as he pulled off his shirt and flung it on the ground.

"Nothing." James shook his head, trying to rid himself of fanciful thoughts involving confessing his feelings and making declarations as the candlelight flickered over his and Sebastian's skin.

Sebastian put a hand on his hip and raised his brows. "Need help getting undressed?"

"I've got it." James got to work on his shirt buttons. The vintage clothes were growing on him, a sure sign that nothing about this situation was right.

Sebastian wiggled out of his slim-cut jeans and perfectly fitting underwear before stepping gracefully into the bath. He moaned obscenely as he lowered himself into the sweet lavender-and-vanilla-scented water.

"You sure you want me joining you two?" James joked.

"Yes." Sebastian flashed his signature sly smile. "It can be a threesome: you, me, and the bath."

"You're hopeless," James muttered as he climbed in.

They settled at opposite ends of the clawfoot tub, facing each other. James spread his legs around Sebastian, who placed his in James's lap. James reached under the water and absently began rubbing Sebastian's foot, working the arch.

Despite Sebastian's comment, the bath didn't feel overtly sexual. He and Sebastian had physical chemistry for days, but they had other kinds of chemistry too. James had never felt so good in quiet moments with someone. Hazel came close. The two of them were often on the same wavelength, but that came from a lifetime of friendship. He and Sebastian just clicked.

James let his mind wander as he worked on Sebastian's other foot. Sebastian leaned his head back, eyes closed, as if he were falling asleep.

"What if magic is more important than life?" James asked after a while.

Sebastian picked up his head. "Huh?"

"What if it's just magical energy the curse is using to stabilize the veins rather than magical life energy."

Sebastian's brow furrowed. "But then why would Stephen think there was a life cost to be paid?"

"I don't know, maybe because the cost of the curse is forfeiting your life, as in your ability to live how and where you want. But life might not be the literal cost of the curse. Life energy and magical energy are linked. I mean, it's how you can accidentally kill yourself overdoing a spell, but what if—as far as the curse is concerned—life doesn't matter, only magic."

The furrow in Sebastian's brow deepened. "I don't get what you mean."

"The only living things with magical energy are people, but what if life doesn't matter and we don't need a person to transfer the curse to, just a source of magical energy."

Sebastian took a moment to consider. "I mean, *maybe.*" He sounded skeptical. "But if all Sullivan and Selma needed was a source of magical energy, then why fuck around with this horrible business of trapping people here, damning everyone in the family?"

James shifted in the bath, getting stiff after so long in one position. Sebastian moved out of his way, and they swapped places with their legs, so James now had his feet in Sebastian's lap. He let out a small, contented sigh when Sebastian started rubbing his feet.

"Back in nineteen forty, there wouldn't have been any magical energy sources for Selma or Sullivan to utilize," James explained. "Magical power—as in the kind that generates electricity—didn't kick off until the fifties, and even then, it wasn't viable on a small scale like it is now."

Sebastian perked up, his posture straightening, hands unmoving on James's foot. "You can't just plug a battery into the curse, James."

"I know. This property drains them all dry. But I think that points to my theory being on the right track. The veins need energy. Hell, they *are* magical energy. Of course that's what's needed to stabilize them. I doubt the imbalance would notice if a human life were involved or not."

"Okay." Sebastian resumed rubbing. "Say that's true. It still doesn't help. Leeching off a living person is the only way to feed the veins magical energy over a prolonged period. No battery would last long enough to replace us. They all drain instantly. While me staying alive provides renewed energy to feed the veins as long as I don't drain myself to death."

"You're right. A battery wouldn't last." James smiled. "But a fuel cell might."

CHAPTER TWENTY-FOUR

Excitement built inside James, starting in his stomach and rising rapidly. "Magical energy is stable in a fuel cell. It's trapped, and the only way to get it out is the spell they teach technicians."

"Okay, and?" Sebastian seemed to be catching James's excitement, his gaze sharp and mouth set in anticipation.

"And," James continued, "magic in a battery is meant to be used, so of course, it leaks out when the veins here pull on it. But I bet a fuel cell wouldn't drain, not right away. They also hold much more power than even the biggest battery. If we could get the curse to link to a fuel cell instead of us, I bet it would sustain the imbalance just as well as a living person."

Sebastian's eyes widened. "For how long?"

"I have no idea, but it's not like it's taking that much energy from you, and I haven't noticed it taking anything from me, so hopefully, a fuel cell would last a year or even longer."

"And then what? Keep changing out fuel cells?"

James admitted that was a catch. "Well, yeah, but it's better than us being stuck here. It would free us to get help. Find someone who can sort out a permanent solution to the imbalance."

Sebastian's hands had stopped their massaging, his full attention on the conversation. "Even if all that's true, James, how will we transfer the curse? You can't bleed inanimate objects. The curse and the transfer spell are both grounded in blood magic."

James chewed on his lip. "The thing about blood magic," he said slowly. "Is that it's not always the blood that's needed, per se. It's the *magic* in your blood. You can't bleed an inanimate object, but you can leach a fuel cell. If it's all about magical energy, same difference."

Sebastian shrugged. "I mean, sure. It sounds like good logic. You know more about magical power than I do, Mr. Electrician. We might as well give it a try. It can't go worse than our last attempt."

In James's opinion, things could always go worse, but he chose to keep that to himself. He doubted there would be any dangerous repercussions to trying this out and failing. He might not even have a panic attack this time.

"The only thing is," he did have to admit, "fuel cells are expensive. I had to take out a business loan to get the ones for Gray Electrical."

"Oh, we'll be fine." Sebastian waved his concern away. "I'll send a letter to my lawyer."

James narrowed his eyes. "You have one hundred to two hundred grand to spare, do you?"

"*That* expensive? Damn." Sebastian winced, then braced himself. "No, it's fine." He squeezed James's feet to accentuate the point. "I have stock in Nelson Power. Worst comes to worst, maybe I can cash some in for a fuel cell. I hold too many shares for them to say no to a deal. Actually, I wonder if I could get a discount."

James was shocked. "You own that much of the company?"

"Yeah. It's been in the family since they incorporated." Sebastian gave him a significant look. "Nelson Storm—the big pain in the ass who ran off after ruining everything with his brother

Sullivan—*Nelson Power*, founded by a revolutionary magical theorist. Same guy."

"No fucking way." James had always assumed Nelson was a last name.

"Yeah, how else do you think I'm so loaded? Selma weaseled a healthy portion of the company's initial shares out of her son before she died. We've been living off it for generations. Keeps me rolling in high-end dildos and organic, sustainably produced goods."

"Oh my god." James splashed Sebastian, sending bubbles into the air between them.

Sebastian splashed back with an evil grin. "I can't believe me saying the word dildo makes you blush."

"There's no need to keep saying it," James grumbled.

Sebastian pushed James's legs off his lap and stalked toward him on his hands and knees. "Dildo," he muttered, his face an inch from James's.

"Nightmare," James whispered back.

"But I'm your nightmare." Sebastian's eyes flashed, and he captured James's mouth in a filthy kiss.

Sebastian wrote to his lawyer, requesting the most powerful fuel cell available. He seemed confident in leaving the details of the deal to the lawyer's discretion, only adding that he'd like the fuel cell delivered as soon as possible. It was a waiting game after that.

James and Sebastian fell into a domestic routine, gardening and making jam, spending hours in the kitchen cooking and laughing. No one came out to Storm House to check on James. He didn't bring it up, and neither did Sebastian. There was nothing they could do about it.

James missed his old habits and going to work. Sebastian's life was full of things James wanted in addition to what he already had, not in place of everything else, but when he could forget about that, he felt good.

The clothes Sebastian had ordered for James arrived half a week later. He'd bought more than James would have asked for. The clothes were nice, good quality, and maybe even *high-end*, given Sebastian's comments. It was nice to not have to wear Stephen's clothes, and James couldn't pretend he didn't notice the way Sebastian eyed him in his new shirts. His leather jacket was still wherever Sebastian had squirreled it away. James hadn't seen it since he'd lent it to Sebastian after breaking the tongue binding, but Sebastian had bought him a nice black bomber jacket and several hoodies, so he couldn't complain.

The fuel cell arrived a week later. The delivery driver was wholeheartedly confused when he pulled up to the house and not impressed that Sebastian wouldn't let him back up the driveway.

"Just stop there," Sebastian shouted. The truck's cab was still beyond the property line and, therefore, not at risk of having its battery drained.

"You could have moved this truck." The driver said as he climbed out of the cab, indicating James's abandoned vehicle. "It's nearly impossible for me to maneuver."

"Sorry," James said without feeling. He was too anxious to find out if his theory was correct to care about a truck that was impossible for him to move anyway.

The driver lowered the fuel cell onto the driveway. The metal cylinder hummed with power, the indicator lights on the side glowing green. It was as tall as Sebastian, bigger than the ones at Gray Electrical, and wide enough that James couldn't wrap his arms around it and have his hands touch on the other side.

"Sign this, please." The driver thrust a pile of papers at Sebastian.

He did and handed the top paper back. "Thank you so much."

The man scowled as he got back in his truck and left. Sebastian locked the gate behind him.

James's attention returned to the indicator on the fuel cell. "Doesn't look like it's losing any power."

"Hell yeah." Sebastian slung an arm around his shoulders. "I got a deal on the thing too. The trust manager is really earning his keep."

"Nice for some." James still couldn't believe Sebastian owned part of one of the wealthiest companies in the country.

Sebastian circled the fuel cell, then looked expectantly at James. "So are we just going to look at it, or what?"

James crossed his arms. "For now. I want to make sure it's not draining before we haul it all the way to the clearing."

"In that case, can we get back to the garden and check on it later?" Sebastian came closer and leaned his head on James's shoulder.

"I want to watch it." It wasn't like James could do anything to stop the magical energy from leeching away if it started happening. He needed to feel like he was doing something regardless and didn't want to miss any changes in case they told him something helpful about how the energy imbalance worked. "You can go back to gardening if you're bored."

"Okay." Sebastian straightened. "Let's move it before dark though. Assuming it hasn't died by then."

The fuel cell didn't die. James stared at it for two hours before he went to go find Sebastian, and when the two of them returned to the driveway, everything was fine.

Moving the thing was a pain. James wished he'd left his dolly at Sebastian's place the day he'd used it weeks ago, trying to set up the generator—which was essentially a big battery and not a source of energy like the fuel cell. That day felt like a million years ago.

Sebastian had an old wooden cart that would hold the fuel cell fine. The only problem was getting it inside. James had to use a spell to manipulate the air and levitate the fuel cell into the cart. With such a heavy object, it was a costly spell, and he let out a grunt of exertion as it landed safely on the creaking wood.

It took both of them pushing to get the cart moving, and James had to use more magic to stabilize the fuel cell to keep it from falling as they moved over the uneven ground. They made slow progress. Miss Moo barely looked up from her grazing as they passed.

The woods looked less foreboding during the day. James wouldn't go as far as to say they were welcoming, but at least there were fewer shades. The sun moved in and out from behind fast-moving clouds, and even with the shadows under the canopy, any shades wouldn't be able to move around very freely.

Just as they were entering the trees, James noticed something off to his right that he'd missed in the dark. A small cemetery was tucked into the trees, surrounded by an iron fence, with a smaller version of the front gate standing open. There were five head-stones clustered toward the back of the plot.

"Meet my relatives," Sebastian said dryly, but James caught a tightness in his tone.

James had never seen a private cemetery like this. True, he'd never been to a property the size of Storm House before, but still, it seemed creepy. Not that he was the most comfortable with death, so maybe that was on him. "Is your uncle buried here?"

"Yeah, Stephen is the one in front." Sebastian pointed to the newest-looking headstone. "He never left."

A chill went down James's spine. It was haunting to think the people the curse claimed couldn't even escape the house in death. James slid his arm around Sebastian's waist and pulled him close. "Did you have to bury him alone?"

"No." Sebastian leaned into his embrace. "An undertaker came out." After another letter to the lawyer, no doubt.

There was a grim silence. James tried not to think about himself or Sebastian joining the cemetery.

"I thought only three people had carried the curse before you," James said after a moment. He didn't want to linger and wasn't sure if Sebastian did either.

"That's right: Sullivan, Simon, and Stephen. Selma is here too." He pointed to the tallest headstone. "And Sullivan's wife decided to be laid to rest with him. Unlike Simon's, who went to join her family in town."

James wondered if the cursed occupants of the cemetery could have been buried anywhere else or if, even in death, they were prevented from leaving the property's boundary.

Sebastian slipped out from James's hold. "Come on. Let's get this thing in place."

They made it to the clearing, where James used more magic to position the fuel cell. It looked strange in the middle of the forest. A bird landed on top, pecked at the metal, and flew off. The good news was it still hadn't lost any power.

Sebastian grabbed James's hand. "Let's rest up before we do this."

Back at the house, James ate his fill to replenish his energy, and then laid down to try and sleep, but he was nervous. He wanted this to work so badly.

Sebastian seemed to be in the same boat. He was quieter than usual, staying close to James, his body restless. They curled up together, and James was glad for the comfort.

Eventually, they fell asleep, and when Sebastian roused him again, it was past the middle of the night.

"It's two-thirty," Sebastian whispered. "Let's have some coffee and head out."

They each brought an oil lamp as they headed outside. Not a single shade so much as swooped near them as they crossed the property.

When they reached the clearing, James rushed to the fuel cell. The glowing indicator still said it was full. He could feel the power thrumming within and breathed out in relief.

"James." Sebastian's uncertain voice cut across the quiet night even though it was barely above a whisper.

"Hm?" He turned to see Sebastian looking upward.

James followed his gaze. No wonder there hadn't been any shades pestering them on the way over. They were all here. Hundreds of sets of eyes peered down from the treetops. Even the sky above the clearing was blocked out by wispy bodies and blinking onyx eyes.

"Fuck," James muttered.

"They were waiting," Sebastian whispered back. "Why would they be waiting?"

James tried not to let the alarm in Sebastian's voice get to him. He glanced at the fuel cell. Did the shades know what it was? They must be able to sense the magic within, but why had it drawn them? Sweat dampened his palms as uncertainty threatened to overwhelm him.

He had to stay calm. The shades' behavior didn't matter. They had to do this. The shades' presence could mean they were onto something. The beasts responded to activity in the veins if what Sebastian said was correct. Hopefully, that meant the fuel cell was what they needed.

"Let's hurry." James pulled off his shirt and picked up the knife.

"They're going to pounce." Sebastian pulled his shirt over his head. "No way they don't come for us."

"Unless you want to do the spell during the day, we don't have a choice." James tried to convince himself they wouldn't be swarmed and overpowered by the shades as soon as they started the spell.

Sebastian clenched his balled-up shirt. "We aren't risking doing it during the day."

James respected Sebastian's unflinching resolve. He wouldn't risk hurting an innocent person, even if it meant risking himself instead. He was a good man. James just hoped this plan was enough to help him.

James performed the linking spell. He was driving the transfer magic this time since he was the one who could access the magical energy inside the fuel cell. They were going to try and transfer the curse from both of them this time, not just from James. The fuel cell held way more magical energy than a person did, so there was no reason—theoretically—that it shouldn't be able to take on the curse for them both.

Once linked, James bled Sebastian, then himself, reciting the incantation and collecting their blood in a bowl. The magic formed a haze around his mind once again. He managed to focus through it, concentrating on the tasks he needed to complete, but as his surroundings blurred, he prayed the shades stayed back.

The first step was done. It was time to 'bleed' the fuel cell. James picked up the cord that was normally plugged into the car or generator being refueled. He positioned the end over the bowl Sebastian held and cast the same refueling spell he'd done hundreds of times for customers at Gray Electrical, only this time, he coaxed out as little energy as possible.

It worked beautifully. Energy began to flow out of the fuel cell in a steady trickle. James stopped the flow after a few seconds, only needing a small amount to mix with the blood.

A green glow lit the blood in the bowl. The mixture became sludgy as it swirled counterclockwise of its own accord. James took a breath and plunged his fingers into the glowing blood. He painted the symbols on the fuel cell above the indicator lights. Somehow, it was creepier to see the bloody lines on the polished metal than on the cow.

Once the symbols were complete, James summoned another light flow of energy from the fuel cell. He said the last of Selma's incantation in a fevered tone, unable to slow the words as they came out. Sweat prickled at his brow. He could feel his own energy flagging.

And then it was done. The energy in the bloody bowl flared brightly. Light shot up the cord and into the fuel cell. The whole thing pulsed green, lighting the clearing in a sickly throbbing display. Then the light sucked back in on itself and a loud boom rocked the earth, sending James and Sebastian flying backward. The knife slipped from James's hand as he was thrown into a tree with enough force to knock the wind from his lungs. Sebastian cried out and the shades above them shrieked. The beasts had been blown back as well, their bodies swirling uncontrollably through the night sky.

Silence fell. Both oil lamps had been blown out. James struggled to get to his feet, but a moment later, Sebastian was there, pulling him up.

"Come on. Let's run before they get back."

James spared one look at the fuel cell. The indicator lights glowed just as before. It hummed happily.

Sebastian yanked on his arm and they ran through the trees, but they couldn't outpace the shades. The horde descended upon them just as they reached the tree line. The sheer number of bodies assaulting them knocked them to the ground like a tidal wave. Sebastian swore as his hand was ripped from James's grip.

James was crushed into the dirt as shades bore down on him. It was getting hard to breathe under the weight. Why couldn't the beasts turn into shadows when he needed them to?

There was no way to get up. There were too many. James was exhausted from all the magic he'd done, but he'd die if he did nothing and let the shades crush him. He managed to get a hand under himself. He couldn't push up, the pressure was too much, but he could wipe the blood from above his heart, breaking his link to Sebastian.

"James!" Sebastian yelled, likely feeling the lost connection, but James didn't respond. He didn't want them linked in case this went badly.

It was even harder to breathe. He was being crushed, his

vision darkening at the edges as the shades pressed him into the earth.

With the last of his strength, James summoned light. Not just a small flicker but a blinding flash even brighter than the one he'd summoned under the house weeks ago.

The shades closest to him burst into shadow and disappeared. Screeches filled the air. James heard Sebastian shouting but couldn't make out his words. It was too much. He was fading fast. He was no longer being crushed, but he was blinded by light and too weak to move.

His thoughts blurred and everything went black.

CHAPTER TWENTY-FIVE

A FAINT VOICE called out to James. He couldn't focus on it, no matter how hard he tried. He was cold, his body wracked with shivers. He didn't know what was happening.

"James, James, please," the voice said.

James groaned. He was lying somewhere soft. At last, he was able to open his eyes. Sebastian hovered over him, worry lining his dirt-smudged face.

"James!" Sebastian reached out and cupped his cheeks.

James was unable to move, wrapped tight in a cocoon of blankets. Another shiver raced up and down his body.

"Here, you need to drink some water." Sebastian left his side.

James was able to track his movement without turning his head. Sebastian grabbed a water bottle from his dresser, then returned to the bed. He lifted James's head and helped him drink.

James made a small sound in response and had another sip.

Once he'd finished the water, Sebastian laid his head back down and curled around him, holding on through the bedspread. "You scared the shit out of me," Sebastian whispered, managing to sound pissed off and devastated at the same time.

"Sorry," James croaked.

"Ssh." Sebastian put a finger to his lips. "Rest. And promise not to do that again. You should have left us linked. Then you wouldn't be in this state."

Maybe not, but then he'd have drained them both. Even if sharing the burden meant they wouldn't have ended up in as severe of a condition as James was in now, there was a good chance they'd have both been too weak to move, making it impossible to get back to the house before the shades regrouped.

James didn't say any of this. Sebastian probably knew it to be true and was just scared by the risk James had taken.

Once his shivers stopped, and he was starting to sweat from the combined warmth of Sebastian, the blankets, and the fire, Sebastian let him sit up.

James looked down at himself. "I got dirt all over your bed."

"Don't care. I wasn't putting you in the bath unconscious." Sebastian's voice wavered. He crossed his arms like he was hugging himself, frowning severely.

James brushed his fingers along Sebastian's arm. "I'm sorry I made you worry."

"You didn't make me worry. You made me terrified." Sebastian closed his eyes for a moment. "I'm so glad you're okay."

James nodded, too choked up for words.

With a swift kiss on the cheek, Sebastian left the bedroom. He returned with an unseemly amount of food, and James ate almost all of it. He then promptly passed out, falling into a deep, dreamless sleep.

HE WOKE to find Sebastian curled up in the dirty bed with him, stroking his hair.

"Good morning, sunshine," Sebastian whispered, his tone playful.

"Is it morning?" James glanced out the window. The light didn't seem right.

"More like late afternoon."

James stretched. He felt worlds better, even if he could sleep another eight to ten hours, no problem. While the thought was tempting, sleep would have to wait.

He gripped Sebastian's hand. "We need to see if it worked."

Sebastian squeezed back. "Yeah, I've been dying to test it, but I couldn't leave you here."

"I'm good." James sat up, pulling Sebastian with him. "Let's go."

They detoured for a quick shower and got dressed in clean clothes. Sebastian shrugged James's leather jacket on over his T-shirt.

"Been wondering where that was."

"I'm borrowing it." Sebastian gave him a look, brows arched and as smug as can be.

James laughed. "Keep it." He'd never complain about the sight of Sebastian in his clothes.

"I think I will." Sebastian smiled like nothing could make him happier. James's heart pounded, and his chest felt like bursting.

James and Sebastian hurried outside and walked briskly across the yard toward the trees. Sunset wasn't far off, and James planned to be somewhere shades couldn't get to him by the time night fell. Whether that was back in the house or somewhere else, he didn't dare hope.

James wanted to check the fuel cell before testing if they were free. If it had lost too much power, they could have a serious problem, whether they were free or not. They needed to know that the fuel cell would hold the veins stable for an extended period. If it was draining too quickly, they couldn't leave and risk the massive explosion the Storms had been fighting off for decades.

The sight of the unchanged indicator lights on the fuel cell gave James a rush of relief. Everything seemed fine. The fuel cell didn't look like it had been damaged by the blast or the magic they'd unleashed on it.

He gripped Sebastian's hand. "This is good."

Sebastian grinned so wide his dimples took on new levels of adorableness. "And while that blast wasn't so fun in the moment, it makes me think this fucking worked."

They dashed back across the property to the gate. For the first time, the sight of the iron bars didn't make James frown.

Sebastian unlocked the gate. "Are you ready?"

"Are *you* ready?" James was giddy, now completely blinded by hope. He didn't bother to try and keep it in check.

Even if the worst happened and they were still trapped, he didn't think he'd break down. Not this time. Not when he had Sebastian with him every step of the way. Not when he'd been able to pick himself up last time and find a new plan. Surely, he could do that again if he had to. He wouldn't give up on Sebastian or himself, and he certainly wasn't giving up on the chance of them together, away from this place.

He held out his hand, and Sebastian took it. They walked forward, each with their other hand outstretched. Nothing slammed into them, and before James knew it, they were past the boundary. Another few steps, and they were risking walking right out into the road.

"Oh my god," Sebastian choked out. "*James!*"

He crushed Sebastian into a hug. "We did it."

"I can't—can't believe— Is this really happening?" Sebastian pulled back and looked around. He didn't let go of James as tears welled in his eyes.

"You're free." James squeezed him tight.

Sebastian smiled, and it lit his whole face. He pulled James into him, crashing their mouths together. They kissed frantically until Sebastian began to laugh between panting breaths. "James Gray, you're fucking brilliant."

"I don't know." He was hot from embarrassment but couldn't hold back his smile. "I'm just an electrician."

Sebastian swatted his shoulder. "You're a hell of a lot more than that." He looked back at the house, seeming lost for a second. "What do we do now?"

"Whatever we want." James gripped Sebastian's shoulders. "You can do whatever you want, Sebastian. Fly to Paris. Or New York. Go anywhere. Do anything." He could undoubtedly afford it.

A slight frown pulled at Sebastian's lips. "But what about you?"

"Me?" James glanced at his truck. "I've got a bunch of people to apologize to."

"But what do you *want* to do?" Sebastian's gaze landed on the truck, his uncertainty solidifying. He took a step back from James. "Go back to your life, I guess?"

"Sure, I like my life. But if I could pick anything?" James paused, feeling foolish, even though he knew he needed to take this plunge. "The thing I'd do first is take you on a date. Ask you out to dinner and show you the best night Moonlight Falls has to offer. And maybe that's not much next to Paris, um." He faltered.

Sebastian's face was unreadable. "You're the one who brought up Paris. Not me."

"Right." James pushed his nerves away. "I don't care about traveling. I'm sure it's nice, but it's not what I want right now. I want to take you on a date."

"A date?" Sebastian echoed like he couldn't believe it. "After being stuck with me for weeks, you aren't sick of me? You're not relieved to make your escape? You're going to ask me on a date?"

James nodded and held his breath, trying not to worry he'd just messed everything up.

They stared at each other.

"Well, I'm waiting," Sebastian taunted, that evil grin making an appearance.

"Waiting?" James squeaked.

Sebastian folded his arms across his chest and raised a brow expectantly. "For you to ask me out."

"You absolute nightmare," James muttered as relief flooded him. He cleared his throat, his face flaming. "Sebastian, would you like to go out with me?"

Sebastian's face lit with happy surprise, pretending to be shocked by the question even when the joy in his eyes seemed real. The silliness made James smile just as widely. "Yes," Sebastian said. "I'd love to go out with you."

"Perfect. How about I take you out to dinner? If you're free?" James added, to which Sebastian nodded enthusiastically. "Excellent." He grabbed Sebastian's hand and said more seriously, "I don't want to go back to my life exactly as it was before. I won't pretend getting trapped was a good thing, but parts of the last two weeks have been better than anything I can remember, and I want to see where this goes between us."

Sebastian's silliness gave way to a tender smile, one that brightened his eyes and softened his features. "Then a date is the perfect place to start."

The End

JAMES AND SEBASTIAN'S story continues in *Moonlight Falls Book Two: The Cursed Sebastian Storm*. For Sebastian, getting free is only the beginning...

LOOKING for even more of James and Sebastian? Don't miss *In the Garden*, a steamy bonus scene exclusive to my newsletter subscribers. Join now and see what James and Sebastian got up to while waiting for the fuel cell to be delivered.

HAVE you read Eli and Parker's story? *The Fall of Elijah Gray* is a stand-alone prequel novella to the Moonlight Falls trilogy, available now.

WANT TO KEEP IN TOUCH? Join my reader group on Facebook, Colette Rivera's Coven!

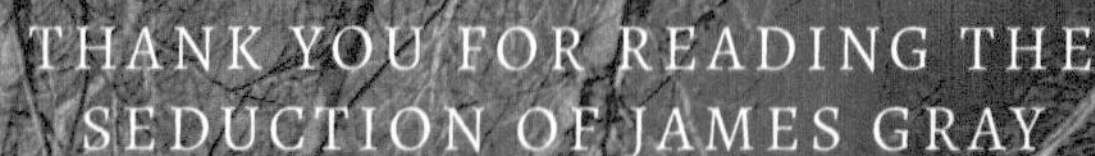

I hoped you enjoyed the beginning of James and Sebastian's story.

Reviews are invaluable to authors. Please consider leaving a review for *The Seduction of James Gray* on your favorite review site or the site where you purchased this book to help others find magical books they'll love.

THE CURSED SEBASTIAN STORM

Some magic changes you forever.

Sebastian Storm didn't dare to dream of a future beyond Storm House. He never hoped James Gray might want to keep him. But it seems that's exactly what James plans to do.

Too bad they won't last. No one ever picks Sebastian and he can't see why James would be any different, especially when Sebastian is keeping a secret he dreads having to reveal.

But he can't keep it to himself when the curse that's haunted him his whole life isn't done with him.

Sebastian should have known escaping wouldn't be easy but he never expected the curse to grow, or to face worse things outside Storm House's walls. Shades are wreaking havoc on Moonlight Falls as something even more sinister builds beneath the surface.

With so much at stake, Sebastian has to risk everything. He needs to know if James can be the one good thing in his life that lasts.

To find out if they can stand together when things get worse, not better. And just maybe they'll be able to build a future out of the rubble.

ACKNOWLEDGMENTS

I would like to thank Abbie Nicole for her excellent editing and attention to detail. I really enjoyed working on this series with you.

Many thanks to Sleepy Fox Studio for the gorgeous cover design. I absolutely love the creepy vibe of the shades and James in his electrician's outfit. You really brought this book to life.

As always, thank you to TK for your love and support. I could not build these magic worlds without you.

And thank you to all my readers. I appreciate every one of you. Your excitement for my stories and kind messages keep me going.

ABOUT THE AUTHOR

Colette is an author of queer paranormal romance novels. She loves to write couples who take care of each other and show their soft sides when in love. Sugar and spice are key ingredients in all her books. She's an avid PNR reader and loves all things magic. Colette once lived in the US but now calls New Zealand home. As a bisexual she has to resist making all her characters bi. When she succeeds you'll find a variety of representation in her books.

Colette can be found on Instagram @colette_rivera and on Facebook under Colette Rivera Author. She can also be found on her website coletterivera.com where you can sign up to her newsletter for bonus scenes and updates.

MOONLIGHT FALLS

The Fall of Elijah Gray

The Seduction of James Gray
The Cursed Sebastian Storm
The Heart of Moonlight Falls